DOWNEAST JUSTICE

BY

WAYNE P. LIBHART

Also by the Author

The Jury is Out
and
The Jury is Excused

For my mother,
still going strong at one hundred and one.

ROLOGUE

All of the pews in Saint Jude's Episcopal Church on Kimball Road in Northeast Harbor were full. That would not be thought unusual these days, even in late August when the 'summer people' are still in town in large numbers. But the day was Thursday, and the service was one of Christian Burial for one of those 'summer people' — Gordon Fairbanks, Esq. Mr. Fairbanks was well known in the village of Northeast Harbor, having been one of the preeminent sailboat skippers at the yacht club. Always the picture of health, his death at the age of fifty two came as a complete shock to all of his friends. Perhaps the brief announcement in the *New York Times* best summarized the circumstances.

> Northeast Harbor, Maine. Gordon A. Fairbanks, Esq. died Monday at his summer home in Northeast Harbor. He was 52. Mr. Fairbanks was the senior partner in Fairbanks & Burke, a prestigious Wall Street law firm specializing in corporate mergers.
>
> Mr. Fairbanks leaves a widow, Bethany Carleton Fairbanks; two sons, Gordon A. Fairbanks Jr. Esq. and Brandon C. Fairbanks, and two grandchildren. Mr. Fairbanks and his wife lived in Greenwich, Connecticut.
>
> It was reported that Mr. Fairbanks died of a heart attack, but now that report has been put in doubt. The death was unattended, and as is customary in such case, the Maine State Police have taken custody of the body and will only say that the investigation into the cause of Mr. Fairbanks' death is ongoing.

That report was well known to those attending the funeral. By then the family knew that an autopsy had been ordered by the police. It was completed the evening of the day Gordon Fairbanks died, but they had been unable to obtain a copy of it, nor had they been able to get an oral report from the State's medical examiner. Because of his obvious good health, everyone close to Fairbanks felt sure that he hadn't died from a heart attack as was first reported. Yet those same people found it hard to believe that he'd been murdered.

Why — why they asked — would anyone want to murder Gordon Fairbanks? He had a great many friends and no known enemies. That question was especially difficult for his wife, Beth Fairbanks. She was in Seattle at the time with their youngest son, Brandon, and his family, helping out with her second grandson who had just been born. She asked herself that question over and over as she flew back to Maine from Washington State. She, too, was very sure that her husband had not died from a heart attack. She was with her husband when he had his annual physical the week before she left for Seattle and heard his doctor give him a clean bill of health. But she could not begin to answer the question of who would have wanted to murder her husband.

$\mathcal{C}$HAPTER $\mathcal{O}$NE

It was an early morning in May. The bright sun, already up above the islands in the bay, promised a nice day. Gordon Fairbanks was sitting on the bench at the shore end of the Carleton pier which extended well out into Somes Sound. He was watching sea gulls catching the discarded bait a lobsterman threw overboard as he went about pulling his traps.

"Hi, Gordon," a cheery voice called from behind him.

Gordon turned around and looked up the path to see his young associate, Cece Tandy waving at him.

"Glad to see you still alive..." he teased." Thought you might sleep all day."

"I'm going for my run."

"Okay. I'll have breakfast ready when you're back," he called to her, watching as Cece ran gracefully back up the path and out of sight.

He had turned to watch and was now facing the old Carleton Cottage, his back resting on the latticed rail that Beth had insisted Harvey Lunt, the Carleton's caretaker, erect all along the pier when their two boys were young. The day was warm for the first of May, the sky cloudless, a gentle breeze coming down the Sound. *Sea Chaser*, Gordon's new Hinckley was tied to the float at the end of the pier, begging to be taken out for a sail. Harvey had just finished painting a fresh coat of white on the trim of Carleton Cottage. It now glistened in the sun, contrasting nicely with the weathered gray of the Maine cedar shingles. The lawn was beginning to green, the forsythia already in bloom, the narcissus budding and ready to burst into flower. It was a soothing sight and, for the moment, it lifted Gordon's spirits.

Having Carleton Cottage with all of it amenities at his disposal should have made him happy and satisfied with life. At that moment Gordon wasn't at all happy. Perhaps more accurately, he wasn't happy with himself. He had flown up to Northeast Harbor in his firm's Learjet on the pretext that he needed peace and quiet while he finalized the extremely complicated bank merger agreement his firm had been working on for the past several months. That had some basis in truth, but he had come to realize that he was in a mid-life crisis and that he had to try to decide the direction he wanted his life to take. He hoped that spending the weekend in the quiet environment of Northeast Harbor might allow him to think the problem through.

Beth wanted badly to come up to Maine with him because it was her favorite place. When he told her he wanted to be alone so he could concentrate on some important work, she reluctantly agreed to stay home. Beth had sensed for some time that Gordon was deeply troubled but she couldn't discover the cause. From the time they first married, Gordon shared his innermost feelings with her. She had tried, but was unable to lead their talks around to a discussion of his problem, or problems. He would simply insist that, other than the merger which was giving him fits, he had no real problems. Beth knew better. She was sure her husband still loved her deeply. She didn't believe that the merger he was working on was the problem either, even if it wasn't going well. Every merger he had been involved with over the years had problems.

Even though Beth believed strongly that married partners should never have secrets from each other, for the first time in their marriage she doing just that. She couldn't bring herself to tell her husband what her doctor had told her that very week — that her cancer was incurable and that in all probability she would not live out the year. When she first learned of it, Beth told Gordon that she had ovarian cancer and it could be treated. After the operation and the course of radiation were completed, she told him that the cancer was in remission — which it was, temporarily. A few months later her doctor told her that it had spread into the lymph glands and it was just a question of time for her.

Feeling the latticework pressing against his back brought Gordon's mind back to the time it was first put in place. He married Beth, she was a Carleton then, in June after she graduated from Wellesley. He had just finished his first year at Harvard Law School. He remembered how happy he was back then. They had lived in a small third floor apartment in Medford. Gordon Junior — Andy — had been born in the middle of his last year of law school. He was doing very well at the Law School and was assured of a good position when he got his JD. The involvement of the United States in the war in Vietnam was coming to an end and he knew he wouldn't have to go into the Army. He was a very happy man.

After he passed the bar exams in New York, he went to work as an associate at Sullivan & Cromwell. By then, he and Beth were living in Greenwich, Connecticut in the rather modest home given to them as a wedding present by Beth's parents. Brandon, his second son, was born the next year. During those years. they traveled up to Maine to be with Beth's parents only for long weekends and on Gordon's short vacations — always taken the last two weeks in August. When the boys were 4 and 6, Beth insisted that she and the boys needed to be away from Greenwich and she started spending the entire summer in Northeast Harbor. By then Gordon was allowed three weeks vacation. Those vacations were very special. They were long enough so he could relax and enjoy his family away from the City and away from the practice of law. The lack of quality time with Beth and especially his boys was the prime reason he and his friend and classmate, Kevin Burke, left Sullivan & Cromwell and started their own firm. Gordon became determined that somehow he would find the time to be with his boys as they grew up. The pain he felt from his father never having time for him as he grew up still hurt. He was determined that his boys would never feel the anguish he had felt when he learned for the first time that his father had been having an affair with another woman. He could still feel the pain he felt watching his mother trying to cope.

So how to explain his present feelings? Was this yet another of his rebellions? His mind went back to his days at Harvard College when he was involved with the anti-war movement. He had been suffering through writing his honors thesis. He was attempting to critique America's constitutional requirement that civilians have the ultimate control over the military and how it affected the conduct of that war. When he first started to write, he was convinced that the system had no flaw — that history proved a democracy couldn't survive unless civilians controlled the armed forces. Then he began to learn from the professor who was supervising his thesis writing that President Johnson had hands on control of the war in Vietnam and was probably responsible for most of the military mistakes had been made there. He changed the direction of his thesis in midstream and the result was a mass of contradictions. Beth came along and saved him — then they were married.

He regretted that his time with them was limited to weekends and vacations. He tried very hard to make those quality times but he knew he failed in that promise to himself. It was Beth who took them to their Little League games and cheered them on. She was the taxi who took them to their private school in Greenwich. She was the one who helped them with their studies. She was the one whose shoulder they cried on when they had disappointments. The boys loved Beth then as a mother and adored her now as a true friend. He felt sure that Brandy loved him as a father, but Andy — was a question.

Gordon knew his feelings for his wife back then were not only of true love but Beth was his best friend, as well. He was extremely proud of her. She was the one their friends gravitated to at parties. She was the one whose friends called when they needed advice and help through their troubles. She had backed him completely when he made the hard decision to leave Sullivan & Cromwell and risk making it on his own.

But it was different then. Their sexual encounters he remembered were nothing short of fantastic and always afterwards they would lie holding each other until they either resumed their play or went off to sleep. For the past few months they simply went to bed and held each other — caressing and kissing — but further he could not go.

Gordon remembered those early years as gloriously happy ones. By the time Brandon was a senior in high school, Beth was diagnosed with rheumatoid arthritis and it had steadily gotten worse. When it got so bad that their love making always ended in great pain for her, Gordon began to limit them. Occasionally Beth would insist, telling him that she wanted him to love her completely and that she could stand the pain. His pent-up desire always led to a violent explosion, but Beth would be in tears and his ecstasy quickly turned to remorse.

About that time, Gordon began to make frequent trips to visit his mother in Saint Albans, Vermont where he grew up. His memories of the town were bitter sweet. It was there he had met his first love, Kelley Morse. That affair ended when the two were in college. For a long time after his father died in an automobile accident in which Josephine Morse, Kelley's mother, also died, visiting Vermont had been extremely difficult for him. Fortunately, a couple of years after the accident, Celia Fairbanks, Gordon's mother, married Jack Morse, Kelley's father. Celia's renewed happiness made his visits to Saint Albans pleasant again. Still, because of the rapid pace of his life, for many years

Gordon's visits to Vermont were infrequent. Infrequent until Gordon learned Kelley Morse had returned to Saint Albans. On one of his rare visits he found Kelley had been hired as a professor of history at UVM (University of Vermont) in Burlington, and was living with her father and stepmother. That discovery coincided with Beth's developing physical problems.

During their senior year at Bellows Free Academy, Gordon and Kelley had finally given in to their desires and became lovers. They had been close friends since they were teens and both were convinced they would marry someday. After they graduated, Kelley went to Mount Holyoke and he to Harvard. As often happens with young love, distance caused other flirtations, at least for Gordon. By the time their parents were killed, they had broken up.

For years however, Kelley's love for Gordon remained strong, even through her short marriage. As the visits to Vermont increased, Gordon found that Kelley was still as sexually attractive as she was in high school. It seemed inevitable that the two would renew their old relationship.

After each visit and their wild sexual encounters, Gordon was consumed with guilt. He had never felt guilt over bedding his college friend, Sarah Rosen. They both knew that was going nowhere. But he knew that Kelley still loved him and would marry him if she could. He kept asking himself if he was simply using her, or whether he still loved her?

Could a man love two women at the same time? Gordon's answer was that he could — he in fact did. But he worried constantly that Beth would learn of his renewed sexual interest in his first love, and he didn't want to make her life any more miserable than it was with her sickness. He knew he had to talk it out with Kelley, even though he knew she understood — she knew he would never leave Beth. To complicate matters, Kelley had become very close to Beth. It started when the Morses began to take their annual vacations in Northeast Harbor. The two women found that they had much in common, and Kelley began to visit Beth quite frequently. Gordon couldn't bring himself to give up the great pleasure of being with Kelley and the trysts continued.

It was inevitable that Beth would learn what was going on between them. Several months went by before Beth asked to accompany Gordon on a visit to Saint Albans, and on the drive back to Maine she asked the obvious question.

"You still have feelings for Kelley, don't you?"

"Yes... why do you ask?"

"It shows. And she's still in love with you...I don't blame you, Gordon. Kelley is a sweetheart. And I'm only too well aware that I can no longer satisfy your needs. If you have to have someone, I'd rather it be Kelley than anyone else."

They were about to pass a rest stop and Gordon drove into it and found a place away from the other cars.

"Darling, I can't hide anything from you," Gordon told her as he drew her into his arms. " I love you so much...I don't want to hurt you."

Beth gave him a long kiss. She knew that he was telling her the truth. He had answered her genuinely and without guile. For that at least he could be proud.

On the other hand, he was sure that Beth did not know about Sarah Rosen. He had been extremely careful to hide it from her. That relationship had ended late last winter and he had no desire to renew it. It had never troubled him with genuine feelings of guilt. Sarah was a real friend, but he never loved her, though he suspected she loved him. And he felt that he wasn't taking advantage of her. Sarah initiated their renewed relationship and she knew it would never be anything more than it was — a mutually satisfying sexual relationship between two old friends.

What was it about his wife that held him so, he wondered. Beth was the first woman he had dated who did not jump into bed with him the first time he had made a serious advance in that direction. The very evening of the day he and Sarah Rosen made love — celebrating his acceptance at the Law School — he had driven out to Wellesley to see Beth. She called him saying that they needed to talk about his thesis which, on impulse, he had given her to read. He didn't expect a critical analysis but he hoped she would at least be able to correct the grammar. As soon as he settled onto a couch in the reception area of her dorm, Beth handed him back her copy of his thesis, almost every page marked in red ink.

Gordon looked at it and then at her and said, " Beth, you forgot to stitch this up after you performed surgery on it."

Beth laughed her engaging laugh and replied, "It's now strong enough to survive without stitches."

It was then that Gordon knew that he was hooked. He had dated better looking women — Kelley for one. Beth was in snug jeans which showed off her long legs and her close fitting sweater accentuated her firm breasts. When she laughed at his comment, her blue eyes sparkled and her long braid swished from side to side. Gordon wanted to jump up and hold her close and kiss her. He didn't dare.

Gordon spent the next three afternoons with Beth and together they completely rewrote his thesis. When it was finished he felt that it finally was a good piece of work, and it was — it got him his *Summa*. Gordon wasn't surprised at Beth's writing and editing skills — she was an English major. What did surprise him was her keen intelligence. She had quickly grasped what he had wanted to argue in the thesis. She excised the many conflicts in his thoughts and organized the work so that it became cogent. Without his telling her, she recognized that he had changed the direction of his argument in midstream. He had already decided that he would only marry a woman of intellect so that was a factor. Sarah Rosen was very intelligent, as well, but his feelings for her, even then, were completely distinguishable.

During the next three weeks Gordon was with Beth almost every day. His final exams were finished and there was nothing to do but wait for graduation. Beth, however, had all her exams still facing her. Often their dates were spent with her studying and him reading Updike's latest novel, *Couples*. They did take time to compete in a set of tennis on most of those occasions. Beth said it cleared her mind so she could go back to her studying. Gordon remembered how frustrated he was that he never was able to beat her. So Beth filled another of the requirements in his desires for a wife — she was a superb athlete.

Gordon had been avoiding the fact that nagged him most, but he had to factor it in to his analysis. Beth's family had money — lots of it. How much he had never realized until both her parents died five years ago. Since Beth was an only child she had inherited the entire estate — at least that which was left after the government had taken its huge bite. He knew that Beth was well aware that someday she'd be rich but she never talked about it. Even after the estates were settled, her friends had no idea what she was worth. Her parents never gave any indication of their wealth either. Still, Gordon knew that they were well off from the beginning.

As evidence, there was the new Thunderbird convertible Beth had at Wellesley, the very valuable home in Greenwich they visited on a weekend and the summer place in Maine she took him to after his graduation. When they first met, Gordon had no idea how he was going to pay for his law school tuition. Beth had learned that it was a problem when he called her to cancel a date, saying he had to meet the financial aid lady at the Law School.

"Gordon, you haven't told me why you made the visit to the financial aids office at the Law School..." Beth asked soon after they were together the next day.

"It isn't a pleasant subject..."

"Tell me anyway."

"Okay. You know my dad was a doctor so you must think my family can help me through school. Well, he's dead..."

"Oh. I'm so sorry..."

"It's Okay, Beth. He was killed when I was a freshman. Car accident. He was with my high school sweetheart's mother. She was killed too. Any money he had is in trust for Mom. Harvard has been awfully good to me...full scholarship. I'm hoping for the same at the Law School. I'm sure of a loan anyway. And I have my summer job in Saint Albans. I'll make it."

"I'm sure you will," Beth agreed.

Beth had told him about the family's cottage in Northeast Harbor, Maine and about the wonderful times she had there summers; sailing, playing tennis and partying. Gordon was dying to sail again. The summer spent sailing with Kelley on Lake Champlain had given him the bug and he had never lost it. So when Beth invited him to Maine for a week after graduation before he went back to his summer job in Saint Albans, he eagerly accepted.

Looking up at the cottage now brought back memories of that wonderful week. The cottage hadn't changed much. It had been re-shingled last year and the pier rebuilt, but it was essentially the same old cottage. That was the week that he first knew he had fallen in love with Beth. He realized that love was not simply prompted by his desire for her. It was certainly something deeper than that. Beth had fascinated him from the first time they met — the way she moved when they played tennis, her agility in tending sails, the way she held him when they danced — all convinced him that she was the one who could fulfill all his desires.

One evening they walked to a small party with some of her friends and on the way back to the cottage they stopped often to hold each other close and kiss. His libido had been on overdrive and he wanted to have sex so badly he threw caution to the winds and started to unbutton her blouse.

"Gordon, please don't," she said, pulling his hand away.

"Sorry, Beth...you are driving me up a wall, I want you so bad..."

"I have the same desire, darling. But I also have this crazy old fashioned notion that I want to be a virgin when I marry that 'right one for me.'"

"Okay...I understand..."

"I have this dream that I will have a marriage just like my parents have."

"My parents had that chance but my father destroyed it. I want that kind of marriage too."

Oh God, Gordon thought, how I've screwed up that promise!

On the last day of that short visit, Mr. Carleton — Gordon couldn't bring himself to call him Bill as he suggested — asked him if they could have a short talk. They went out to sit on the large porch overlooking the sound. Bill told Gordon how pleased he was that he was about to go to Harvard Law School, and that he probably didn't yet realize how getting a degree from Harvard Law would open many doors for him. Then he told him that Beth had shared the problem of his financial needs with him and he wanted to make him a proposition — he would finance his attendance at the Law School and no repayment would be required until he was well established after graduating. Gordon told him he couldn't do that — it was just too much. Mr. Carleton then asked if he had a financial package in place that would assure he would be able to complete his studies and Gordon had to admit he didn't.

"That settles it then," Bill Carleton had said. "Tell Harvard you have secured a loan elsewhere. I'll have our lawyer draw up papers for you to sign and set up an account from which you can draw funds as you need them. I've observed you closely all week here and I'm convinced you are a good risk. No one who takes to sailing as you do can be anything else."

The last was said with a laugh followed by a handshake. Gordon still remembered that conversation and how happy he had been that his financial worries were over. Now, he wondered how much the fact that Beth's family money had influenced his decision to ask her to marry him. It was after all, the last item on his list of qualifications for a wife.

They exchanged letters that summer and took up where they left off when they both returned to their studies in the fall. At Christmas, Gordon gave Beth a ring and they were married after she graduated from Wellesley that spring.

Gordon had excelled at the Law School, making Law Review at the end of his first year. He was offered a summer job at Sullivan & Cromwell in New York City that spring and worked there that summer. They had the home in Greenwich which had come as a wedding present — Beth was pregnant — Sullivan & Cromwell had offered him a job on graduation. Beth had been happy to be in Greenwich near her friends for nine months of the year but, when June arrived, she wanted to be with the boys at Carleton Cottage. After a couple of years Gordon agreed. He was working the long hours associates at the huge New York law firms all worked, piling up the billable hours required to become someday a partner. He would manage a long weekend or two during the summer and spent his two weeks vacation in Maine just before Beth, the boys and the Carletons returned to Greenwich.

$\mathscr{C}$HAPTER $\mathscr{T}$WO

Gordon was interrupted in his reverie by suddenly becoming aware that Harvey Lunt was standing there in front of him.

"Good mornin' Mr. Fairbanks," he said.

Good morning Harvey," he replied. "Why can't you call me Gordon after all these years? As far as I'm concerned, you're part of the family. "

"Thank you for that, but I jest can't. Habit ya know."

"Okay, but please try. What's on your mind?"

"I was wonderin' if I need to get the housekeeper in. You've got a guest.."

"Oh, it's only Cece. You know...my associate. Came up with me to help with a project we're working on. Her family's cottage on the Pond isn't open yet. That won't be necessary, Harvey. Thanks for asking, though."

"Jest thought I'd ask. I'll get back to my painting."

Gordon watched as his caretaker walked briskly back to the cottage. He was aware that Harvey was especially fond of Beth and he wondered if the visit was to let him know that his young woman house guest was noticed. Well, Beth knew that she was there with him, so no need to worry. He quickly resumed his reverie.

Those times in Maine were always a joy for him. He remembered the wonderful sails in the stiff breezes of late August, the lobster bakes, the parties, going mountain climbing with Beth and the boys, teaching the boys to sail, swim, and play tennis. Remembering those days now brought back his joy with a rush of feeling. How could he not now be completely satisfied with his life, he wondered.

The answer was obvious. Gordon knew only too well that the cause of most of his friends' mid-life crises were always in some way related to sex. His life was truly happy back then and he knew that being completely satisfied with the sex Beth gave him was a large part of it. He knew that he possessed an inordinate sexual drive, but even when his times with Beth slowed almost to a standstill, between Kelley and Sarah, he was kept satisfied in that regard. Yet they were all aging.

When his friends divorced they, without exception, had a younger woman on the string. He had always thought that was rather foolish, especially when he thought that his friends were swapping good for bad and he resolved it wouldn't happen to him. That was his thinking until Cece came along.

What was it about young women, he wondered. Well, for one thing, young nubile women are extremely attractive to men of any age. He remembered Beth when she was young. She had remained a virgin until their wedding night. He thought back to that night now. They had been married at Saint Judes in Northeast Harbor and the Carletons made sure that they had the cottage all to themselves after the wedding. Gordon had been worried about his wedding night. He remembered only too well the first time he had intercourse with Kelley, and then Sarah. Their pain on his entering them left a lasting unhappy feeling of guilt. And, on both of those occasions, he hadn't been able to wait for them and he left them unfulfilled. He was determined that wouldn't happen on his wedding night.

Gordon could bring it back as if it were yesterday. They were in the Carleton's huge bedroom on the second floor of the cottage. There was a full moon and they could see the waters of the sound almost as well as in the day. Gordon could see Beth even now, standing naked near the picture window in the moonlight. Her leftover tan darkened her wonderful body and only the parts which had been covered by her skimpy bikini showed white. She seemed to be daring him to pick her up and throw her on the bed. He had done just that and after a bit of play he had entered her without any sign of pain, even though the telltale signs were there on the sheet afterward, confirming that Beth was indeed a virgin. It had been perfect. He made her do most of the thrusting, fearing that he would climax too soon. When they climaxed together Beth had held him inside her, kissing him and thanking him over and over. Until Beth developed her rheumatoid arthritis, she had enjoyed their love making as much as he, often initiating it. Sometimes on weekends and especially when they were in Maine, they would spend hours in bed together, caressing each other and playing their games. They became experts in knowing each others needs and on those occasions they would routinely reach climax together, often having orgasms more than once. It was extremely satisfying for both of them.

Gordon was only too well aware that his sexual drive had not declined as he grew older. He had no problem taking care of two women. Even though his activities at home were in decline, his first straying wasn't at all planned. It started when he was still with Sullivan & Cromwell. Actually, it all started when Sarah Rosen had undressed him in Lowell House that spring afternoon just before his Harvard graduation, and then seduced him into taking her virginity. Gordon had suspected that Sarah was in love with him for some time before that. She knew that he didn't reciprocate her love and that he thought too much of her ever to have taken the lead to having intercourse. Sarah knew that Gordon had become accustomed to women falling for him quickly and completely from the spring of his freshman year when he and his roommate Jeff had begun their quest to see how many women they could conquer before the end of the semester. Thinking about it then, he decided it was something done as a final goodbye, the end of a college friendship occasioned by their going their different ways.

Why did he think that Sarah was 'different' back then, Gordon wondered. He didn't see her as sexy then. But with her, the conversation was always interesting and lively. Even though she didn't turn him on and he knew he wasn't in love with her, he 'liked' Sarah more than anyone he had met up to that point in his young life. Yes, he thought, 'liked' — not infatuated with, as he was with Kelley Morse. They both knew that their friendship, no matter the extent, would never lead to marriage because Sarah was determined to marry a Jewish man. She had made that plain to him often enough. Certainly their first sexual encounter was a celebration — a product of the time. They both were about to graduate and thought they would never see each other again. Sarah simply wanted something to remember him by. As far as he was concerned, that was a one-time thing, confirmed by the fact that after it was interrupted by Beth's phone call, Sarah made no attempt to see Gordon alone again.

Was it fate that they did meet again? Gordon had been working on a corporate merger with one of the senior partners at Cromwell, and that involved sessions with executives from the corporation they were representing. Gordon learned from mutual friends that Sarah had received her MBA from Wharton. He did not know then that she had chosen Wharton over Harvard Business School because she had learned about

Beth and didn't want to be at the "B School' when Gordon was at the Law School. He lost track of her after that. When he walked into the client corporation's board room for an early session on the proposed merger, there Sarah was, sitting with one of the senior vice-presidents. During the break they happily brought each other up-to-date on their lives. Sarah told him she was still looking for the Jew of her dreams and seemed genuinely pleased that Gordon was doing so well with his life.

They saw each other often during the many months it took to work out the details of that merger. Sarah told Gordon that she had a small apartment in up-town Manhattan, was beginning to have a good income and that she was thoroughly enjoying life. During that time they often had lunch together, neither made any move to see the other outside of their work. When Beth moved to Maine during that summer and Sarah learned of the fact, she invited Gordon to have dinner with her at her apartment after they had finished a long day's work. With some trepidation, fearing where it might lead, Gordon accepted. He knew how much his being faithful meant to Beth, and to himself for that matter, but he rationalized she wouldn't mind his having dinner with an old friend from college — wouldn't mind if that was all that it was, a dinner date.

That wasn't the way it turned out, of course. It had been a long day. They both had a double Manhattan while Sarah was cooking their dinner. There was wine with dinner and they had a brandy afterward. Gordon made the mistake of saying he dreaded the train ride back to Greenwich and when Sarah insisted, he agreed to spend the night at her apartment. There was only one bedroom and Gordon intended to sleep on the couch in the living room.

When Gordon told Sarah of his intentions, she said, "Gordon, that's silly. We'll sleep together. You know I haven't the slightest intention of breaking up your marriage. And you want me as badly as I want you."

Sarah slipped out of her clothes and then she began to undress him. Sarah had developed into a mature woman since the last time he had seen her naked. Her dark skin was even darker, he suspected from the tanning salon in her athletic club. Her body felt firm as he took her into his arms.

"You look great," he told her.

"I've been working out on the nautilus for years now," she told him. " It helps the mind as much as the body. You should try it."

"I'm still in pretty good shape," Gordon said as he lifted her up and dropped her on her bed."

As soon as he joined her on her bed, Sarah was all over him, kissing, rubbing and exploring with her tongue. When they finally joined, it was done with such ease that Gordon wanted to ask who she had been with over the years. It didn't matter. Whoever it was had taught her well. They spent the night with little sleep.

After that, they spent many nights together while Beth was in Maine. Gordon was troubled at first. Thoughts of his father's affair and how it had devastated his mother were constantly on his mind. But he wasn't in love with Sarah as his father was with Jo Morse. Sarah never told Gordon she was in love with him. No one would be hurt. It was a friendship — not a relationship — between two mature adults who enjoyed each other's company very much — and the great sex. Gordon now knew that was a complete rationalization. It wasn't him, or Beth for that matter, who was hurting.

By the time Gordon decided to leave Sullivan & Cromwell and form a partnership with his old classmate, Kevin Burke, Sarah had already set up her own business as a consultant to companies engaged in mergers. She saved as much of her income as she could and made good investments with those savings. She also had the benefit of an inheritance from her frugal father. Since Fairbanks & Burke specialized in corporate mergers, it was natural that Sarah was often involved with their work, usually as a result of a recommendation from their firm. It wasn't patronage — Sarah had the experience and expertise to make a real contribution to the process and her clients loved her. Still, it produced the result Gordon desired. Their sexual needs were satisfied whenever that could be accomplished without giving anyone cause to notice. The firm maintained an apartment in uptown Manhattan within walking distance of Sarah's. Outwardly it was for times when the partners had late and early meetings in the city and it facilitated those events. Gordon was constantly amazed at how gullible Beth was in accepting without question his need to stay in the city those many nights. Now he wondered if she had known all along and was just being Beth. They were both extremely careful and it was easy for anyone exercising care to hide away in New York City. It was years before Kevin Burke learned the depth of their relationship.

Gordon wondered what Sarah would have done if she learned he had renewed his relationship with Kelley Morse. Thank God, he thought she never found out. He was sure it would be the end of their relationship. She would know that it wasn't simply a mutual desire for sex, as was theirs. And thank God, he added, Kelley hasn't learned about Sarah. Gordon told both women that he not only was married to Beth, but he loved her deeply and would never leave her. Still, when he thought about it, he often was filled with feelings of guilt and he hated himself, especially now that Beth wasn't well and he knew that she was suffering.

By the nineties, Fairbanks & Burke was flourishing. It had tried to avoid becoming very large, but the need to satisfy the ever-growing demand for their services led to their hiring several additional associates every year. Burke was the partner in charge of hiring and his recommendations were always followed. When he returned from interviews at Harvard in 1997 he was ecstatic. He told Gordon that with luck they might finally hire a woman who not only had an outstanding mind, but also was a raving beauty — a description he rarely used. She had completed her second year at Harvard Law and agreed to work for them that summer. Her name was Carol Coffin Tandy but she went by the name of Cece — C. C. Tandy. She was from Cape Elizabeth, a suburb of Portland, Maine. That summer she worked for Kevin, and Gordon rarely saw her. But Kevin was right, Cece was as he described her. She was hired as an associate when she received her JD from Harvard the following spring and was assigned to assist Gordon whose workload was out of hand.

Gordon was then working on a merger of two New England banks, Northeast Holdings and ConnTrust and it had been giving his firm fits. Sarah was engaged by ConnTrust to assist it in the process and had observed Gordon and Cece together during the many meetings between the lawyers for the two banks. She had sensed immediately that Gordon was really taken with Cece. Sarah had never given Gordon even a hint that she was jealous of Beth. But when Gordon, on one of their evenings together after both had too much to drink, foolishly told her how much he admired his new associate, Cece Tandy, she had immediately exploded in a tirade.

"You idiot," she yelled at him, her eyes full of anger. " You have everything in the world a man could want. A wife who adores you. Two wonderful sons you should be proud of. A wonderful daughter-in-law and an adorable grandson. An extremely successful law practice. All the toys any man could want or use. All the sex you need or want.What in hell is the matter with you Gordon Fairbanks?"

Then she burst into sobs. Gordon had never seen her so angry.

When she calmed down a bit he said, " Sarah darling, all I said was that I admired my new associate. I didn't say I'm in love with her."

That triggered another outburst.

"Oh shit you don't! I'm not so naive that I haven't noticed. Your eyes are constantly on her. I've never seen you treat any of your associates with so much deference. Don't tell me you're not in love with her. It was written all over your face when you just mentioned her name!"

Gordon left immediately for the firm's apartment, saying he was terribly tired and they had a big day in front of them. In fact, he was just as angry as Sarah was but he wasn't about to let her see it. At that point in time he thought he was the only one who had an inkling what his feelings for Cece were. How had Sarah known? He knew he had to be more careful in showing his emotions. Cece didn't seem to notice that he was infatuated with her. At the moment he had to be satisfied with just being near her. He didn't want to do anything that would cause her to reject him.

That thought turned Gordon's mind back to Beth. His love for her through all the years seemed to get stronger and now that he sensed that her time might be limited, he was determined to do nothing to make those years unhappy. He had made that promise to himself when Beth's doctor in Ellsworth had first discovered on her annual visit the previous fall that she had cancer in her ovaries. Her doctor in New York had not seen the early abdominal swelling and missed it. Even though it is extremely difficult to detect, Gordon still blamed him for not finding it earlier. Her Maine doctor had immediately removed the ovaries, the fallopian tubes, the diseased parts of the abdomen and the uterus. She had radiation every few weeks and was on cytotoxic drugs. Beth told him that the prognosis was good. She was her usual upbeat self and was handling her situation much better than Gordon. Their sex life had ended and his trysts with Kelley now left him feeling more guilty after every encounter. Though Beth knew it was happening and wasn't making a large issue of it, he knew down deep it must hurt her terribly. And if he now turned his attention to a young woman, it would not only be Beth but also Kelley who would be hurt. What was the fatal flaw he saw in himself? Was it from his father's genes?

Gordon's reverie was interrupted again when he saw Cece running down the long driveway and enter the Carleton cottage. He had said he would have her breakfast waiting when she returned from her morning jog and he hadn't even put the coffee on. He had only gotten a glimpse of her but it made his desire rise just the same. She was in scanty running shorts, her blouse wet through and tight around her ample breasts, her nipples showing through. Cece was the sexiest woman he had ever known.

"Oh my God," he said out loud. "What a fool I am..."

CHAPTER THREE

The proposed merger of ConnTrust with Northeast Holdings had problems that wouldn't quit. Every time Gordon thought he had gotten the merger back on track something else came up to derail it. Gordon had reached that point in his career where the practice of law wasn't fun anymore. He couldn't believe he was burnt out in his early fifties. He promised himself, that if he ever got these companies merged, he was going to take a long vacation. He had been promising Beth a tour of Europe for years. The last time he had made the promise Beth had said that she wouldn't live long enough to see that happen — that he was too involved with his work to ever take a long vacation. That was before Gordon learned that she had cancer and he knew that if he was going to keep that promise, he would have to begin arranging it soon.

But he knew he couldn't make definite plans until the merger was set. It was originally supposed to have been finalized by the end of July. Shortly after taking on ConnTrust as a client, Gordon realized that its president, Ralph Ralston, was one of the most difficult men he had ever worked for. Ralston had been a medical doctor before he left his practice to run the bank. He had the arrogance of some of the doctors Gordon knew but he also had the aggressive instincts of most of the successful CEO's he had worked for. Ralston had begun purchasing shares in ConnTrust at the same time he started his medical practice in Torrington, Connecticut. He didn't have a specialty and he didn't like the income a general practice produced. As soon as he had acquired enough shares of the bank to be listened too, Ralston demanded a place on its board of directors. Two years later he became its CEO.

Gordon's new Hinckley had just been commissioned the weekend in May when Gordon first brought Cece up to Maine with him. Tiger Wass, Gordon's boat captain, had come up from Medford, Massachusetts for the weekend. He was in his third year at Tufts' Medical School. Gordon hadn't realized at the time that Cece and Tiger had been committed to one another since the previous summer. They had first met when Cece made a brief visit to Carleton Cottage at the end of the summer between her second and third year of law school — when Gordon invited her to visit after she finished her internship at Fairbanks & Burke. They became better acquainted the following summer. Both were determined to finish graduate school and for years had not allowed themselves to become deeply involved with members of the opposite sex. That resolve dissolved for both of them almost from the first time they met. The attraction for one another was magnetic. They tried to slow the process without success. For some reason neither could explain, they hid the fact that they were dating from Gordon. For the past several years, Tiger had spent his summers working on Gordon's sailboat. In past years he slept aboard the old Hinckley. Now Gordon provided an apartment for him in Manset, a village of Southwest Harbor across the Sound from Northeast Harbor. When Cece visited the Island, she stayed at her parent's cottage on Long Pond. Their few times together that first summer were evenings spent at that cottage. Neither of them were interested in seeing any of the movies which were showing or spending the evening at one of the many local pubs. They preferred to swim in the pond, make a meal together, talk and enjoy each other's company. They continued to date when they returned to the Boston area in the fall — Cece for her final year at Harvard Law and Tiger for his second year at Tufts Medical. The pressure of their studies limited their dating but they talked every day by phone. By spring they both realized that they had fallen totally in love.

Gordon was completely unaware of this fact as he planned that May weekend. He knew, of course, that the two had become acquainted when they sailed with him on the occasions Cece had been on the Island the previous summer. But they never gave him the slightest indication that they were any more than casual friends. As the years passed, Gordon always got his way with any women he set his sights on. He thought that would be so with Cece, if he gave it enough time. Taking her to Maine each weekend for work and then relaxing with her while they sailed was part of a plan to accomplish that.

The breeze in Somes Sound on that mid-May day was light when Gordon, Cece and Tiger left the pier at Carleton Cottage, but as soon as they were out of the Sound, it quickened. The previous summer Gordon had asked Tiger to teach Cece the rudiments of sailing and she was becoming quite proficient. Cece was soon in love with sailing. She liked being in the sun and being on the boat quickened the time it took her to get a dark brown.

When she appeared in a full swimsuit the first time they went out sailing Gordon asked, "Don't you have a bikini, Cece?"

"Well, yes..."

"I wish you'd wear it the next time out."

That was her usual attire for future outings on *Sea Chaser*. If it got cold in late afternoon, Cece pulled on a sweatshirt but her legs never seemed to get cold. Gordon thought that Cece was trying to please him and it made him happy. Actually, it was Tiger she was pleasing.

"You seem to enjoy sailing," Gordon told her as they walked up the pier after *Sea Chaser* had been tied.

"Wonderful! I loved every moment of it," she replied.

"Do you think we can make a sailor out of her, Tiger?" he asked.

"I'm not sure," Tiger answered. " Lawyers are very difficult people to teach anything to..."

Tiger had said this with a big smile looking directly at Cece. When he saw that Cece thought he meant it he quickly added, " Only kidding, Cece. You are doing just fine."

Her frown turned to a broad smile. Cece had never before felt so overpowered by a man. She couldn't believe that a man his size could be so agile. He moved quickly around the deck of the boat, anticipating every move Gordon wanted him to make. He always had the sheets ready when they were going to come about. He never had to be asked to trim the sails. When Gordon tired of the helm, using the electric winches to trim the sails, Tiger could man the helm without any help. It seemed to Cece that he was part of *Sea Chaser*. His rugged face was already tan, even though Cece knew Tiger hadn't seen much sun all winter while he was at Tufts. This part of the man she saw only on the boat. Ashore he was always so gentle and unassuming that, when she later learned about his exploits in the Vietnam War from his friends, she found them hard to believe.

Gordon's desire for Cece grew stronger as every week went by but every subtle invitation to take her to lunch or dinner when they were in the City during the week was rebuffed. Seeing her in her bikini on *Sea Chaser* was driving him crazy with desire. By the middle of August he found his mind in constant turmoil. The merger business with Ralph Ralston had him in a constant state of anger. The breakup with Sarah left him sexually frustrated. He hadn't been with Kelley. The pressure of work on the merger, had prevented visits to Vermont. He had no desire to visit anyway. Cece had all of his attention.

Gordon was in the habit of having a scotch highball each evening before dinner, but he hardly ever abused alcohol. He didn't smoke. He had tried pot in college and hated it. His one vice was women. Even in his early fifties his drive hadn't seemed to lessen. He had spent that day on and off the phone with Ralph Ralston. By nightfall he was so angry with the man that he was ready to terminate his firm's representation of ConnTrust. To try to cure his anger, Gordon spent the evening drinking Chevas Regal.

As he sat on the verandah of Carleton Cottage, his thoughts again turned to Cece. He could close his eyes and see her beautiful face, her tanned body. He tried to imagine what making love to her would be like. Finally he decided to pay her a visit at the cottage on Long Pond. He knew that her parents were away on their annual trip to the Maritimes. It was 11 p.m. He was sure it would be a safe visit.

Normally Gordon drove his old 1960 Ford station wagon when he was on the Island. It was a custom of the 'summer people' to drive nice old cars. But he decided to take his Mercedes convertible instead. It was a warm evening, The moon was full. He thought he might entice Cece to go for a ride up Cadillac Mountain. Or anywhere she might want to go for that matter. As he drove onto Great Neck Road, he had sobered up a bit and began to have second thoughts about the adventure he planned. As he approached the Tandy place he decided to park the Mercedes at the top of the driveway and walk down to the cottage. He saw that the lights were on in the kitchen and also in what he thought might be a back bedroom. Good, he thought, she must still be awake. The back door was open so he opened the screen door and walked in. Hearing nothing, he decided to explore the back of the cottage. As he approached the bedroom where he had seen the light, he saw that Cece was lying on the bed, completely naked, reading.

He had about lost his nerve and started to turn back when Cece saw him standing in the hallway. She jumped out of her bed and started to pull on a robe.

"Gordon!" she shouted. " What in the world are you doing here?" Gordon just stood there grinning and teetering back and forth.

"Gordon?"

"Warm night, Cece." he slurred. " Nice night for a beautiful lady to go for a ride in my convertible."

With that Gordon reached out and pulled at Cece's robe. As she struggled to get it away from him, Tiger appeared, dripping wet from his evening swim. Gordon was shocked to see him. He released the robe and fell back against the door jamb.

"Mr. Fairbanks!" Tiger shouted. " What the hell are you doing?"

Gordon didn't answer. He turned and went down the hall to the kitchen where Tiger stopped him and made him sit in a kitchen chair.

"Get some clothes on, Cece," Tiger said. "He can't drive in the condition he's in. We've got to take him home."

"Tiger, I'm sorry..." Gordon slurred. " Too much...too much..."

"It's Okay Mr. Fairbanks. It's Okay."

"I can drive," Gordon said as he tried to get up.

He didn't make it, and sat back down. Cece was soon dressed and in the kitchen. Tiger pulled Gordon up and they each got an arm over a shoulder and walked Gordon to Tiger's old Bronco. They folded him into the passenger's seat and headed to Northeast Harbor and Carleton Cottage. As they neared the town, they met a Mount Desert police cruiser coming their way at a high rate of speed, it's blue lights flashing.

"Think of the trouble you'd be in if we'd let you drive," Tiger said to Gordon.

Gordon only grunted. They drove in the long driveway to the cottage. The Fairbanks caretaker, Harvey Lunt, was standing at the entrance of the cottage.

"Heard him drive out," Harvey told them. " I came up to see if anythin' was wrong. From the empty bottle of scotch on the coffee table, I thought I might have to go fetch him back from someplace. You saved me the trouble."

"I'll be Okay," Gordon told them. " Just leave me be..."

He tried to get out of the Bronco but fell back. Tiger and Harvey helped him into the cottage and to his bedroom on the first floor.

"He'll be all right," Harvey told them. " You two run along. I'll take over from here. Mr. Fairbanks don't often have too much but when he does..."

When Gordon woke from a bad dream it was the middle of the morning. Even though Harvey had left the windows of the bedroom wide open, he was sweating. He sat up and promptly lay back down. His head was spinning. As he lay there trying to get himself together, the events of the previous evening came back to him in a rush. 'What a fool I made of myself!' he thought. 'What a God damn fool!'

During all of his life, Gordon Fairbanks had never been completely depressed. There had been sad times — when his father died leaving his mother in shock, when he wanted Kelley back and couldn't have her, when Sarah Rosen drove him away. But he knew he had led a charmed life and there had been nothing before to get really depressed about. Now he realized Beth wouldn't be with him much longer. Sarah was out of his life and had left a void. Kelley...what was he to do about Kelley? And now he had made a fool of himself with Cece.

Then there was the confrontation with Ralph Ralston. He was failing in that as well, and it could lead to real trouble, both for him and his firm.

As he painfully pulled himself up on the bed he looked at himself in the mirror. He didn't like what he saw.

"You'd be better off dead!" he said to the image.

If it was a death wish, it was fulfilled in little more than a week.

CHAPTER FOUR

Gordon Fairbanks died in late August, the time of year when most of his friends were on vacation. Somehow Andy Fairbanks — Gordon Andrews Fairbanks Jr. — had managed to find them all and give them the sad news. They came from far and wide in large numbers to attend the funeral.

From the time Beth Fairbanks first received the sad news, she showed the grit she was made of. She was in the nursery at her sons home, gently rocking her new grandson while Norma was fixing dinner.

When the phone rang Beth answered it and Andy said," Mom, I have bad news..."

"Something has happened to your father!" Beth broke in.

"Yes, Mom. Harvey found him this morning on his boat. They think he had a heart attack."

"Oh my God! My God! Wait, let me get Brandy."

The baby was asleep. Beth put him gently in his bassinet, called for Brandy to please pick up the phone. When Brandy came on the line, Beth replaced the phone and collapsed on the bed beside the bassinet, sobbing quietly.

Brandon had always been much closer to his father than Andy and the news, coming so suddenly, put him in a state of shock. As he attempted to hold back his tears he choked up and couldn't talk. Andy immediately began telling his brother about the funeral arrangements he had made and asking for his approval. Brandy could only say 'fine' or 'okay,' as Andy went over each of the details. Andy had already dispatched the law firm's jet to Seattle to bring him and Beth east. The pilot would call when he arrived. Brandy said that he and his mother would need a little time to get ready. He had to arrange for help for Norma while he was away. They would be as quick as they could. The call ended on that promise.

For the past week, Brandy had been elated with the safe arrival of his second son. Now, after hanging up the phone, Brandy slumped into a kitchen chair, trying to control his compulsive sobs. Norma heard enough of the conversation to know that Gordon had died and she ran to the nursery to be with Beth and the baby.

Beth had regained her composure by the time Brandy joined them in the nursery. She found herself consoling the two young people. The only other time Beth lost her composure was at the funeral when her husband's partner, Kevin Burke gave the eulogy. Kevin had the gift of the Irish and the philosophy of his Catholic upbringing. He celebrated his friend's life by reciting his accomplishments and relating many of the amusing times they had spent together. There was a mixture of laughter and sobs among the audience as he finished with a final amusing story. Beth strongly approved but she couldn't hold back her tears.

Celia, Jack, and Kelley Morse were in Maine on their annual vacation, staying at Kimball Terrace Inn in Northeast Harbor. Knowing that they were family, their waitress gave them the bad news while they were lunching on the terrace. All three left immediately for Carleton Cottage to help Harvey Lunt get ready for the family's arrival. In late afternoon, Kelley drove up to the Bar Harbor Airport to meet Beth and Brandy. When Kelley saw Beth she was immediately in tears. They embraced for a long moment, neither able to speak. The short trip to Carleton Cottage was over before they were able to control their emotions and talk to each other.

Andy had invited all those attending his father's funeral to come to Carleton Cottage for brunch. There were well over one hundred people who accepted the invitation. The brunch was spectacular. Harvey Lunt had been able to get the local catering service, on short notice, to provide a sumptuous lunch — lobster rolls, crab rolls, sandwiches of every kind imaginable, and a choice of a great many deserts. Harvey opened the Fairbanks bar and served those who desired something stronger than the punch the ladies of the service provided.

Had the circumstance been different, the mood of those present might have been to continue the celebration of the life of Gordon Fairbanks as Kevin Burke had suggested in his eulogy. The knowledge that Gordon Fairbanks might have been murdered hung over the group like a pall, and many of the conversations were in muted voices, relating the rumors which were already making the rounds.

Celia and Beth found a great deal of mutual support just being together in their sorrow, as they sat chatting on the verandah of Carleton Cottage. Neither felt the need for food after the ordeal of the funeral. Celia was amazed at the vitality Beth seemed to exhibit. She knew that Beth was fighting cancer and she suspected that her illness was terminal. She knew better than anyone that her son had given Beth good cause to leave him long ago. It was obvious to Celia however, that Beth was still devoted to her son. Her love shone through her tears like rays of sun. Celia wondered if the Fairbanks men were all alike. Did they all feel the need to have more than one woman at their beck and call? Were they all doomed to an early death?

"You seem to be doing awfully well," Celia told her. " I wish I could say the same."

"I just try to remember all the good times we had together," Beth replied. " Your son has made my life worth living. I loved Gordon so much..."

Beth paused and both women were silent for a long time. What Beth had said turned Celia's mind back to her husband's death so many years ago. She too had loved her husband until the day he died. She too had ample reason not to. Celia had not thought about those sad times for a long time, but at that moment, they completely occupied her thoughts.

Gordon had been a sophomore at Harvard at the time of his father James's death. The family had moved to Saint Albans, Vermont after James finished his residency to live on Celia's parents old hardscrabble farm. Soon James, had developed a busy medical practice in Saint Albans. Even though James was never able to openly reciprocate her show of love for him, she thought — up until the end — that he loved her but he just wasn't capable of showing it.

Celia and James met while they were both at Tufts College. She knew back then that James wanted to avoid going into the Army during WW II at any cost, but she didn't know until much later that the reason he had insisted on marrying her before she graduated from college was to start a family and thus avoid the draft. She later suspected that was the prime reason he went to medical school.

By the time James had his degree in medicine, the war was over. By then, Celia's parents were both gone and they left the farm to her. During those years, James spent very little time with her and Gordon.

His excuse was that he had to be available to see his patients on a moments notice — it was a requirement of a small town general practitioner. As the US became involved in the Vietnam War, James formed an anti-war group and spent his evenings going about the area talking at anti-war meetings. Celia wasn't happy with these activities, but she remembered the poverty she had endured growing up on her family's farm and James was a good provider, so she didn't complain. Celia had loved animals, especially horses, since she was a child. Knowing this, and perhaps as a consolation for his absence, James had bought her and Gordon two beautiful Morgan horses which provided constant enjoyment for them.

The farm next to the Fairbanks' was owned by Jack and Josephine Morse. Jack was a veterinarian, so it was natural that they quickly became friends when the Morse's bought their farm and moved in. The Morse's also owned Morgan horses, and had a beautiful daughter, Kelley, who was the same age as Gordon. With the exception of James, the families spent a lot of time together. Gordon and Kelley became fierce competitors at the horse shows. As they grew older, Gordon and Kelley extended that competition to the tennis court and on the ski slopes. They were soon inseparable. About the time the two were seniors in high school, James took a sudden interest in horses. He bought a Morgan for himself and joined the families on their weekend rides. Celia welcomed the change in her husband's interests and didn't question his reason.

Jo Morse was a registered nurse. After she completed training, Jack convinced her not to take a position at the local hospital so she could assist him in his busy veterinary practice. Shortly after James joined the family riding group, his nurse retired and he convinced Jo to take her place. Jack wasn't happy to hear that, but Celia thought nothing of it. Jo told her she was tired of treating animals and wanted to go back to nursing people. Celia thought she had a solid marriage, but Jack had begun to suspect that his had problems. Celia had long since gotten used to James being out most evenings and never being overly loving towards her. Still, neither had any idea that their mates were sexually involved until the afternoon they were killed in an automobile accident.

It was a Wednesday afternoon, saved by James for house calls. That afternoon the two had gone to spend the afternoon at a motel in

Swanton, far enough away as to be safe. They stayed too long, and James pushing his car to the limit, lost control on a patch of ice. They hit a large boulder and both were killed instantly. Those memories caused Celia tears to start again.

Celia's unhappy thoughts were thankfully interrupted when Beth said, " Do you know Sarah Rosen?"

"I've never met her," Celia replied.

"That's her with Kevin. Isn't she attractive?" Beth asked.

"Gordon told me that Kevin had finally found a woman who interested him. I'm happy for him. His divorce was such a difficult time for him... Kevin rented a cottage on the back side of the Island for the summer. She has been with him here on the Island every weekend helping on the firm's latest merger. Gordon told me that she is an expert on the economics of mergers and often works for his clients."

Celia did have a vague recollection of hearing the name before. Her memory was then prompted. Gordon had told her he had met a wonderful Jewish girl by that name when he was at Harvard. She wondered if she was the same person. Her idle gaze focused on Sarah. She was indeed attractive. Her dark skin, deep brown eyes, black hair, her rather thin but well proportioned body now clothed in black, all came together to produce a striking figure.

As Celia watched, Sarah had turned to go back into the cottage. Kelley Morse had been walking towards her and it seemed to Celia that Sarah was deliberately trying to avoid Kelley. If that were so, she failed. Kelley followed Sarah into the cottage and Celia saw that they were engaged in conversation.

"Sarah, why are you avoiding me?" Kelley asked.

"I'm not avoiding you, Kelley." Sarah answered. " It's just that..."

Sarah broke into tears and walked away, leaving Kelley standing there wondering why this woman who seemed to be so tough was acting the way she was. Obviously, something was bothering her badly. Kelley knew that Gordon had, what he called a platonic relationship, with her while they were in college. She also knew that the relationship had been resumed a few years back but Gordon had told her on the one occasion the subject had come up that it was no longer platonic. Their consensual sex was simply that. Gordon insisted that they were not lovers — only friends who enjoyed sex. Gordon knew the admission hurt Kelley deeply and he was careful never to mention it again. Kelley realized that the sex was a larger player in the relationship than Gordon would admit, even to himself. But she also knew by then that, for some reason Gordon had never explained, the relationship had ended.

Kelley was standing by the huge bay window in the large living room of Carleton Cottage absently gazing out at the waters of the Sound. Several minutes passed as she watched a small sailboat barreling along before a stiff breeze. Her thoughts turned to a day on Lake Champlain when she and Gordon had gone sailing. They both were back in Saint Albans for the summer after their junior year at college. By then, her father had married Celia and that had brought Gordon back into her life — at least for that summer. There had been a good breeze but at noon it quit. They were well out on the lake and the sun was hot. Both were in skimpy swim suits. They had spent the week haying on both farms, getting in the winter feed for their horses, so they were already well tanned. In a few days they would return to college and they planned to spend those last few days together. Gordon dropped the sails and they lay back on the boat cushions to relax and wait for the breeze to freshen.

Their high school friendship had first been renewed that summer while they accompanied their parents on weekend horseback riding treks. Kelley's love for Gordon had remained strong and she was slow to forgive him for breaking his promise to remain faithful to her while they were away at different colleges. That afternoon, as she lay on the boat cushions looking idly at Gordon's trim body, she felt a sudden surge of desire remembering the time they both lost their virginity. It was on the night they graduated from Bellows Free Academy. During the summer, Kelley had slowly come to realize she was still in love with Gordon but she doubted he loved her. Being with him while they hayed the farms and watching his almost naked body as they worked often filled her with desire. Her desire that day, seeing him in his skimpy bikini was overpowering. The sun had turned his blond hair almost white. His deep blue eyes seemed even more blue in the dark tan of his face. 'Adonis', she thought as she as she looked at Gordon lying half asleep on the opposite cushion. 'Adonis is the only way I can describe him.'

Gordon sensed Kelley's feelings but, even though his desire was as strong as hers, he was determined that he wasn't going to hurt her again. He knew he wasn't ready to commit himself to any woman at that point in his life and he wondered if his feelings for Kelley were of real love or just of passion. Tired of wrestling with his emotions, he sat up.

"Let's have some lunch," he suggested.

"I'm ready," Kelley answered. 'More than ready,' she thought, 'but not for food.'

Kelley retrieved the cooler from the cuddy and they ate, silently enjoying the lunch Kelley had prepared. When they finished, Gordon got up, stretched and then pulled off his bikini, stood on the rail and jumped into the lake.

"Come on in, Kelley," he shouted as he came to the surface. " The water's great."

Kelley quickly slipped out of her bikini and jumped in after him. Gordon chased her around the boat and when he caught her, he held her tightly to him, treading water, kissing her. Gordon climbed into the boat and then pulled Kelley back in, as well. Without either saying a word, they were immediately on the boat cushions, pumping in unison and climaxing together.

Remembering that day prompted Kelley's thoughts to turn to the night before Gordon died. She, her father and Celia, had been in Northeast Harbor only a few days on their August vacation. She hadn't seen very much of Gordon because he had been working into the nights, putting the final touches on a bank merger he told her was driving him up a wall. Now with him gone forever, Kelley begrudged even more the loss of their usual times together while she and the Morses were in Maine on vacation. But that day he had called and invited her to join him at Carleton Cottage at noon. He told her his group was going sailing to celebrate being finally done with the work on the merger and he wanted her to come along. Kelley quickly agreed. She was sure she would always remember that wonderful afternoon sailing, taking turns at the wheel with Gordon. Now she was sorry that she had not joined Gordon for the lobster dinner he had planned after their return from the day's sail, but she had promised to be with Celia and Jack that evening.

Kelley was thankful that Gordon insisted she return to Carleton Cottage later that evening. The others had left when she came aboard

Sea Chaser. It was soon apparent that Gordon was more despondent than when she had left him earlier that day. Except for the time years before when he returned to Saint Albans for his father's funeral, Kelley had never seen Gordon so down.

The night was warm and they decided to have a drink on the forward deck. It was obvious to Kelley that Gordon already had more than the two drinks he usually allowed himself, but he wasn't drunk. She asked him why he seemed so sad but he wouldn't answer. He just looked at her and took another sip of his drink.

Kelley wanted very much to change his mood so she started teasing him. Gordon quickly threw off his shorts, she followed suit and they were in each other's arms. Soon they brought the cockpit cushions up to the cabin trunk and immediately they were together. Kelley had never seen Gordon so passionate, even when they were very young. Afterwards, they stayed together for a long while, entwined in each others arms. Kelley was hoping that Gordon was cured of his despondency, but he wasn't. When they returned to the cabin, he told her he loved her and wished she could stay but it was time for her to go back to her motel.

When the rumors started that Gordon hadn't died of a heart attack but that he had been poisoned, Kelley didn't believe them. She was convinced that, if he died from being poisoned, he had taken it himself. Now that thought came back strongly. 'Oh my God' she thought, 'I hope he wasn't despondent over me!'

Kelley was startled out of her reverie by suddenly realizing that Sarah had returned and was standing beside her.

"Kelley, can we talk?" Sarah asked in a low voice.

"Sure," Kelley agreed. " Let's take a walk down to the pier."

They walked in silence down the path to the pier and sat on the bench at the head of the pier before either spoke.

"Kelley, they say that Gordon was murdered...," Sarah started.

"I can't believe that, Sarah," Kelley interrupted.

"Why?"

"What would be anyone's motive to murder Gordon? They know it wasn't a robbery. Nothing was missing. Gordon's wallet had his usual stash of cash — over a thousand dollars. His Rolex was on his wrist. His huge diamond ring on his finger."

"Tiger had a motive," Sarah insisted.

"Oh my God, Sarah! I can't believe it! Gordon's paying Tiger's tuition at medical school. Tiger adores him as if he was his father..."

"But Tiger is in love with Cece, Kelley."

"I know that. So...?"

"Gordon was...screwing her."

"How do you know that?"

"Two or three weeks ago, I was talking to the man we rent our cottage from. He knows we are friends of Gordon's and he's an awful gossip. He asked how Gordon was. I told him he was fine. Then he asked if Gordon was in trouble. I told him no. Then he said that he heard on his police scanner a call for the Mount Desert Police to respond to a call that there was a fight at the Tandy cottage."

"So..."

"Then he told me that the Tandy neighbors heard Tiger shouting at Gordon and then a short while later, they saw Tiger's car drive up the driveway and out the Great Neck Road. By the time the police arrived, they were gone but Gordon's Mercedes convertible was still in the upper parking lot. He wanted to know what I knew about it and I told him 'nothing.' "

"Sarah, I didn't see any sign of a problem when we were with all of them on *Sea Chaser* Friday. I can't believe it!"

"You'll see..." Sarah told her angrily, and walked quickly back up the path to the cottage.

CHAPTER FIVE

Cece awoke from a deep sleep with a start. The beam of a strong flashlight was sweeping her bedroom. As she started to sit up, Tiger's arm, which had been wrapped tightly around her, fell away as he too woke up. The beam stopped full on her face and she closed her eyes, blinded for the moment. She was aware that Tiger was now fully awake and starting to get out of bed. She heard a sickening thud and Tiger fell back on the bed. The beam of the light turned to him and she could see blood gushing from the top of his head.

"For Christ's sake, what did you do that for? " the voice behind the light demanded.

"He was coming at me, God damn it! What did you expect me to do?" the other voice shouted back.

"Bullshit! Back off for Christ's sake..." the first voice ordered.

Cece had found the light switch near the headboard of the bed and turned on the lamp on the bed stand. Standing in front of her was a large man in dark clothes with an automatic pistol glistening in his right hand. He quickly pulled a badge from his belt, showed it to her and said,

"Maine State Police. Don't move."

Both Cece and Tiger were completely naked. Cece ignored the man, jumped up from the bed, ran to the bathroom, grabbed a towel and the first aid box from the medicine cabinet and returned to Tiger who was now regaining consciousness. The two men — Cece now realized they were both police officers — stood beside the bed immobile, saying nothing. Cece soon had the blood slowed to a trickle and Tiger was able to sit up.

"You monster!" Cece shouted, glaring at the officer who had administered the blow, "Tiger's head is going to need several stitches to close that wound and it won't wait!"

"Okay...Okay, Miss Tandy. Get some clothes on and we'll get him to the hospital."

Cece dressed quickly and then helped Tiger into his clothes. The four then left the Tandy cottage. Waiting near the open back door to the cottage were two more men in civilian clothes, whom Cece knew must also be State Police officers. The smaller of the two showed her his badge and told her she had to stay outside while they searched the cottage.

"Do you have a search warrant?" Cece asked.

"We do..." the office answered, but didn't offer to show it to her.

"Am I under arrest? " she then asked.

"Not unless you refuse to cooperate," he answered.

"If I'm not under arrest, I'm going in the other cruiser with Tiger. Your cohort over there could have killed him and I'm going to see that they get him medical attention."

The older man, the one who had shown the light in her eyes and who Cece later learned was Sergeant Robert Tardif, told the officer to let her get into the cruiser with Mr. Wass. He ordered the other two officers to stay there and carry out the search as planned. The unmarked cruiser made a fast trip to the Maine Coast Memorial Hospital in Ellsworth. It was 4 a.m. on a Sunday and there was no traffic on the road. The cruiser was flashing the blue lights on its dashboard just the same.

The hospital's emergency room staff had been alerted by the Hancock County dispatcher and were waiting for their arrival. The emergency room doctor irrigated the wound and then sutured it with ten stitches. He told Sergeant Tardif that Mr. Wass should not be subjected to any kind of pressure, such as questioning for 24 hours. When Tardif started to object, the doctor told him that if he wouldn't agree he'd simply not release him from the hospital. With that, he got Tardif's reluctant agreement.

The four then proceeded to the Hancock County Sheriff's Office — the SO — on State Street in Ellsworth. The county dispatcher was called on the radio and had a room with a cot in it waiting for Tiger — Adam Wass — and he was taken there by one of the deputies. During the trip up to Ellsworth from the Tandy cottage Cece tried to remember what she had learned in her course on criminal law during her first year at law school which might help in her present situation. By the time Sergeant Tardif and his assistant, Corporal Nick Carsillo, had brought her into the Sheriff's conference room, she was ready for them.

"Miss Tandy, we simply want to ask you some questions, " Tardif told her.

"Am I under arrest? " Cece responded.

"No, but we have reason to believe that you might be able to answer some questions we have surrounding the death of Gordon Fairbanks. You worked for him, right?"

"I will not answer any questions without my lawyer present," she answered.

"But you are a lawyer," Tardif said in an annoyed voice,

"True, but I know better than to represent myself in any legal matter,"

"Okay. Who is your lawyer?"

"My parents have had Mr. Hardy do some work for them and I would like to call him."

"We'll call him for you. Nick, give Dan Hardy a call and ask him if he'll be good enough to come up and be with Miss Tandy while we ask her some questions."

Carsillo left on his mission and while they waited, Cece decided to ask Sergeant Tardif questions of her own.

"Do you have an arrest warrant for me?"

"No, ma'am."

"May I see the search warrant then?"

"Yes ma'am. I should have given it to you. I'm sorry...but in the haste to get Mr. Wass to the doctor I overlooked it."

Tardif handed Cece a copy of the search warrant and she read it carefully. It was issued that Saturday by a judge of the Maine District Court. It required the server to search the premises owned by Wexford and Rachel Tandy situated in the town of Mount Desert at Long Pond. The search was to be for drugs of any kind, especially barbiturates; hypodermic needles, syringes, aspirators or anything used in applying drugs; any papers or documents pertaining to the merger of a company known as Northeast Holdings with a company known as ConnTrust; and any computers, floppy discs, CD ROMs, or lap-tops and any related equipment found on the premises.

Although Cece was totally surprised by the disclosure that the police suspected that Gordon Fairbanks' murder was somehow connected with the merger she had been working on with him all summer, she didn't let it show.

"All right," she said when she had finished reading. " The basic warrant appears to be valid on its face but obviously I don't know what you told the judge to get it. Anyway, it isn't an arrest warrant. What right do you have to hold me?"

"Basically, the AG's office decided to do it this way as a courtesy to you and your family. We think we can make an arrest on probable cause. That wouldn't require a warrant as you know. If we have to, we will. We were hoping you would answer our questions so that wouldn't be necessary."

Cece felt her anger rising again. One thing she knew for certain — neither she nor Tiger murdered Gordon Fairbanks. They had seen him —alive and well — the evening he died. She and Tiger had spent the rest of the evening together at the Tandy cottage, as they had done all that week. She was tempted to make a strong assertion to that effect, but she knew once she had made it, she would have difficulty refusing to answer the questions that would follow. There was no telling where they would lead. She knew from her criminal law course at the Law School that innocent answers could be taken out of context and on several occasions such answers had been used to convict an innocent person. She would wait until Mr. Hardy arrived.

Cece asked if she could be with Mr. Wass but she was refused. She was worried that he would start talking without a lawyer present to represent him. He wasn't under arrest, as far as she knew, and they didn't have to give him the Miranda warning until he was in custody. Of course he was in custody — they both were. She was tempted to start to leave and force the issue. Recently, courts in most jurisdictions have ruled that the magic words — 'you're under arrest' — had to be said in order to trigger the requirement that the police must give the Miranda warning to a person before they questioned him. That fiction has been the court's way of making inroads on the Miranda rule. Tiger was studying to be a medical doctor and she assumed he didn't know anything about that. To him everything was black and white. She could only hope that the police would follow the doctor's orders.

After a half hour or so, Nick Carsillo brought Dan Hardy in the room. Dan remembered Cece from the time he met with her parents in his office in Ellsworth the previous year. She wasn't a young woman any man would easily forget. He had spoken briefly with Carsillo, who he had known from the time he was a State Police patrol officer years ago. Carsillio had given him the basic information as to why Cece was there. He asked Sergeant Tardif to allow him to speak with Cece alone.

After they both left, Cece turned to Dan Hardy and said, " Mr. Hardy, I hope you will represent me. I don't know what this is all about. I don't even know if I need a lawyer, but if I do, I want you."

"I'll be happy to represent you, Miss Tandy. From what I've been told, the police don't as yet have any real suspects in the Fairbanks death. They say they know for sure it was murder. And they are on to something that seems to involve you." he answered.

"Mr. Hardy, I'm sure all your clients charged with a crime tell you the same thing but I'm going to say it anyway — if Gordon was murdered I did not have anything to do with it. Nor did Mr. Wass. Nor did we have anything to do with whoever did do it — if in fact it was murder. I have a great deal of trouble thinking in those terms. But I do know how important it is for a client to be honest with her lawyer. What I'm telling you is the truth."

"I appreciate your telling me that, Miss Tandy. It helps. It helps a lot. But I have to tell you that I have a self-imposed rule which I follow religiously, even though my clients usually come to hate it. I have a rule that I must assume that my client is guilty of the charge even when I feel sure they are telling me the truth when they deny it. Any lawyer who doesn't have that rule and follow it completely is asking for trouble. Can you live with that?"

"I don't like it, Mr. Hardy, but I can't quarrel with it. I can see the reason for it. And I want you to represent me."

"Good. First off, I'm much happier when my clients call me Dan."

"Okay. Then I'm Cece."

"Fair enough. I have a second rule which is almost as important. I never — repeat never — let my client talk to the police. Most often I come into a case too late to prevent that, so I'm happy you called. These Maine State Police detectives are very clever people. They know from experience that a person accused of a crime usually thinks he or she can tell the police a story that will exonerate them. If in fact they are involved, it usually has the opposite result."

"Okay. I have no problem with that."

"They may decide to arrest you, as I suspect they have already suggested to you, but from my limited conversation with Corporal Carsillo, I doubt they will. They don't have a warrant and they don't seem to have enough evidence to make a probable cause arrest."

"You're right. The suggestion was made. And I hope you are right that they won't follow it through."

"That settles it then. I'll tell them you refuse to talk to them. Sergeant Tardif won't be surprised. He has had me on the defense's side before and he knows my rule."

"Dan, I'm really worried about Tiger Wass..."

"I know Tiger Wass. Watched him grow up in Southwest Harbor. A real fine young man."

"They have him here..."

"I know. They told me."

"He needs a lawyer."

"It can't be me. I'm sure you remember the Brutten rule, the one basically preventing a lawyer representing two people charged with the same crime?"

"Vaguely. Would it make any difference if we were married?"

"Are you?"

"Yes. We were married by a justice of the peace in Bangor the day I started my vacation over a week ago. We haven't told anyone because we want to have a proper wedding in the spring. I hope you won't tell anyone."

"Fine. I'm happy to know that and I won't divulge it to anyone without your permission. Still, it would be better if Tiger had his own lawyer from the beginning."

"Can you recommend one?"

"There is a young lawyer in Southwest Harbor who I have a great deal of confidence in. His name is Ian Campbell."

"Can we get a message to Tiger to call him?"

"Under the circumstances I can arrange a meeting as soon as Tiger agrees to have Ian as his lawyer."

"Okay. You can tell Mr. Campbell that my family will guarantee he'll be paid and I'll have a retainer for you as well, as soon as we are out of here."

"That will be fine. I have no problem with it. I have worked for your folks often."

Dan Hardy left to speak with Tiger. It was good that Tiger knew both Dan and Ian Campbell well or he would have refused to let Dan ask Ian to represent him. He told them he hadn't done anything wrong and felt he shouldn't have to pay a lawyer to represent him. It wasn't until Dan Hardy told him that Cece insisted on it that he agreed. In less than a half hour Ian Campbell arrived at the SO and Dan filled him in on what he had been told by Nick Carsillo. Then Ian spoke with Tiger. After they had reviewed the few facts as they knew them, Tiger was happy to instruct Ian to tell the detectives that he too would not speak with them.

Sergeant Tardif had anticipated that once the two suspects had retained attorneys, especially ones with the reputations of Hardy and Campbell, that he would not be interviewing either of them. He had called his superior to get further instructions and was prepared for the meeting with the two lawyers. As he anticipated, they told him that their clients declined to talk to him at that time, but perhaps they might later as more was known about the matter.

"Okay then. I'll just have to do what I have to do," Tardif told them.

"Sergeant, you and I go back a long way," Dan responded. " I know I don't have to remind you that police officers are not completely immune from civil damages when they make a false arrest. The US constitution and the Federal Civil Rights Act provide a remedy for that. Unless you have a lot of information we don't know about, you don't have a basis for a probable cause arrest. By the way, I'd like to see the affidavit the search warrant was based on."

"There isn't one."

"The rule requires it..."

"Not if there is recorded testimony before the judge."

"Well, let us hear the record..."

"No record. It was a court reporter and she hasn't transcribed it yet."

That of course was permissible and the lawyers were stymied.

"Okay. Tell us the gist of what was testified to. I suppose you were there and it was under oath."

"I was there. It was my testimony. My boss has instructed me not to divulge the information so my hands are tied. Sorry..."

"I'll bet you are. Where is the inventory of what was taken from the Tandy cottage?" Ian Campbell asked.

"I don't have a copy of it yet. As far as I know, our people are still there. I'll have a copy for you both tomorrow. I'll see to it," Tardif promised.

"The ball is still in your court, Sergeant," Dan Hardy said. " What are you going to do with our clients?"

"Your clients are free to go. But tell them not to leave the area."

"Sergeant, you know you can't make that order and we won't promise you they will stay here. We will know where they are though," Campbell responded.

The lawyers and their clients left the Hancock SO about 8 a.m. that Sunday morning. Dan Hardy took Cece home in his car so he could talk to her and try to get a handle on the situation. Ian Campbell did the same with Tiger Wass. When the two lawyers had obtained all the information surrounding the death of Gordon Fairbanks known to their clients, they were as much in the dark as they had been before the conversations took place. Two things they did know, however. First, that somehow the merger of ConnTrust and Northeast Holdings was involved; secondly, their clients were prime suspects. Further, they knew that Sergeant Tardif was a veteran detective and their clients would not be suspects unless he had some information that tied them to the crime. Beyond that, they were clueless.

*C*HAPTER *S*IX

Four days had passed since the Tandy cottage was invaded by the Maine State Police when Cece's parents, Wexford and Rachel Tandy, returned to their cottage on Long Pond after their annual vacation in Nova Scotia. They were shocked to learn of the events of the past days. Soon their shock turned to anger and then worry. They couldn't believe that the police thought their daughter was somehow involved with her boss' murder. They insisted on seeing Dan Hardy right away and he scheduled a late appointment at his office that same day. Hardy was unable to give them any more details on the matter than had their daughter. He suggested it might be well not to wait for the police to act and for them to engage a private investigator to get to the bottom of the situation. Dan told them that the money might be wasted if Cece were not charged. Wexford Tandy's response was that if Dan felt it was needed 'to go for it.'

Dan's old friend, Detective Joe Goldberg was on the case from that day forward. For the next three days Goldberg worked solely on the matter. He took advantage of the many friendships made when he was still an active Maine State Police detective and was able to get bits and pieces of information from that source. He also developed some information on his own. Then he called and told Dan Hardy he needed to meet with him, Ian and Kara Campbell — Tiger's lawyers and Cece, Dan's client. The meeting was set up for the following day.

When the group was ready, Goldberg told them that he had, with some difficulty, been able to talk to Sergeant Tardif. Tardiff was reluctant to talk because he didn't want to say anything which might lead to a lawsuit against him or his fellow officers for the unnecessary beating they had given Tiger Wass. When Joe told him that wasn't in the cards, Tardif relented.

"With the promise that we would not disclose its contents to the media, I was allowed to read the autopsy report," Goldberg told the group. " The state's medical examiner, also a pathologist, was of the opinion that Mr. Fairbanks had died from a lethal dose of a barbiturate.

The blood study disclosed the concentrated presence of a barbiturate in Fairbanks' blood and that had given him the lead he needed to make further tests. Those tests confirmed his original hypothesis that the cause of death was the ingestion or injection of a lethal dose of a barbiturate. He couldn't be sure which one or how it was administered. The blood alcohol level was 0.29 — very high, and when a barbiturate is combined with alcohol, it increases the drugs' toxicity and it acts much faster. Further tests will be conducted, but the preliminary report predicted that the barbiturate was ultra-short acting and probably sodium pentothal."

"What exactly is sodium pentothal?" Kara Campbell asked.

"It's a barbiturate often used in small doses by dentists to put people to sleep for dental work. Veterinarians use it in larger doses to put animals to death. And it is used on death row in states which allow the death sentence," Joe Goldberg answered.

"So given that one wanted to murder a person by using a lethal dose of a barbiturate either by injection or ingestion, and that person made a search for something which might be readily available, that product would be a natural?" Dan asked.

"Right," Joe responded. " The problem would be in obtaining it in its ultra-fast acting form."

"But who would want to murder Gordon Fairbanks?" Ian asked. "Do the police have any leads on the question of motive?"

"The only thing I've been able to piece together is that they have at least two theories. One is that they believe, even though Mr. Fairbanks' marriage was a good one, on the surface at least, that he had on-going affairs with at least two women. In Maine, when they have that kind of information, they always assume that the murderer may have a motive somehow connected to it. Eighty percent of murders in Maine are caused by a domestic quarrel of some kind. I couldn't learn who the women were or where Tardif got that information.

"Tardif's second theory involves Mr. Fairbanks' work. He has been getting a lot of information on the legal work Mr. Fairbanks was doing at the time of his death. Yesterday they seemed excited about a breakthrough there. So far I'm in the dark as to what that is all about."

"I think I can answer that," Cece told them. "Our firm has been working on a corporate merger that has had a lot of problems. Gordon

Fairbanks' wife has cancer and it may be short term so he wanted to spend a lot of time in Maine this summer to be with her. The merger had a deadline to meet. He decided that we'd come up Fridays and work until Saturday afternoons on the merger. Then we'd have the rest of the weekend to play."

"Does that explain why Mr. Fairbanks' partner, Mr. Burke and a woman by the name of Sarah Rosen have been up here as well?" Joe Goldberg asked.

"Partially," Cece answered.

"I'm hoping that you and Tiger will tell me all you know about Mr. Fairbanks and the situation he was in this summer, whether or not you deem it significant," Joe encouraged them.

"Well, Sarah Rosen is an expert in corporate mergers and works for our client ConnTrust," Cece told him.

"And Mr. Burke?" Joe asked. " Is he working on it as well? I've been told that they have rented a cottage in Sawyer's Cove for the summer and stayed there when they were up here."

"That is true." Cece reluctantly agreed.

"Miss Tandy. It's important," Joe urged.

"Cece, please tell us all you know, or suspect for that matter, " Dan added. " And under the circumstances, you don't have to worry about client privilege so long as you are just giving us general information which is already known by the public."

"Okay. I have to be careful not to disclose privileged information beyond that, however. I don't like gossip and I hate to repeat it. Beside, I work with both of them. Okay? Anyway, Mr. Burke had been going through a very bitter divorce in Connecticut for the past couple of years. It dragged on forever and he told me that when his wife — ex-wife — was through with him he was basically broke."

"And Miss Rosen — or is it Mrs. Rosen?" Joe persisted.

"It's Miss Rosen. She told me that she and Kevin like each other a lot but that is as far as it goes. She told me that they will never marry because Kevin is a Catholic. They seem very devoted to one another though."

"Go on," Joe urged.

"I can't remember now who told me — I think it was Kevin — Gordon was a classmate of Sarah Rosen's at Harvard..." Cece started.

"I hate this..."

"Please go on." Joe instructed.

"Okay. Kevin said that he started his own relationship with Sarah after she and Gordon had a bad disagreement and broke up last winter."

"That could be one of the affairs Sergeant Tardif was talking about," Joe suggested. "Tell us what you can about the legal work."

"The merger was basically Gordon's responsibility but Sarah asked that Kevin be brought in on it when the going got rough."

"Can you give us any more information as to what the problems were?" Dan asked.

"Well, as you know, the exact details are privileged information. I can tell you only who the parties are and what is known by the public," Cece said. " It started out as a merger but the parties kept changing their minds as new information was provided. It looked for a while as if it would end up in a leveraged buy-out. The parties came to agreement about two weeks ago and the merger was announced the day before Gordon died. Our client is ConnTrust, a small bank whose main office is in Torrington, Connecticut. The other party is Northeast Holdings, a bank holding company centered in Worcester, Massachusetts."

"Why was there so much secrecy?" Joe asked.

"If the word leaked out that these two banks were contemplating a merger, there would be very serious problems for whoever was responsible. There is always a price differential in these matters which can produce a very nice profit for a person with knowledge of the facts who takes a major position in one of the companies before the merger is announced."

"Position in either?"

"Position in either. Long position in ConnTrust and short in Northeast Holdings was the way it worked out. If a trader took either position and the merger went forward, he could make a lot of money."

"Okay. I guess we understand. Tell us everything you remember about the day Mr. Fairbanks was murdered. The police say you both were with him during that day and into the evening," Joe instructed.

"That is true," Cece responded. " The merger with all the proper disclosures had been announced to the public the day before. Our group was joined by Ralph Ralston, the president of ConnTrust and one of its principal stockholders. He appeared to me to be awfully antsy... more nervous than usual. He flew up from Connecticut after the merger was announced. He said he wanted to be with his lawyers in case he needed them. So we stood by the phone until noon that day in case there was any problem. It was a Monday, the 24th of August, right? There was a good breeze and Gordon was fierce to go out on *Sea Chaser*, his sailboat. Tiger had her ready and we came down on the pier and we all went out. Mr. Ralston was with us. Kelley Morse was already on the boat with Tiger, waiting for us."

"It was very warm as you may recall and Gordon was soon after you to change into your bikini," Tiger said to Cece. Turning to the others, he said, " He loved to have her on the fo'castle deck sunning herself. Shit, so do I...Sorry, Mrs. Campbell."

"No problem Tiger. And it's Kara, Okay?" Kara Campbell said with a laugh.

"Okay, Kara," Tiger continued. "We had a great sail all afternoon until the breeze lessened. When the wind had died completely and we brought in the sails, we came back to the Carleton Cottage pier under power. Cece and I planned to go back to my apartment in Manset where I was going to boil some lobsters for dinner."

Cece took up the narrative.

"I may as well tell you that I have known for a long time that Gordon — how do I say it — really liked me? No, it's much stronger than that — had a real desire for me. He was always giving me things. Then he started asking me to go to dinner with him after work when we stayed late at the office in the city. I went a couple of times and then, when he invited me to the firm's apartment afterwards for a drink, I refused. I tried to make an excuse but he wouldn't take no for an answer. Finally, he suggested that a partnership in his firm would be very lucrative for me. That's when I told him straight out that if going to bed with him was the *quid pro quo*, I would be looking for another firm to work for. For a moment he was so angry he couldn't speak. Then he calmed down and he apologized profusely. Said he couldn't stand not to have me work for him so he could see me every day.

"Then there was the incident recently when Gordon had too much to drink and made a visit to my family's cottage on Long Pond in the middle of the night. I don't know what would have happened if Tiger hadn't been there..."

"Were there repercussions from that?" Dan asked.

"He apologized the next day...Said he didn't realize Tiger and I were intimate...That if he couldn't have me, he couldn't think of anyone he'd rather have me than Tiger," Cece answered.

"Anyway," Tiger resumed, " Gordon wanted us all to stay and have dinner with him on the boat. He said that Harvey — Harvey Lunt, his caretaker — would have lobsters waiting on the pier. Gordon had been sleeping on the boat while Beth was in Seattle — said he hadn't been sleeping well lately but sleeps like a baby on *Sea Chaser*."

"Beth was in Seattle with Brandon and his wife Norma, helping with their new baby boy," Cece explained.

"Cece and I knew that Gordon had been extremely upset about something during the past week, but we didn't know why," Tiger said.

"Gordon was a very private person. He rarely showed any emotion but several little things he said that week gave us that impression." Cece added. " Kelley left us as soon as we were at the pier, making an excuse that she had promised her father and Celia she'd have dinner with them. I knew something was bothering her but I don't know what it was. Kevin wanted to stay but Sarah insisted that they had a reservation at the Asticou for dinner. She seemed really upset too, but again I don't remember anything that happened that afternoon which could have caused it. So just Mr. Ralston, Tiger and I stayed."

"We had a great meal up on deck and a lot of good talk," Tiger continued. "Until this summer, I've never known Gordon to be a heavy drinker but that night he had several highballs. We watched one of the reddest sunsets I have ever seen. 'It went down in flames,' Gordon said. Then he added something really strange — he said, ' Just like me.' We passed it off. As I said, Gordon had a lot to drink and I guess we were afraid he was going to get morbid — like he got sometimes recently when he has had too much,"

"We had already cleaned up after dinner, so we told him we'd see him in the morning," Cece continued. " We expected that Ralph Ralston would leave with us but he said he had something private he wanted to discuss with Gordon and he'd stay awhile. We left for Manset in Tiger's Whaler."

"What time did you leave?" Joe asked.

"It must have been a little after 9 p.m. Maybe a little later."

"Tardif says it was after midnight," Joe said.

"No way!" Cece disagreed. " Tiger and I were having our midnight swim in Long Pond at midnight. Its become a ritual ever since we've been together."

"Where the hell is Tardif getting this information from?" Tiger demanded.

"I think it is from Harvey Lunt. He lives in the Carleton Cottage boat house near the pier," Joe suggested.

"That has to be it," Ian agreed. " But there are three hours between nine and midnight..."

"Right. I knew I had to talk to Harvey myself and I tracked him down Friday. He wouldn't talk to me. Said that Andy...Gordon's oldest son...told him not to speak with anyone about the case unless he was present. Even to the police, he said. Tardif put short shrift to that, I'll bet. I gave him my card and asked him to call if he changed his mind...told him it was extremely important for Cece and Tiger. Saturday he called and said he had an errand to run in Ellsworth that afternoon and could we meet some place out of the way. We made the arrangement and met at the city's boat launch area on the Union River.

"It seems Harvey had been stewing ever since I tried to talk to him. He's a true downeaster. Andy made a mistake giving him that order. Harvey said if Andy finds out he talked to me he'd probably get fired. He says he's ready to retire anyway. He heard that the police 'raided' — his words — the Tandy cottage and brought Cece and Tiger in. He was furious about that. And he was worried that he may have had something to do with it. He's liked Tiger a lot, ever since Gordon Fairbanks hired him years ago as a 'boat boy,' as he called him. And he thinks he likes Cece, even though he's only really seen her this summer. I take it, he takes his time deciding on his likes and dislikes. Anyway, it was he who told Tardif that Tiger and Cece had been with Gordon that evening. He was in his apartment on the second floor of the old boathouse while you folks were eating your lobsters. He left to go to visit his sister and her husband in Hancock and got back about eleven. He told the police that he noticed that Tiger's Whaler was still at the float on the opposite side from *Sea Chaser.* Now he isn't sure it was the Whaler and he isn't sure if the boat was tied up or just going by. It was dark and his eyesight isn't what it used to be. He said that now he had thought about it, it didn't sound like Tiger's outboard engine. It was a lot quieter. And he now isn't even sure that the boat was close to the float. All he is sure of at this point is that there was a small boat in the vicinity. He hasn't told the police about his doubts yet. He went to bed and right to sleep. But something else bothered him. On his return, he was sure he saw a car without lights on coming out of the Carleton Cottage entrance as he came around the bend of the road. It quickly disappeared and he wondered if he had been seeing things.

"He slept fitfully the rest of the night. He kept wondering about the car. He had a feeling something was wrong. He got up at daybreak as he usually does and he decided to check on Gordon before he got his breakfast. He went down the pier to the float and went aboard *Sea Chaser* where he found Gordon in his bunk. He called his name but he didn't get a response. He went to him and shook him. Gordon felt cold and he knew that he was dead. Harvey's cheeks became wet as he described the scene. He ran back to his apartment and called the Mount Desert PD. The dispatcher told him to go back and stand by the scene and make sure no one got on the boat and that an officer would be there right away. He did as he was told. Chief Jackson and one of his officers were there almost as soon as he was back to the *Sea Chaser*. It was an unattended death. The police now are being very careful whenever a person dies unattended. Harvey spent the morning answering questions, first to the Mount Desert Police Department — the Mount Desert PD — and then the State Police. They insisted that the body be taken to Bangor for an autopsy.

"The reason Harvey called was he wanted me to know that he wasn't sure it was Tiger's Whaler he had seen and heard that night. He wanted to know if he should tell Sergeant Tardif about his doubts and I encouraged him to do so, but to be sure not to imply to him in any way that I'd told him to change his story. He said he wouldn't tell them he had talked to me. I said he shouldn't lie and he laughed. Said it wasn't something he could do."

"I'm trying to think..." Tiger said. " Another small boat near the pier about midnight. Quiet engine...There must be a hundred in the area...My guess is that it was just passing by. There are a lot of young people who like to take a boat ride up the Sound at night. No telling who it was."

"Right," Joe agreed. " It's like looking for the proverbial needle in a hay stack. And that is what they are doing now. They have had a diver searching the bottom near the pier but I don't know what success they have had, if any."

"I wonder why Sergeant Tardif thinks I'm involved?" Cece asked. " Why do you suppose he mentioned to you that he knew I had been flying up here with Gordon every weekend?"

"I got the distinct impression that Tardif thinks you and Gordon were having an affair," Joe answered.

Cece looked at Tiger and said, " Tell them about that visit."

"All right," Tiger said. " Gordon had too much to drink one night and made a visit to Cece's parent's cottage on Long Pond. He didn't know I was there. I came back from a swim just as he came into the bedroom. Cece was naked and Gordon had started to grab her. That's when I stopped him. We decided to take him home...He wasn't fit to drive. I think someone in a nearby cottage called the Mount Desert PD because we met a cruiser heading in that direction going fast with its blue lights flashing as we were going to the Cottage."

"The police have that information, I'm sure," Joe said. " Tardif alluded to a call from a neighbor. He thinks it was more than that...That you could have found out Gordon was involved with Cece and taken revenge."

"No way!" Tiger exclaimed. " It wasn't a big deal. It was exactly as I said."

"Anything more about the merger, Cece?" Dan asked.

"I got a call from Gordon's secretary Saturday morning," Cece told them. "She had been told to call me to make sure I would be in the office tomorrow. She also wanted me to find Kevin Burke and make sure he'd be there, as well."

"I haven't been able to locate Mr. Burke," Joe said.

"I have not seen him, or Sarah Rosen, since the funeral. I called the number at the cottage they were renting in Sawyer's Cove and got no answer," Cece added. " Then Tiger and I went over to the cottage in Sawyer's Cove and it was obvious that they had packed up and left."

"Did Mr. Fairbanks secretary say why they were anxious to have you back to work tomorrow?" Dan asked.

"Yes she did," Cece said reluctantly. " This is between us, okay? I don't think it is privileged. She said that Ralph Ralston called and was very upset. He wanted to be sure that Kevin, Sarah and I would be in the office the next morning. He told her that two investigators from the SEC — Securities and Exchange Commission — had visited him and served a subpoena on him. They then left a list of documents they wanted and a list of questions they wanted answered right away. Ralston had gone back to Torrington right after the funeral and had been told by his people that they were certain the stockholders of both companies would approve the merger. Then out of the blue the investigators from the SEC appeared and left the list of questions. He didn't like what they were asking and he wanted direction from the attorneys. One of the partners at the firm, Melvin Rex, spoke to him and told him to get the answers together but not to give them to the investigators until Mr. Burke reviewed them. He told him he expected him back the day after Labor Day."

"Do you have any idea what the questions were?" Dan asked.

"No. She didn't say. I doubt she knew. I'm sure you know that what we had been working on all summer was not only to finalize the agreement to merge but also was putting together the disclosure material that the SEC requires before the merger can be approved. So most of that is now public information. Every shareholder gets a copy of the disclosure with the request for a proxy giving the shareholder's consent to the merger."

"So they must want something else?"

"Not necessarily," Cece disagreed. " The disclosure has to be completely accurate in every detail. If, for example, accepted accounting principals were not used in the financials — the required financial data — and not disclosed and the SEC learned of it, that could trigger an investigation."

"I know nothing about the stock market," Kara Campbell said. "Can you explain to me again how someone with prior knowledge of a merger can make a profit by buying or selling stock in the company?"

"Sure," Cece said. " Now that it is public knowledge I can use our client's merger as an example. The directors of Northeast Holdings decided they wanted to own ConnTrust, okay? ConnTrust's directors were willing to merge so long as the merger was tax free and they got a good price. After a lot of negotiations, Northeast Holdings offered a one-for-one stock exchange, okay? Northeast's stock was selling on the NASDAQ market at $45 a share when negotiations started and at $47 when the agreement was reached. ConnTrust stock was selling on the NASDAQ Small-cap market at $35 a share when it all started and at $39 a share when the agreement was reached. Bank stocks have been having a run up for the past couple of years, so there was nothing to lead the ordinary investor to believe that a merger between the two was imminent. You can understand that if you had a stock worth $39 a share one day and the next day it was worth $47 a share you've made a nice overnight profit. Of course the resulting stock would probably lose a point or two due to earnings dilution, but you'd still be way ahead."

"I see," Kara said. " So if you knew those facts — especially that Northeast Holdings was going to pay a premium for the ConnTrust shares — you could buy at $39 and sell at $47 making a profit of $8 a share, right?"

"Right," Cece agreed. " Except you'd expect a drop in price due to earnings dilution. That is where selling short would come in."

"That certainly adds another dimension to this case," Joe said. "So far my list of possible motives has been short — real short. Tardif seemed sure that the murder was related to a lover's quarrel and I have been proceeding along the same line. So far that has left me with a lot of possibilities and no answers. Now it seems I need to find out if the merger you were working on is somehow involved with Mr. Fairbanks' murder. That could get real sticky."

"Maybe your friend Tardif is misleading you, Joe," Dan suggested. " Why did he include the items of papers and records of any legal work in his search warrant if he wasn't privy to information along that line?"

"I'll bet that the SEC investigation is known to him," Ian added.

"We certainly need to get to the bottom of that, and soon," Kara agreed.

"Right," Joe agreed. " So Miss Tandy, that settles the question of whether or not you stay here as Tardif suggested. You are not under arrest so you can go back to New York. When you get to see the questions from the SEC they may shed a lot of light on the situation."

"Then I'll go back to New York. Tiger is due back at Tufts Medical School..." Cece started.

"He can go too...so long as we always know where we can find you both on a moments notice, " Ian answered.

It was decided that they would leave immediately for Boston in Tiger's car. Cece would then fly to New York and call Dan as soon as she had any information she thought important. The meeting ended with a host of questions but no answers to any of them. For the first time in his career as a detective, Joe Goldberg found himself involved in a complicated financial investigation and he felt completely adrift.

CHAPTER SEVEN

Tiger was quiet as he drove his battered Ford Bronco down Interstate 95 on the way to Boston late Labor Day afternoon. Traffic was heavier than he had ever seen it. The tires on the old Ford had barely passed inspection nearly a year ago so he stayed well within the speed limit and watched the traffic pass him by. He could see that Cece was still very apprehensive and didn't feel like carrying on a conversation so they drove along in silence. Whatever had caused the police to suspect that she and Tiger were involved with the murder, she knew intuitively, had to be connected with the merger of ConnTrust with Northeast Holdings. But how? There were a great many possibilities, and since she did not have any idea who the players were, let alone what their motives might be, she could only turn them over in her mind, one after the other, all to no avail.

When Cece was packing to leave she had discovered that her IBM lap-top was missing. She had searched the cottage completely. When Tiger arrived from his apartment in Southwest where he had been packing up to leave for the winter, he searched the place again. They then were sure that the police had taken the lap-top when they made their search in the middle of that night, which now seemed like an eternity ago. Cece called Dan to report the missing computer. He told her that he would get a copy of the search team's inventory from the search of the Tandy cottage and confirm whether or not the police had seized the lap-top. Dan wanted to know what was on the hard drive of the lap-top. Cece told him that all the documents of the merger were on it as well as a lot of other legal work. She added that the police didn't have her password so she doubted they could access her work. Dan quickly disabused her of that belief. He told her that the police had access to experts who could find the password quickly and that they undoubtedly had accessed her hard drive already.

"A penny for your thoughts, darling," Tiger said, after they had driven in silence for a long time.

"Oh, I was just thinking about my lap-top. Every document we produced during the long negotiations over the merger is on it.' "

"So?"

"Well, I was trying to think of everything that happened during those long negotiations which caused changes to be made in those documents. What was it that might give the police a clue...one that would lead them to suspect that the merger was somehow involved with Gordon's murder..."

"And?"

"There isn't anything I can think of. I remember asking Gordon if all merger negotiations had as many twists and turns as this one had and he assured me that this one had fewer, if anything."

Tiger had come to understand Cece very well during the few years he had known her. Seldom did she seem to be troubled. When she was, she seemed to go into a cocoon and when that happened it was best not to try to carry on a conversation. He asked no more questions and they returned to their silent ride. By dark they were at Logan Airport in Boston. Tiger tried again to convince Cece to stay with him at their apartment in Medford that night and fly down to New York in the morning, but Cece wanted to be able to be in Fairbanks & Burke's office as early in the morning as she could. She said she was hoping to arrive before any of the lawyers who had worked on the merger with Gordon, because there was something she wanted to check out. She bought her ticket on the shuttle, gave him a passionate kiss and ran to catch the plane. Tiger was a natural optimist. He hardly knew the meaning of the word worry. But seeing the tears in her eyes as she ran to catch the shuttle made his stomach churn. He hated to see her so upset. Then the thought struck him — if somehow he lost Cece, his life wouldn't be worth living.

After a sleepless night, Cece arrived at the offices of Fairbanks & Burke about 5 a.m. She found that she was the only lawyer there. She went immediately to Gordon's office and tried her key. The door was locked and her key wouldn't open it. There was a sign scotch-taped to it stating simply 'No Admittance.' She next went to her own office. Her door also had a 'No Admittance' sign taped to it. She tried her key and it too failed.

Cece was now sure that the police had something factual that tied the merger the firm had been working on to Gordon's murder. And she knew that she was a prime suspect. She went back to the elevator and down two flights to the firm's main entrance, hoping to find someone there.

Her entrance key had worked on the top floor so she wasn't surprised that it still worked here. She let herself in and was quickly joined by the night security guard. Even though Cece had seen the man often when she came in early, he still demanded to see her Fairbanks & Burke identification. After he read her name, he told her he'd been instructed to tell her that her office had been secured and that she should use another office which had been assigned to her. He led her to an office in the section where the paralegals worked, opened it and gave her a key tagged with her name and then left.

Cece went in and sat at the small desk where she tried to collect her thoughts. She wanted to call Dan Hardy but remembered that the firm's telephone system would automatically make a record of the call. She then realized that all her personal things had been placed in the small room. She went to her file cabinet and started looking through it for her files. There were only a few. She had been working for several months only on the ConnTrust merger but none of her files on it were there. Cece then sat down at the computer and booted it up. She searched for her ConnTrust files on its hard drive. There were none. They obviously had been deleted. Then she tried to access the firm's main- frame in an attempt to retrieve the ConnTrust files from it but, either the main-frame had not been booted up after the long weekend or her computer wasn't connected to it. She had left the office open and suddenly she realized that someone was walking down the hall.

"Cece? " a voice asked.

She turned to see Kevin Burke standing there.

"Yes...Well, good morning sir," she greeted him.

"Cece, please ...Why can't you just call me by my name?" Kevin said, his face full of his handsome Irish smile.

"Good morning, Kevin," she smiled back.

Kevin put his finger to his lips, took a pencil from her desk, wrote something on a note pad and handed it to her. 'Don't talk — office bugged.' she read.

"Have you had breakfast?" Kevin asked.

"No, not even coffee," Cece answered.

"I'm on my way down to the street — care to join me?"

"I'd love too."

They left the office, closing the door behind them, walked to the elevator and went down to the street floor without speaking. Kevin led them to a coffee shop over on Fifth Avenue where he was sure they would not be seen by others from the office on their way to work. They found a booth in the back. A waitress appeared shortly and they ordered.

"I'm glad you are here," Cece told Kevin. " I had a call from Gordon's secretary at my folk's cottage Saturday morning telling me that Melvin Rex wanted me to be sure to be back this morning. She also asked me to find you and give you the same message. She said she'd been calling the number for the cottage you were renting in Sawyer's Cove and hadn't gotten an answer. Tiger and I also went over there but there was no sign of life."

"Sarah and I left soon after we arrived at the Carleton Cottage for the brunch following the funeral. She was terribly upset. She didn't want to talk to Beth. All she wanted to do was to leave the Island. Our summer's rent was up in a couple of days anyway. We decided we'd drive up to Saint Andrews in New Brunswick and stay at the Algonquin Hotel until Labor Day and then drive back to New York that day," Kevin explained.

"So you don't know what happened to Tiger and me Saturday night?" she asked.

"No. What happened?"

"Tiger and I were at my folks cottage on Long Pond. In the middle of the night the Maine State Police burst in on us. Said they had a search warrant. They took my lap-top. The warrant allowed a search for any papers about the ConnTrust merger but I didn't think that would include my computer."

"My God! I didn't realize it had gone that far so quickly."

"The police tried to question us. I guess it was about Gordon's death. I'm not sure. They never got very far."

"Why?"

"By then we knew Gordon had been murdered and I wasn't about to answer any questions without a lawyer."

"You found out for certain that Gordon was murdered ?"

"Well, the police are sure he was murdered and that was the reason they gave for breaking into my folks' cottage on Long Pond."

"So you got a lawyer..."

"Right. I called my folks' lawyer in Southwest Harbor. Dan Hardy is his name. Mr. Hardy came immediately up to the jail in Ellsworth where they had taken us. Apparently they knew that they didn't have a basis to arrest us and they let us go."

Cece stopped and looked at Burke directly and said, " Kevin — we had nothing to do with Gordon's death."

"Cece, I believe you. But what in the hell is going on?"

"You know as much as I do. Probably more. Why do you think that office was bugged?"

"I talked with Melvin last night when I got back to New York. There was a message on my answering machine saying it was urgent, and for me to call him when I got back...no matter what time it was, he said. I called him and he immediately said we needed to meet right then. I asked why and he said 'Can't talk now. Meet me at our usual lunch place' and he hung up.

"I met Melvin about a half hour later. I've never seen him so upset. He said that he and his wife had planned to spend a few days in Maine after the funeral but he got a call from his secretary at their motel saying the firm needed him back in New York. He flew back that afternoon. Investigators from the SEC had been at the office that day demanding to see the records of the ConnTrust — Northeast Holdings merger. They had a search warrant from the Federal District Court. The next morning the SEC people were joined by agents from the FBI..."

"The FBI? I don't understand..." Cece interrupted.

"Melvin says they wouldn't talk to anyone at the firm, but he has figured out that the FBI must be in on it under the RICO law."

"RICO?" Cece asked.

"Racketeer Influenced and Corrupt Organizations Act."

"Yes, I know. Melvin thinks RICO can be used in this situation? "

"He thinks so. They are using it more and more in cases where they can prove that the company itself was involved in defrauding consumers...investors...whatever."

"Okay. Go on, please."

"By the second day they had copies of everything the firm had. In the meantime, Ralph Ralston was calling every half hour, totally out of it. 'Why didn't my office know where I was? His office was being 'raided' and he wanted to know what the hell was going on. He'd hired us on our reputation for doing things right. What the hell had gone wrong?' And on and on. Melvin ended up not taking his calls."

"So what do they think went wrong?"

"That's what Melvin wanted to know. I'll tell you the same thing I told him — I haven't a clue. And that, young lady is the truth."

"Where do we go from here? What's next?" Cece asked.

"Knowing your work habits, I knew you'd be in the office early today, so I came in hoping to get some ideas from you."

"Kevin, even though you came in on this merger late, I'm sure you know everything I know about it."

"Fair enough, Cece. But Gordon seemed not himself that last week when we were all in Maine waiting for the news of the merger to be released. Something was bothering him — something bad enough so he was unable to hide it like he usually could."

"You noticed that too?"

"I thought he might have said something to you. I know he trusted you completely."

"Well, I think he started to. I had gone to Carleton Cottage early that last day. Gordon wanted to fix us eggs Benedict. He loved to cook breakfast, you know..."

"Especially for you..."

Cece blushed and went on, " We had finished breakfast and were cleaning up. He seemed nervous...said he'd been up most of the night going over the final disclosure materials on the merger. We finished cleaning up and Gordon poured himself another coffee and we sat on the porch waiting for everyone to arrive. He was in deep thought for a while and then he turned to me and said ' Cece, there is something you should know... in case I'm not around...' That got me on the edge of my seat. Just then Ralph Ralston came up the steps. Said he'd rung the front bell but when no one answered he came around back. Gordon never had a chance to finish what he was about to tell me. I haven't told anyone about it, but I've been wondering about it ever since."

Kevin thought about what Cece had said for a minute or two and then said, " I'll bet the clue to what he was about to tell you is somewhere in those disclosure papers. We've got our work cut out for us. We've got to go over them carefully and find it."

They talked for a while longer discussing their strategy. They decided that until they had more information they would keep what they had just talked about completely to themselves. They would go back to the office separately. Cece first and then Kevin would follow in ten minutes or so. A meeting of the firm's executive committee was scheduled for 8 a.m. Kevin should learn something at that meeting. He had an appointment with Ralph Ralston at ten a.m. and he was sure he'd be given ConnTrust's spin on the matter. They would meet at Cece's apartment that evening at seven p.m. Until then they would keep their mouths shut and their ears open.

The meeting with Kevin had a calming effect on Cece. Clearly he trusted her and she trusted him as well. That was the best news she had in days. Still, she knew her problems were far from being solved.

CHAPTER EIGHT

Tiger Wass was no stranger to flying. He had been with a Marine Medevac team from the time he had graduated from the Navy hospitalman school he had been sent to after he completed his Navy boot training. He had been in the air often after that. Yet his head was full of worry as he watched the shuttle to New York take off from Logan, climb steeply up from the runway and disappear into the clouds. He wasn't worried about Cece being aboard the jet. Tiger knew that flying was safer than any other mode of travel. It was a worry engendered by her mood on their trip down from Maine that afternoon. Until then, he hadn't been inordinately upset by the events of the past week and a half. He had never been a worrier. He had a simple faith that problems in life would work themselves out, given time. Tiger still felt sure that Sergeant Tardif and his crew would soon learn that they were barking up the wrong tree and they would look back on these days in later years with some amusement. It was comforting for him to know that neither of them had any involvement with Gordon's death. Yet, because Cece was so worried about the situation, he now had second thoughts. There had to be another problem to cause her that worry, but what it was he had no idea.

As Tiger pulled the last bag of luggage out of the back of his Bronco he noticed in the dim light a canvas boat bag partially hidden behind the spare tire. It took a moment for him to remember how it came to be there. The State Police had released *Sea Chaser* from their custody the previous Saturday and Andy called him from New York with the request that he take her to Hinckley's yard for her winter's storage. As he motored over to Southwest Harbor from Northeast Harbor, he remembered that he needed to make a final check of the boat to make sure Harvey Lunt had removed all of Gordon's things.

After he had secured *Sea Chaser* to the inner Hinckley dock he began a thorough check of the boat. The task was quickly completed. Apparently Harvey had done his work well. Then Tiger remembered the secret storage compartment he had installed at Gordon's request soon after the boat was built. Gordon wanted a place he could safely store the Ruger P85 pistol he kept on board, as well as a supply of cash for emergencies, so Tiger built a small compartment under the storage cabinet in the forward head. The front of the compartment was built to look like a solid bulkhead. The small front piece was released by a button hidden well back on the top of the cabinet. Tiger pushed the release button and opened the compartment. There was the P85, a wad of bills in an elastic band and under them he recognized Gordon's lap-top. He left the P85 where it was but took the rest out. Then for some reason, he opened the lap-top and saw a manila envelope with a note on the outside. He read the note, put the envelope back in the lap-top's case, packed it and the money in his backpack, carried it off the boat with him and put it in the back of the Bronco. He had intended to have Cece deliver the cash, lap-top and the envelope to Andy when she returned to the Fairbanks office the next day. With all that happened that day it was no wonder that he had forgotten about them. He took the bag up to his apartment with his last load.

After Tiger stored the left-over food from the Southwest apartment in the refrigerator, turned it on, plugged in the TV, put the travel bags in the bedroom and the apartment more or less squared away, he called Cece's apartment hoping she had arrived safely. She had. She told him that she missed him terribly already and wished she had agreed to his request and stayed in Boston for the night. They were both exhausted from the events of the day so the talk was short, ending with an exchange of love and a promise of a call the next evening. Tiger went to bed and directly to sleep.

Tiger awoke with a start at daybreak. He had remembered what it was that he wanted to tell Cece when they talked the previous evening — that he had found Gordon's lap-top on *Sea Chaser*. He wondered what was in the envelope that was so important that Gordon had hidden it in the secret compartment on the boat. He got up, found the canvas bag, took it to the kitchen table and sat for a time thinking what he should do. He examined the envelope and found that it was not sealed. It was simply held closed by the clasp. He again read the note which had been scotch taped to the outside of the lap-top. He recognized Gordon's bold printing:

WHOEVER FINDS THIS:
PLEASE DELIVER IT TO MY ASSOCIATE
CECE TANDY

Gordon Fairbanks

Tiger's first impulse was to call Cece and tell her what he had found and ask her permission to look inside the envelope. When he had thought about that for a moment he decided that he wanted to know its contents before he talked to her. If it contained bad news, he'd be able to decide how best to tell her. He opened the clasp, took the contents out in order and laid them on the table. He read the first one. It was a typewritten letter to Cece.

"Dear Cece,
        By the time you see these papers you may know all the details in them. If you don't, use them as you feel necessary. I have complete faith and trust in you,
        If you know the details and these papers in your judgment are unnecessary, please destroy them.
        Keep the lap-top.
                                I love you.
                                Gordon."

The next page was a photocopy of a typewritten letter. There was no date or heading.
        He read:

"Dear Ralph,
        I feel the need to memorialize our private conversation of Tuesday last.
        At that time the problems of the merger seemed to be solved. You had been insisting that the merger use the 'pooling accounting' method. You took the position that you would not be able to sell a major portion of your stock in the combined company for two years under APB 16 and the SEC rules. Northeast insisted that the 'purchase accounting' method be used because it wanted to avoid accounting for

goodwill.

In explaining why you agreed to Northeast's requirement you told me that you have a promise in writing from
John Gropus, Northeast's president that he will arrange to
buy your stock at the expected increased price and pay for it
soon after the merger is complete but that he would delay the
actual transfer of the stock on the company's books for two
years.

I told you then that you must not do that. First, it is
wrong because it is unfair to the other stockholders. Second,
it is illegal. If the SEC learns about the arrangement you will
go to jail for a long time.

I will keep a copy of this advice privately.

Gordon
Gordon Fairbanks, Esq."
Attorney for ConnTrust

Tiger was mystified by the legalese in the letter but he certainly
understood Gordon's advice to his client. He eagerly turned the page
over and went to the next one. It was an original, but again there was
no date or heading. It read:

"Gordon,

I have your last. Destroy any copy you made. Forget
what I told you. I never said it. Destroy this.
Ralph

That was clear enough. Tiger went on to the next page. It was a
photocopy. It read:

"Dear Ralph.

I must assume that you are not taking my advice with
respect to the private agreement you told me about last
month. Regardless of your last direction to me, I won't forget and I insist you do what I directed.

It is obvious I have failed to make you understand the

risk you run. I find it necessary to write to you privately even though I write as corporate counsel. I know it is difficult for a non-lawyer to understand the distinction but I must tell you again that Fairbanks & Burke represent ConnTrust — not Ralph Ralston. I write to you in that capacity.

I have been told by a reliable source in ConnTrust that you are purchasing sizable amounts of ConnTrust stock and 'parking' it. I am also told that you have not filed the required Schedule 13[d] with the SEC.

Since we have discussed the matter on prior occasions, I feel sure you know what you are doing is illegal and that you could end up in jail as did Ivan Boesky.

Be advised that if we at Fairbanks & Burke are not advised that you will make the required filings and abide by the law, we will have no recourse but to withdraw as counsel and report the matter to the SEC.

I will keep a copy of this advice.

> *Gordon*
> Gordon Fairbanks Esq.
> Attorney for ConnTrust "

Again the legalese escaped Tiger but he well understood that the president of ConnTrust was apparently engaged in an activity that was illegal. He turned the page over and went on to the next. It was type-written and again it was an original. It read:

"Gordon,

I insist that you refrain from talking to anyone at ConnTrust other than myself. I want you to destroy all copies of your 'private advice' to me. It is not welcome and I will not tolerate any more of it.

As you are well aware, the merger is something I have been working on for years and it must go forward. Barring unforeseen circumstances, it will be accomplished in a couple of weeks. The parties are so small in the banking industry there should not be any problems. Your firm has finalized the disclosure documents for us and Northeast's are ready.

You will not go to the SEC for two reasons.

The first is that your lady friend, Sarah Rosen, has apparently told the trustee of the trust her father set up for her about the merger and he has purchased a significant amount of our stock for that trust and for his own account.

Secondly, your associate Cece Tandy's father, Wexford Tandy has been buying ConnTrust stock in large amounts. Some for his clients accounts and a lot for himself. I'm sure you see the implications, especially on the second matter. If either comes to light, Fairbanks & Burke is in trouble.

Shall we go to jail together? Don't think for a minute that I won't bring you down with me if you go to the SEC.

I know you will want to destroy this.

Ralph "

Tiger had read enough about the problems created by insider trading for people like Ivan Boesky and Michael Milken to know that the package of letters he had just read suggested that the president of ConnTrust had been engaging in activities which were illegal and serious enough to send him to jail for a long stay.

As he thought about it some more, it became obvious that Ralston had a real motive for murdering Gordon. Ralston was with Gordon when they left *Sea Chaser* the night he died. He knew he had to talk to Cece right then. He dialed her apartment but eventually after four rings he got her answering machine. He left a message for her to call back. He thought about calling her office but for a reason he couldn't explain, he decided it wasn't a good idea. He'd have to wait until Cece called him back.

$\mathcal{C}$HAPTER $\mathcal{N}$INE

$\mathcal{C}$ece's day did not go well. Her intellect told her that the police would soon learn that neither she nor Tiger was involved with Gordon's death, but her intuition told her that the situation they were in would only get worse. Kevin asked her to spend the day going over the disclosure materials the firm had prepared for the merger of ConnTrust in a final effort to determine if anything was astray. When she told him that her computer access to those materials was not available to her in her 'new' office, he took her to his secretary's office where there was an additional work station connected to the firm's mainframe. Cece spent the day doing as he had directed. It was after 6 p.m. before she was finally satisfied she could find nothing wrong in the work the firm had done for the disclosure. She cross-checked and found that everything in the printed materials was backed up by the information given to the firm by Ralph Ralston.

The answering machine was beeping when Cece arrived at her apartment around 6:30 p.m. It was Tiger. She punched the auto-dial number for Tiger's apartment but he didn't answer so she left a message for him to call her. He would be at the medical school library where he usually studied. Cece knew it would be late when he returned the call.

Kevin arrived at Cece's apartment a little before 7 p.m. looking very distraught. As Cece invited him in, he tried to put on his usual happy face but it didn't fool Cece. Without his asking, she poured Kevin a double shot of Bushmills on the rocks. She had observed at Carleton Cottage that he was very fond of Bushmills and had gotten a bottle for just such an occasion. After she poured herself a glass of Chardonnay from the bottle in the fridge, they went into her small living room and sat opposite each other in the only overstuffed chairs. Cece waited expectantly for Kevin to speak.

"Cece, this was not a good day ," he began. " My meeting with Ralph Ralston was like a high stakes poker game. I still can't believe it happened."

"A poker game?" Cece asked.

"Yes, a poker game," Kevin assured her. " As you know, Joyce, my secretary, brought Ralston into my office soon after I gave you your day's task. I'm sure he saw you because the first thing he said was 'Make sure we are not interrupted by anyone and I mean anyone.' No 'Hello Kevin,' no greeting of any kind, just the order. I nodded to Joyce and she left. He sat down and asked why Miss Tandy was 'out front.' I told him you were working on a project for me. I asked if he wanted me to have you come in. He quickly said that was the last thing he wanted. Then he demanded to know why the SEC investigators had served the subpoena on him the day after the merger was announced. I told him I didn't know but if I had a copy of it, I might be able to shed some light on the situation. He quickly produced a copy from his briefcase. I took my time reading it, waiting for a comment from him. I've never known him to be silent for any length of time but he just sat there staring at me.

"The subpoena was an order that he or any senior officer of ConnTrust had toproduce a three page list of documents and within ten days deliver them to the SEC. Using a broad brush, it demanded documents for many different aspects of the merger. It was soon obvious that the investigators were attempting to conceal the real thrust of their investigation, but two items really caught my attention. They were a demand for a list of every stockholder who held more than one percent of ConnTrust stock. Then it requested the dates of acquisition of those shares. As you know, the threshold for most disclosures is a three percent stock holding.

"I laid the papers down and looked at Ralston. Then I asked him if he had any thoughts about the matter. He said he did but they were his thoughts and he would make them known when and if he thought it wise. Then he told me I had not answered his question. I hate arrogance from any source and he had me ready to fight. I told him that there was no way of telling what they were after because the demand included so many aspects of the merger. Then I told him that I was sure of one thing — that if there was a problem it wasn't created by Fairbanks & Burke.

"He leaned forward in his chair and stared at me and said, ' Don't be too sure of that Kevin.' 'Okay,' I said. ' Tell me why you say that.' He said it wasn't the time to disclose that to me. I was ready to show him the door but I knew I had to find out what he was holding back and the only way I could see to do that was to play along with him. Then he said he wanted to go over the list of documents the SEC requested one at a time and discuss in detail any implication that might come from it. You can understand that took the better part of the day."

"Did he mention me again?" Cece asked.

"Yes he did, right at the end of our meeting. He asked me if I were aware that you had been arrested. I told him truthfully I wasn't aware that you had been arrested. Then he said you had been... that your cottage in Maine had been searched and the Maine police were convinced that you and your boyfriend, Tiger, had murdered Gordon.

"I said I doubted that could be possible. I asked him what would have been your motive and he said that your father had been buying significant amounts of ConnTrust stock over the past several months. I asked him if he thought you were involved and he said the answer was obvious. That finally got to me and before I had a chance to tell him that the firm no longer wished to represent ConnTrust he handed me a letter dismissing us as counsel. I read it and thanked him for saving me the trouble of withdrawing. He grabbed his papers and stormed out of my office. Thank God Joyce has the entire meeting on tape."

"Oh my God, Kevin ! Ralston really thinks I — we murdered Gordon," Cece exclaimed. " I had no idea my father was buying ConnTrust stock, but I don't doubt he was. Obviously Ralston was suggesting to you that the police knew about it and that is why we are suspects. Where did he get his information? As far as I know there was nothing about the search at Long Pond in the papers. I'll bet he knows more than he told you."

"I agree. But if your dad was buying stock in ConnTrust it makes a plausible theory...assuming he was acting on advice from you."

"Well, he's wrong — dead wrong!"

"I want to believe that. Cece — is there something there though? Could you have inadvertently said something to you father — or anyone else who might have understood that there was a merger of ConnTrust in the offing? Your father's a stock broker, isn't he?"

Cece jumped up from her chair and went to stand in front of Kevin so she could look him directly in the eyes.

"Kevin — I swear to you that I have not mentioned, inadvertently or otherwise, the merger to anyone," Cece said firmly. " I will take a lie detector test if you like."

"Cece, I believe you — but I had to ask."

"My father's firm has a seat on the New York Stock Exchange and the NASDAQ. He's registered. He specializes in bank stocks. He's done well with them. He knows the banking business and he buys stock in ones which he thinks will be bought out. Buys for himself and his customers."

"But it would have to have been in significant amounts to get the SEC's attention," Kevin pointed out.

"True. He's done well enough to buy significant amounts of stock in ones he is sure will be targets for take-overs. He bought a large amount of People's Heritage stock when it went down to $3 and everyone thought it was going belly up like Maine Savings. He made a bundle on that alone. He could have bought a large amount of ConnTrust if he thought it was going to appreciate significantly, even if he didn't think there was merger in the offing."

"Makes sense. But how would Ralston know your dad's name?"

"He knew his name and the firm's name too. We were talking during a break right after the first time we met. He asked about my family. You know how people do when they first meet, just getting acquainted. I remember how interested he was when I told him my father was broker. He wanted the details — said he always wanted to get into that work. Did you know he was a doctor — medical doctor — before he became president of ConnTrust?" Cece asked.

"Oh yes. It was something he is very proud of. That is where he got the money to buy his ConnTrust stock to start with. He got himself appointed to its board of directors years ago and bought all the stock he could. The banking business always fascinated him. He told me that after ten years of general practice and the limited income from it, he had the choice of going back to medical school and becoming a specialist or changing the direction of his life. He was going through what he called a nasty divorce at the time and it was an easy decision for him."

"How did he keep the stock after the divorce?"

"On one of the sails we had on Gordon's boat he and I had a long talk and I asked him the same question. He said it was easy. He knew his marriage was going down. His wife caught him 'in the act' with his nurse. She made him fire the nurse and that really cost him. They stayed together for a couple of years and she caught him again with another woman. He blamed it all on his wife — said she was frigid, scared to have any more children, the son they had was enough trouble. Anyway, she divorced him and he felt justified in not disclosing the stock ownership. He said her dumb lawyer didn't follow up on the answers he gave on the divorce interrogatories. He told me he's still paying her plenty."

"Sounds like he was proud of it."

"I got that impression too. He'd had a couple of stiff Manhattans with lunch and his tongue was loose. His eyes were on you all the time we talked. Every time you changed your mat to be in the sun, he'd change his position so he could still see you. He asked me if Gordon was sleeping with you and I told him I doubted it. He said Gordon's crazy if he wasn't."

"That's so gross..."

"I've come to know Ralph Ralston very well in the past six months. We spent many evenings together while he was in the city working on the merger with us. At first he didn't let me see the other side of him — always the staid conservative banker type — always politically correct. Then one night after we had a long tiring day, he had several Manhattans and I got to see the other side of him. Underneath his facade, he is really a crude individual. He told me that he grew up desperately poor. His father had deserted his mother when he was a baby. He soon found that he was smarter than the rest of his friends and he made up his mind he was going to be rich. He knew that doctors made a lot of money and he became one only to learn there was a lot more money to be made in business. Along the way he developed a penchant for young women, something he still has. He thought that since I was now single that I should be able to help him find a 'safe' young woman in the city. He was very upset when he learned that I couldn't...or wouldn't. The thing that I was most surprised about was his willingness to break the law. Towards the end of the battle with Northeast Trust he told me he had hired the wrong law firm. He said he should have gotten one which wasn't so tied to doing things according to the rules."

"A real Doctor Jekyll and Mr. Hyde..."

"In spades!"

They talked about the next move. Kevin said that he couldn't see anything they could do but wait and see what came up. Ralston would soon have new counsel, if he didn't have already, and he was sure that they would be hearing from the new lawyers right away. In the meantime the trial lawyers in Fairbanks & Burke had a date with the SEC lawyers in the morning and he was hopeful that they would be able to learn what was going on. Kevin asked Cece to be in early so they could review the rest of the files on the merger and try to discover any problem that the firm might have created outside of the disclosure. He said he was sure it was a fruitless task but it had to be done just in case. Then he told her that he appreciated how she was standing up under the whole mess, bid her good night and took his leave. It was then 9 p.m. Cece punched the auto-dial for Tiger hoping he had returned to his apartment.

All that day Tiger had been turning over in his mind what he should do with the contents of the envelope he had read that morning. He knew that the letters would upset Cece terribly, but he knew she had to be told about them. He had counted the cash — twelve hundred dollars in large bills. He wanted to get it to Andy but he was worried about answering the questions Andy was sure to ask. When he first entered medical school Gordon paid the portion of his tuition at Tufts that wasn't covered by his grants. Gordon continued to do that each year, telling Tiger that he'd keep track of it and some day 'when he was a rich doctor' he could pay it back. When Tiger first went to work for Gordon as his 'boat boy' he slept on Gordon's boat. That was when he had been a student at UMO, seven years ago. By the time *Sea Chaser* was first launched, Harvey Lunt had moved into the boat house where he could watch the boat. Gordon decided it was asking too much of Tiger to require him to sleep aboard. He began to pay the rent for his summer apartment at that time. What Gordon was doing for him always bothered Tiger — until Cece told him that Gordon was earning upwards of two million dollars a year. After mulling it over all day, Tiger decided that he would add the twelve hundred dollars to the account he was keeping of what he owed Gordon and pay it back when he paid the rest of the debt which he assumed was now owed to Gordon's estate.

The decision as to what to do about the letters was harder to reach. Tiger didn't want to talk about them on the phone. He wanted to wait until Cece could read them herself. But he made a habit of never missing a class and he didn't want to take a day and drive to New York. He was still full of indecision when Cece called.

After she told him that she loved him and missed him, Cece told Tiger about the conversation she had with Kevin. Her memory had always been excellent and she was able to repeat the conversation almost verbatim. When she came to the part about her father and whether she might have 'inadvertently' mentioned the ConnTrust merger to him, Tiger knew he had to tell Cece about the letters right then. He didn't want her blindsided in any future conversations with Kevin who now seemed to be her mentor.

When Cece had finished relating the conversation, she asked Tiger, " What do you make of all that?"

"Darling, I'm not a lawyer so the legal stuff is beyond me. But what Mr. Burke told you concerning your dad I understand...wait a minute while I get something."

Tiger put the phone down and retrieved the envelope and took out the letters. Picking the phone up, he told Cece about the secret compartment Gordon had asked him to build on *Sea Chaser* and that he remembered it when he was bringing her to the Hinckley dock for winter storage. He told her what he found when he opened it up. Cece said she wanted him to read the letters to her right then. At that point she didn't care if the SEC investigators might have her telephone tapped.

Tiger read each letter to her in the sequence he had found them. When he had finished there was a long silence on Cece's end of the line and then she asked him to read the letters to her again. When he had finished reading the letters the second time, Cece told him that she had to think about what to do with them. Her initial reaction was that she should have them in New York because she had to show them to Kevin Burke.

"I think you should give that a lot of thought, darling," Tiger said. " First of all, Gordon wanted you to have them — not the firm. How much do you trust Kevin Burke? Suppose he is setting you up somehow."

"Tiger, I've gotten to know Kevin pretty well this summer... and I trust him completely. He's too honest...too sweet to set me up. I'm sure of that."

"Okay, darling. But there are some very weird things going on.

Weird...my God! Someone murdered Gordon and the police suspect us. They have some information that they used to get the search warrant of your folks' cottage at Long Pond. They were specifically looking for papers about the merger. Now Ralston tells Kevin — or at least implies — that you gave your father information about the merger and he bought stock in ConnTrust on the strength of it..."

"And then we murdered Gordon to protect my dad," Cece broke in. " I don't see how that connects."

"If someone were setting you up it might. Cece, I don't think we should discuss this any further on the phone...okay?"

"Okay, I agree. I know one thing though, we have to discuss these new events with our lawyers. I'm going to arrange a meeting with them Saturday. I'll take the 6 o'clock shuttle to Logan Friday night. Can we drive up to Maine early Saturday morning?"

"Can if my Bronco is still running, darling."

"Tiger we have to have a reliable car. We can afford one. Kevin just gave me my annual raise and, after two years here full time, it's a good one. I want you to find us a new four-wheel drive vehicle and I'll arrange the financing."

"But Cece..."

Tiger knew there was no sense in arguing with her and just the thought of a new Ford Bronco got him out of the funk he had been in. He agreed to shop around and call her to make the arrangements when he had found something. He hated the thought that Cece had to be the one to sign the papers but he had to be satisfied with the knowledge that it would not always be that way.

The happy thought of a new vehicle lasted only a moment. It was quickly replaced by worries which now seemed to have a base. Cece's agreement that her father could well have been trading in ConnTrust stock worried him. That Ralston knew about the trading worried him. It didn't seem likely that Ralston had gone to the police with the information, but it was possible. It may have been part of a scheme to cover up his involvement. Or, it could all be a bunch of lies. Tiger slept little that night.

CHAPTER TEN

During the noon break between his Wednesday classes, Tiger called the Ford dealer in Kittery. He wasn't sure what kind of a hassle it would be to buy the new Bronco in Massachusetts and register it in Maine, but he didn't want to face it. The only argument — serious discussion was probably a better word — he and Cece had when they were planning to get married, was where they would live. Tiger had never thought that he could live anywhere except on the Maine coast. Cece had begun to realize that she didn't want her children to grow up in or near New York City — or Portland or any large city for that matter— so it really wasn't an argument. They decided that when Tiger had his MD they would move back to Maine. That depended on his ability to complete his internship at a hospital there. He wanted a family practice specialty and that had to be considered as well. The bottom line was that they would find a town on the Maine coast where they both could work.

The salesman who answered the call told Tiger that the new models were in but, that she had two of last years' Broncos on the lot and she could give him a real good deal on either of them. With the manufacturer's rebate and the dealer' discount, either one could be purchased below the dealer's cost. Tiger told the woman that he'd be in Kittery shortly after 5 p.m. The saleslady agreed to wait for him and not to worry if he got caught in traffic. He called Cece at her office to report. She told him she'd be in the office until 7 p.m., and if he struck a deal to call her. Cece told him she hoped the dealer would accept her Visa Gold card to hold the vehicle until she could be there to sign the paperwork.

Tiger found that one of the Broncos was black and the other a dark green — otherwise they both had the same equipment and the same price tag. After a short hassle, he was offered $1500 for his old Bronco. He was convinced he couldn't do any better and called Cece who quickly agreed. She wanted the green and he the black. They settled on the green since it was going to be she who paid for it. The dealer was willing to take Cece's Visa credit card for the down payment and insisted that Tiger take the car back to Medford. She'd have the paperwork ready when he and Cece came back Saturday morning to finalize the deal. Tiger had a hard time believing how much improved the new Bronco was over his 11 year old model and his trip back to Medford was one of joy.

On Friday evening, Tiger drove to Logan to pick up his wife. As he drove back to the apartment, he demonstrated all the new gadgets on the new vehicle. Cece could have cared less, but she was happy Tiger was so taken with it. They carried Cece's bags up the three flights to their apartment on the run and as soon as they were both inside, without saying a word, they went directly to the small bathroom. In a moment both were undressed and in the shower, laughing as they soaped each other in the cramped space. When neither could wait any longer they toweled each other and jumped into bed where they quickly completed their joyful reunion. After their vigorous encounter ended in mutually satisfying release, Tiger went right to sleep. Cece lay awake thinking how lucky she was to have found Tiger for her husband.

Her mind wandered back to the first time she had seen Tiger. It was that day in August after her summer working at Fairbanks & Burke when Gordon learned she would be at her parents cottage and had invited her over to Northeast Harbor for a sail. Gordon told her that his son, Andy, would be with them. She sensed that was supposed to be an inducement. She had seen Andy often at the office but had never officially met him. The young women lawyers at Fairbanks & Burke were always talking about him and what a great catch he'd be for one of them. It made Cece sick to realize that those women were so determined to reach the top of their profession that they were willing to marry the senior partner's son to get there. It was something she was sure she wouldn't do. Still she was eager to accept Gordon's invitation. She would take it a step at a time.

By late August Tiger was bronze from the sun and sea. He was a big man, at least six two, very broad shoulders, a narrow waist. His hair was so short that it had the appearance of being shaved Marine style, but what there was of it was blond. His face was square and rugged, yet the dimple in his chin and his deep blue eyes which seemed always to twinkle, told her he wasn't so tough. She was fascinated with his grace as he moved around the deck tending sheets, anticipating Gordon's every move. It was as if he was a part of *Sea Chaser*.

After that day's sail, Tiger walked back up the pier with Cece, carrying the canvas tote bags, now containing plastic bags of trash. It was the first time they had had a chance to talk to each other alone. His voice was pleasingly low, his smile irresistible, his presence commanding. He started the conversation by teasing her about something she could not now remember. But remembering the day, Cece realized that she had been captivated by the young man the very first time she met him. There was no comparison between him and Andy Fairbanks. She didn't know it at the time, but the fascination was mutual.

They left for Maine the next morning in time to arrive at the Ford dealer's when it opened up at 7 a.m. As promised, the paperwork had been filled out. In a matter of minutes the papers were signed and they were again on their way. Traffic was heavy with cars flowing into Maine for the weekend so they went by way of the turnpike to Augusta, then the shortcut over to Belfast, then to Ellsworth and down to the Island. They were in Southwest Harbor by 1 p.m. and in Ian Campbell's office at the appointed time.

Dan Hardy, Ian and Kara Campbell, and Joe Goldberg were in the conference room waiting for them. Joe was finishing a sub sandwich so Cece began by telling them what had been going on in the offices of Fairbanks & Burke. She reported that the two days she and Kevin had spent going over the merger materials had confirmed their belief that there was nothing in the disclosure filings with the SEC which would prompt an investigation.

Then she asked if she could make copies of the contents of the envelope Tiger had found. Kara Campbell said she would do it and left for the secretary's office. While that was being done, Tiger told them how he had come by the envelope, the cash and Gordon's lap-top. He told them his current plan for the cash and asked if they approved. They didn't. They told him that in the near future it would have to be turned over to the personal representative of Gordon's estate. Then he asked about the lap-top. That prompted more discussion. Everyone agreed they would like to know what was on its hard drive. By then Kara had copies made and the discussion stopped so they could be read.

When they all had digested the letters, Joe said, " I am now pretty much convinced that the motive for Mr. Fairbanks' murder is some-how connected to the bank merger. Sergeant Tardif could be on a wild goose chase looking for a lover's quarrel motive and I'm sorry to say that is the lead I've been following. As of now I'm changing the direc-tion of my investigation."

"Cece, have you told your dad about Mr. Ralston's charge that on a tip from you he has been buying ConnTrust stock in large amounts ?" Dan asked.

"No, I haven't," Cece answered. "Tiger and I decided that we wouldn't talk to anyone about the case, nor tell anyone about his find-ing the copies of the letters until we had spoken to all of you."

"No one at Fairbanks & Burke either?"

"No...no one. And that bothers me. I wanted desperately to tell Kevin."

Dan again read his copy of the letter to Cece.

"Well, it is clear that Gordon wanted you to have the letters and he gave you authority to do with them as you saw fit," Dan told her.

"I know that," she agreed. " But he also expected me to do what is right. I'm worried about three things. First, I don't want my father dragged into this. Second, I...we all want Gordon's murder solved. Third, I don't want Gordon's firm destroyed by the likes of Ralph Ralston. I think the letters should be shown to Kevin at least, but I real-ly don't know what to do."

"Let's take your worries one by one," Dan said. " First we need to know if your dad was, in fact, buying ConnTrust stock in large amounts."

"Dad's specialty is trading in small bank stocks," Cece replied. "He knows as much about the banking business as most bankers. He has made a good deal of money in recent years picking small local banks he thinks are undervalued on the market from a reading of their annual reports and all the other sources brokers have. Then he makes a study of their management, their reputation in their communities, their financial history, the quality of their loans, their reserves, and their non-performing loans. When he finds one which meets his criteria, he buys and holds the stock until the expected merger takes place. There is a great deal of consolidation of banks going on. He is simply doing what the larger banks are doing. The only difference is that the larger banks are out to buy up the best of the small ones. Dad simply is trading on that knowledge. So — he probably had been buying a lot of ConnTrust stock."

"It would be good if we were sure," Joe said.

"I've been agonizing over that. I certainly could ask him...but should I?" Cece responded. " Maybe I'm being paranoid after being dragged out of bed and off to the jail, but I thought that I shouldn't. I have never mentioned ConnTrust to him...never. It seems to me if I'm ever asked, I should be able to truthfully say I have never talked to him about it...either before or after the merger was announced."

"That makes a lot of sense," Dan said. " I think for today we should proceed with the assumption that Ralston knew your dad had been buying ConnTrust stock. With your permission I will see your dad in a day or two and ask him."

"I was hoping you'd do that, Dan," Cece said. " He knows you and I'm sure you can do it without upsetting him."

"I will do it," Dan agreed. " How does this all fit in to your second worry...Gordon's murder?"

"I wish I knew," Cece answered. " Maybe it's woman's intuition. Maybe its just a crazy notion, but my mind keeps going back to that last night on *Sea Chaser*. What Gordon said when the sun went down in that deep red sky. ' It went down in flames...just like me.' And he had started to tell me something. I know it was not only very important but was also troubling him badly. If it didn't have something to do with the merger, why would he tell me? And why did he want those letters to be given to me?"

"Did anyone but you, Tiger, know about the secret compartment on *Sea Chaser*?" Ian asked.

"No...no one, I'm sure," Tiger answered. " That is why he had me build it instead of the Hinckley people. He told me he wanted a place that was known only to him. I told him that he should build it then and he only laughed."

"So he knew only you would find them and that is why he was sure they would be given to Cece," Ian said.

"Right...but I never thought of that," Tiger said.

"But what did he mean when he said he'd be going down in flames?" Kara asked.

"If we knew that, we'd probably know who killed him," Joe answered.

"So let's skip that worry for the moment and go to the third one, Cece," Dan said. " How much does Kevin Burke know and how is Sarah Rosen involved?"

Cece told them in detail the conversation she had had with Kevin the previous Tuesday. She followed with the details of the discussion with Kevin about the meeting in which Ralston told him that her father was buying ConnTrust on a tip from her and that was what prompted the SEC investigation.

"Now I understand," Dan said. " Did he mention Sarah Rosen?"

"No. And after reading the letters, that really troubles me."

"Why?"

"Well, as I told you last time, Kevin and Sarah were just getting into a relationship. I think so much of Kevin that I have trouble believing that he might know that Sarah is somehow involved and is protecting her."

"Gordon had an ongoing relationship with her for years. Do I remember that right?" Dan asked.

"True. But even though they had broken up, as I understand, in an angry argument, Gordon would still protect her to the fullest extent he could. He was that kind of man."

"Let me throw this out just for discussion," Kara said. " If Gordon thought that Ralston was telling him the truth, and two people, one an associate and one a consultant recommended by the firm, had broken the code of secrecy and traded in their client's stock knowing there was profit to be made, the dilemma he faced might have caused him to say he was 'going down in flames.' "

"That is certainly a possibility," Joe agreed. " But where does it get us?"

"Where is Sarah Rosen?" Kara asked.

"Kevin said she flew out to the west coast as soon as they got back — from Canada — I believe I'm remembering right. Said she had a consulting job out there," Cece answered. " I've been thinking about that too. I wondered why she was so distant the last days we were working on the merger. And I watched her at the funeral and at the brunch afterwards. She acted so strange. I think she was still in love with

Gordon. I know she couldn't stand to talk to me. I know she thought Gordon and I were having an affair. And she wouldn't go near Beth at the brunch. The only one I saw her talk to was Kelley Morse. She and Kevin left early and I know that wasn't like Kevin."

"I can't believe she had anything to do with Gordon's murder," Joe said.

"Why?" Tiger asked.

"I've told the lawyers already. The Maine Game Warden and Marine Patrol divers failed to find a syringe off the Carleton Cottage pier. Tardif is convinced that one was used to inject the sodium pentothal which the police believed was used to kill Gordon Fairbanks."

"So? " Tiger asked.

"Tardif seems sure that a lethal dose of sodium pentothal has to be injected into a person's vein. He says that is the way it is administered in states which use it to carry out death sentences. That means it has to be done by someone with training...someone who could get the needle into a vein."

"That is only partially true," Tiger responded.

"That is why Tardif is convinced that you were the one who injected the lethal dose," Joe said.

"Oh my God!" Cece exclaimed.

"I've suspected that since you told us last week that the pathologist who did the autopsy concluded that Gordon was killed with a lethal injection of a barbiturate. I didn't mention it to Cece because I knew what her reaction would be. But I'm glad it's now out in the open," Tiger responded.

"Well, my reaction was one of surprise," Cece said in a calm voice. "I was with Tiger that entire evening and I know he didn't have anything to do with Gordon's death."

Joe Goldberg and the lawyers had been watching the two closely. Joe had given the lawyers the information he had gotten from Sergeant Tardif as soon as he learned it and asked them not to convey it to their clients. He told them he would like to tell their clients Tardif's theory at their next meeting to give him an opportunity to observe Cece and Tiger as he did so.

Joe had many years of experience interviewing persons charged with crimes and one of his great assets was often being able to tell if one was lying. His technique was to suddenly confront the witness with a known fact and ask him to explain it. Usually, if the person hadn't anticipated that the question would be asked and he wasn't prepared for it, Joe was able to discern whether the person was telling the truth. Later, after this observation, Joe told the lawyers that he couldn't be sure because Tiger had admitted he had thought about the matter and was sure that was what the police were thinking.

"Is that such a big deal...finding a vein and sticking a needle in it?" Ian asked.

"Not if a person knows the basics," Tiger answered. " Student nurses learn how early on. Paramedics can do it. A lot of people can do it."

"Of the people we know who were at Carleton Cottage the day Gordon was murdered, how many could do it?" Dan asked.

"Certainly I could," Tiger said. " And I've been thinking about that question myself. For the past several years Jack and Celia Morse, and Jack's daughter Kelley, have vacationed in Northeast Harbor. I've gotten to know Kelley quite well because she loves to sail and Gordon liked to have her go with us. I know her father, Jack, is a veterinarian. I know that both she and Gordon's mother, Celia, have worked with him in his animal clinic. I assume that all three are capable of injecting a vein. A vein is a vein whether it's in an animal or a human."

"There's another," Cece said. " Ralph Ralston is a medical doctor."

"Oh? How do you know that for sure?" Dan asked.

"He told me himself," Cece replied. " He also told Kevin in more detail. He had a family practice for several years and when his marriage ended he was already a director at ConnTrust where he was investing all his excess earnings. He wanted to change the direction of his life, he told Kevin, and he thought he could make more money in banking."

"Isn't that interesting," Ian mused.

"How easy is it to get sodium pentothal?" Kara asked.

"There are a lot of sources," Tiger said. " As Joe told you the last time we met, the problem is to get it in a lethal dose."

"Tiger, I for one need more information on that drug," Ian said. "It isn't one I've had any cause to research."

"Barbiturates are derived from barbituric acid," Tiger responded.

"There are hundreds of derivatives. Commonly, they are used as sedatives. One of the most common ways to commit suicide in the U.S. is to take an overdose of a barbiturate. You've heard of 'purple hearts,' 'goof balls,' 'downs,' 'blue heaves,' or 'yellow jackets.' They are all barbiturates. They are usually ingested and even in large doses they often don't produce death for some time.

"Tardif is correct about one thing. Pentothal...correct name is thiopental, is the drug usually used in states which execute persons for crimes using the lethal injection method. It is very quick...especially if the person has ingested a quantity of alcohol. It is the favorite for doctors wanting to commit suicide. One source that is perhaps relevant here is that veterinarians commonly carry a lethal dose in their travel bag. If a horse, for example, is down with a broken leg the owner always wants it out of its misery right away...so they usually have it. "

"Well, that is interesting and saves me a lot of time," Joe said. " I was dreading to do more research to get that basic information. "

"Okay," Dan said. " I am trying to visualize what happened. I now have learned that a lethal dose has to be injected into a vein if it is to act quickly. Mr. Fairbanks is on his boat. He's had a lot to drink but I have to assume he hasn't passed out...that if someone tried to stick a needle in him he'd react and make that difficult if not impossible. True?"

"Well, if he was asleep in his bunk....," Ian started. " Isn't that where Harvey Lunt found him?"

"That's right," Joe answered. " If he was passed out it seems an injection would be simple for someone with a minimum of training."

"And if he wasn't passed out?" Dan asked.

"It would be my guess that the person intending to accomplish that mission would slip a 'Mickey' in his drink to get him in that state," Joe answered.

"Joe, was there anything in the autopsy report that suggested that?" Dan asked.

"I'm sorry, I don't remember anything like that but I could have missed it," Joe answered. " I was interested in the cause of death."

"That would limit the suspects to the persons on the boat that evening," Kara observed.

"True, but Mr. Fairbanks could have had a visitor after our clients left," Ian said. "I keep remembering what Harvey told Joe...about seeing the headlights of the car which he thought was coming out of the Carleton Cottage driveway as he came back that night."

"Apparently Tardif doesn't know that the drug could cause death if it were ingested just as well as if it were injected in a vein," Tiger said. " It just wouldn't act as fast. As long as the police think that the drug has to be injected, Cece wouldn't be a suspect. If they knew that the drug could be put in a drink and ingested, she would be in the mix of suspects."

"Good thinking." Joe said. " I certainly won't give him that information."

Then the discussion turned back to the letters Tiger found on the boat and Dan said, " I think it is safe to say at this point at least, there is no legal obligation for Cece to turn the letters over to anyone. There may come a time when to keep them would amount to obstruction of justice, but we are not there yet."

"So what about the lap-top?" Cece asked.

"As of the moment, it is yours Cece," Dan told her.

"I don't know Gordon's password so I don't know if there is anything on it that might help us," Cece said.

"It is extremely important to know, one way or the other," Joe said. " I know a fellow who can find the password rather quickly. I'd like your permission to have him find it for us. He wouldn't have to know anything other than we want the password."

"I agree," Dan said. ' Can we have it, Cece?"

"Certainly," Cece answered. " When we have the password though, I will probably have to interpret Gordon's input. He's given to short sentences and it'll be a lot of legal stuff. Tiger and I can come up next weekend."

The group agreed to meet again the following Saturday right after 1 p.m., unless something came up which required them to meet sooner.

The meeting had taken up most of he afternoon. Cece wanted to drive back to Medford as soon as it was over. She was apprehensive that Sergeant Tardif might appear at any moment with a warrant for their arrest. Tiger told her that was not going to happen — that Dan had told the prosecutor's office that he would produce his client whenever the State wanted him to. All he needed was a day's notice. Dan had reported that Sergeant Tardif seemed satisfied with that promise.

Tiger had called his grandmother when they first arrived in Southwest and she reminded him of his promise that when he came home again he would bring Cece with him to have supper with her in her new home. He told Cece of the invitation and his promise. She reluctantly agreed to stay over as long as they could leave early Sunday morning.

Jessie Wass had been lucky to find a whole fresh haddock at the fish market. She stuffed it with poultry stuffing, covered it with flour, butter, salt and pepper, covered it with milk, and baked it until it began to fall apart. It was the first time Cece had haddock prepared that way. She told Jessie that it was even better than Tiger had predicted and Jessie beamed. She had met Cece only twice before but she knew from the first time they met that Tiger was in love with her. She had told Tiger then that she was impressed. Tiger's response was that he intended to marry her — if she'd have him. Jessie said it wouldn't be a problem — and of course she was right.

Jessie was 64 years old — although she looked to be in her early fifties. Three years earlier she left her job in the hardware store and went to work for a lady across the street as a clerk in her gift shop. Within a year the lady took ill, and Jessie successfully continued to run the shop by herself. When the owner died, she found the local bank was happy to lend her the money to buy the business. She put in many long hours in the summer months but it was profitable. For the first time in her life she was able to have a home of her own. Jessie gave them a tour of the house after supper and Cece complemented Jessie on her taste in furnishing and decorating the home. They chatted away as if they had known each other all their lives. It made Tiger so happy to see how well they got along that he was tempted to tell Jessie that they had secretly married but he knew it would spoil the wedding they planned for the coming June.

It was late evening when they arrived at the Tandy cottage. The air was still warm from the heat of the day and the pond was still at a temperature that they could tolerate for their ritual swim. They didn't stay in the water very long, however. They wrapped themselves in their beach towels when they came out and hugged and kissed until they were warm, then went into the cottage and to bed. The cottage was the first place they had made love and just being there with Cece always turned Tiger on. It was a couple of hours before they both fell asleep, exhausted but completely fulfilled. Knowing that their lawyers and investigator were doing all they could in their behalf was greatly comforting, even though no one could say that real progress was being made in solving Gordon's murder. They both slept through the night for the first time since the police made their visit to the Tandy cottage.

CHAPTER ELEVEN

Joe Goldberg asked Dan to have the lawyers stay for a strategy conference after they met with their clients. He wanted their thoughts about the truthfulness of what Tiger and Cece told them at the meeting and to get direction as to how he should proceed.

"How well do you know your clients?" Joe asked as soon as Cece and Tiger left.

"I've known Tiger most of my life," Ian responded. "I can't say I know him well. He was three years ahead of me at MDI High School. We played on the same teams. But he was a senior and I only a freshman. Cece I met for the first time last week."

"I've known Tiger since he was a baby," Dan said. "He grew up with my boys. He's done really well considering..."

"Tell us..." Joe prompted.

"Tiger was brought up by his grandmother, Jessie Wass. His father got his mother pregnant but joined the Army before he learned of the situation. He was killed in Vietnam. Tiger's mother had taken up with a young man from Bangor just before he was born. I was involved with this so I know the facts. Jessie talked the girl out of having an abortion and I arranged the adoption. He was a close friend of my oldest son and at our house a lot while they were growing up. I've never had any reason to believe that he isn't the totally honest young man he appears to be."

"Well, that helps," Joe said. "Usually — if a person has a dishonest streak — it would be noticed by anyone who has a chance to observe him over time."

"You're saying you can't change a Tiger's spots," Kara suggested. After a moment they all laughed.

"How about Cece, Dan?"

"I only know her parents, and then only as clients. I've done some real estate work for them and prepared their estate plan. From all appearances, they are very fine people."

"Somehow we've got to check out the information on Mr. Tandy's purchases of ConnTrust stock," Joe asserted.

"I can take care of that, I think," Dan said. "I can talk to him. I'll have to make sure that there isn't a conflict of interest ...that he's fully informed."

Other than Dan's self assigned task, the lawyers were at a loss to give Joe further direction and they agreed he should follow his own instincts. They would meet again after Dan had completed his task and see if Joe had anything to report.

Dan was in court all day that Monday and by the time the case he was trying was finished it was too late to call Wexford Tandy. He did not call him at his home for fear of upsetting Rachel, his wife. He was saved the trouble. Wexford was on the phone to Dan's office as it opened Tuesday morning. He spoke to Carrie, Dan's secretary, and insisted that he had to see Dan that day. Carrie was up on everything that went on in Dan's office and knew Dan wanted to see Mr. Tandy, so she promised him he would be able to meet with him when he arrived in Ellsworth that day after lunch.

Carrie brought Mr. Tandy into Dan's office as soon as he arrived in the early afternoon. They shook hands as always and Dan asked Wexford to sit. It was clear from the look on Wexford's face that he was troubled. Dan waited for him to initiate the conversation.

"This is basically about Cece's problem," he said. "And I don't know if I have a problem or not. I didn't want to talk to our firm's lawyer because this may develop into a conflict of interest. I wanted to talk to you to get your thoughts before I did anything further."

"Fine," Dan said, "but I have to be careful it doesn't place me in a conflict situation."

"You mean between my interests and my daughter's?"

"Right."

"I'm comfortable with that. There are none, I assure you."

"Okay then. Go ahead..."

"Late Friday afternoon I had a visit from two government investi-gators who I assumed were from the SEC. I'm sorry to say I was so dis-tracted with the market when they came into my office that at first I did-n't clearly take it all in. They showed me their badges and I asked them to sit and tell me what I could do for them. I've had visits from federal agents like that before...but the subject has always been one of my clients..."

"Let me stop you there, Wexford," Dan interrupted. "As I feared, this may develop into another kind of conflict of interest."

"You're thinking this involves Cece?"

"Right."

"I'm fully aware of that. That's why I'm here. I want to tell you about the visit from the Feds."

"Okay. But first we need to clarify the problem. I represent Cece on a potential murder charge. You have information I need in that regard. I must share it with her so I need your agreement. On the other hand, what you tell me may not be confidential because I can't represent you if there is a conflict."

"I understand that fully and I agree that you can share the information. I know I have no problem with the Feds as you will see when I tell you what happened."

"With that understanding, please go on."

"Well this visit wasn't about a customer of the firm. Up front they told me that they were investigating a complaint the SEC had received anonymously which had alleged there had been insider trading in ConnTrust stock and I might be involved. It's a bank stock traded on the NASDAQ Small-cap market based primarily in Connecticut. Then they told me that since there was a possibility of a criminal charge, they had to read me a warning...I think they called it a Miranda warning."

"That is what it is called," Dan agreed

"Anyway, they read me my rights, as they called it, from a card. I can't remember all of it but I was sure that it was a warning that anything I said could be used against me if charges were brought."

"Right. That's what the warning is supposed to convey."

"Okay. When they finished reading it to me, I told them that I might very well answer their questions because I knew that I hadn't done anything wrong. But first, I told them that I wanted to know more about the complaint. They said they had told me all they could. I've been buying ConnTrust stock for a couple of years now — for myself and for some of my customers. But I knew it had to be me personally who they were interested in. And I'm well aware what a charge of insider trading means. I followed the Boesky case and the Milken case closely. So — I probably shouldn't have — but I was upset at the notion that someone thought I could be involved with insider trading, so I took the initiative."

"What did you do?"

"I immediately took the two of them into my work office, took out my ConnTrust file, laid it on my work table, opened it up and invited them to inspect it."

"Go on..."

"Well, they seemed real surprised. One of them thanked me and said it was the first time since he began work for the Commission that had happened. People they were investigating always needed time to get their records together or some such excuse. They spent a couple of hours going over my records and then they asked if they could copy some of the pages. I pointed to my copier and told them to feel free and they made copies of several pages. My only request was to know which pages they were copying and they complied. When they had finished, they thanked me. It wasn't just pro-forma, they were both really sincere. One of them told me that he hoped that they wouldn't have to make another visit, but that was out of his hands. He asked me please not to destroy any of the papers or alter them in any way. Then he showed me what he called a *subpoena duces tecum*. He said that if I hadn't cooperated as I had done, he'd have served the subpoena and taken all my records concerning ConnTrust."

"What happened next?"

"They left. It was well past closing time. The other brokers and all the secretaries had gone for the weekend. I spent the next hour looking over the pages they had photocopied. It was obvious they were looking at dates. I am pretty meticulous and keep daily notes on stocks I am interested in and I date each entry I make as I follow the stocks. I also chart those stocks and they made a copy of my chart on ConnTrust as well as all the pages recording my purchases of that stock. For a couple of my customers I had made a written analysis of the merits of ConnTrust from the past three years and set out the reasons I thought that it was an excellent candidate for acquisition. It was dated well before I started buying the stock for my own account. They took a copy of that as well."

"So you are telling me that you could document the fact that you had been following ConnTrust for how long?"

"Three years at least."

"And when did you start acquiring it?"

"About two years ago."

"You bought for your own account?"

"My own and two of my customers who are willing to take a position in a stock that may or may not increase very much in value. I have done pretty well by them and they have faith in me."

"What would be the total purchases?"

"About 15,000 shares. Average cost about $30 per share."

"What percentage of the total outstanding stock?"

"A little over one percent if my figures are correct."

"Are you aware of the kind of legal work your daughter does?"

"Yes, Fairbanks & Burke specialize in mergers and acquisitions."

"Right."

"Oh my God! Why didn't I make that connection! Cece was working on that merger."

"So, are you telling me that you and Cece have never discussed her work specifically? More to the point, you never discussed the merger of ConnTrust with Northeast Holdings?"

"I am telling you that...I will say it positively. I have never discussed specifically any work Cece was doing and I certainly never discussed the ConnTrust merger with her, or anyone at her firm for that matter."

"The police think that merger had something to do with Mr. Fairbanks' murder."

"Oh my God! ...but I don't get the connection."

"At this point neither do we. We simply don't have enough information. One could speculate and that leads to all kinds of theories."

"Like what?"

"Suppose for the moment that I am the investigator in charge of solving the Fairbanks murder — that I had information that Fairbanks had been working on the ConnTrust merger. Assume I also had information that the SEC had an anonymous tip that there had been a lot of trading in the stock in the few months prior to the pending merger and before the information had been released to the public. Finally, suppose that the informer said that the trading was based on insider information. A knowledgeable investigator would assume that information had to have come from someone in the know. Insider trading is a serious crime and I understand the SEC investigators are very good. So assume that Gordon Fairbanks knew that news of the merger had leaked and that insider trading had been going on. If the source of the leak was someone in his firm, he had a duty to disclose it to the SEC. If he didn't, and it was discovered by the authorities, his firm could be charged, as well. If it was the firm's client, he had an even larger problem because of attorney-client privilege, but he still would be required to disclose it. From all I've been able to learn, Mr. Fairbanks was the kind of lawyer who would follow that requirement, no matter how much he would like to avoid it. So I would have to assume that if that inside trader knew Mr. Fairbanks was about to disclose the facts to the SEC, he — she — had a motive to murder Mr. Fairbanks."

Tandy had been listening carefully and was thoughtful for a moment before he responded.

"I understand all that, but how does it involve me? I'm sure Mr. Fairbanks didn't know that I was purchasing ConnTrust stock let alone have reason to believe I had insider information."

"But we have to assume that the police know your daughter was actively involved with that merger."

"And they assume she told me about it!"

"We think that is the what they think."

"And she murdered her boss to protect herself and her father! That's crazy!"

"That would be their theory."

"Well it didn't happen," Wexford said in great anger. "What should I do now?"

"If I were you, I'd find an attorney who works in the securities area and put him on retainer."

"You can't represent me?"

"Wexford, I can't — for two reasons. First, I represent Cece and if the police try to tie the merger of ConnTrust to Mr. Fairbanks murder, it is a definite conflict...."

"I understand..."

"And the second reason is that if the SEC brings an action, you need someone who specializes in that area of law."

"But you do a lot of criminal law work..."

"True, but the SEC rarely brings criminal charges and I can't see that they would here. They usually bring a civil action seeking monetary damages."

"Then that is what I'll do as soon as I get back to Portland. Thank you for seeing me so quickly. I feel better just talking to you. I certainly am happy that you are representing Cece."

"I need copies of the records that the SEC took from you and permission to use them in Cece's case."

"You have permission. I brought you a set," Wexford said, handing Dan the copies.

"Thanks. That is a great help. I hope you don't mind, but I need your permission in writing confirming that I can share what you have just told me with Cece and the others we have working on it."

"You must have a form I can sign..."

"I do."

Dan filled out his standard release form. After Wexford had read it, he signed it and thanked Dan again for seeing him on short notice. Then they said their good-byes.

'If he's telling me the truth, what he says will be a great help,' Dan told himself. 'If he's lying, Cece is in deep trouble.'

CHAPTER TWELVE

As soon as Wexford Tandy left Dan's office that afternoon Dan called Carrie on the intercom and instructed her to hold his calls. He didn't want to be disturbed no matter who it was. Carrie had saved the afternoon for his appointment with Tandy so he had the rest of it to himself. Dan sat leaning back in his leather chair, going over in his mind everything he knew about the Fairbanks murder. That took only a few minutes. Then he reviewed all he knew about his client, Cece. Dan learned early on that a trial lawyer had to know everything he could learn about his client, otherwise he wouldn't be prepared for every eventuality. This is especially true in a criminal case. So far he'd had extended talks with Cece only on those three recent occasions. Still, he had already formed an opinion that she wasn't capable of being involved in a murder. Realizing where that could lead, he started to play devil's advocate with himself.

In his almost twenty years of practicing law in downeast Maine, Dan had developed a reputation not only as an excellent trial lawyer but also as an excellent civil lawyer. Some of his attorney friends would say without hesitation that he was the best trial lawyer in the state. He was blessed with an excellent mind and a fantastic memory, both of which are essential ingredients for a successful trial law practice. The subject of his trials ran the gamut from divorces to murder. He quickly learned that his success at trial depended not only upon how well he was prepared but also how well he was able to understand people — witnesses certainly, but also the clients, the jurors, the opposing lawyer, and even the judge.

As he began to focus his attention on developing that ability he found that it demanded a lot of study, insight and thought. Perhaps most importantly, it demanded keen observation. Dan began to make it a practice to observe people closely, to listen to them carefully when they spoke, to compare what they said to what he knew to be facts, to look for compassion, intellect, judgment, arrogance or humility — everything he could know about the person. He found that often he could predict with accuracy what a person would do in any given situation. It had stood him well in his trial work and in his general practice of law.

Dan had been completely honest when he told Cece when they first talked at the Hancock Sheriff's office that, in preparing for a criminal case, he always assumed that his client was guilty. It, however, didn't affect what he kept to himself — his real judgment on the issue. He simply wanted his client to know that in preparing the matter for trial he always assumed his client was guilty. He had found that the warning prepared the client for hard questions without losing their trust in the process.

Dan's first impression of Cece was very positive. He had judged correctly that she was about 28 years old, well educated, and quite mature. One would expect that a person would have become quite mature at that age, yet Cece seemed mature way beyond her years. She was in the most serious crisis of her young life, yet she was handling the situation surprisingly well. True, she was a lawyer but she had no criminal law experience. Most young lawyers in that circumstance, especially if they thought they were being unjustly accused of a crime, would have answered any question the police put to them. They would fear that not talking to the police would be taken as a sign of guilt and usually, they'd be quite right. But Dan knew from experience that if a person is guilty of a crime it was much more likely he will try to convince the police that he isn't guilty by giving them what he believes is a plausible story. Many a criminal has sealed his fate with that act.

Dan learned that from the beginning of the interview Cece had with Sergeant Tardif, she had not played that game. She simply asked to speak with her lawyer. That act made Dan believe that she was capable of making intelligent decisions while she was under stress. It was a decision that demanded courage. At the same time she was also concerned about Tiger talking to the police and her next request was that a lawyer be obtained for him. That was good thinking, as well. As expected, however, Sergeant Tardif told Joe Goldberg that his clients had to be hiding something from the police, otherwise they would have told him their story right then and there. That assessment most often would have merit, but again, it depended on the person. Dan's question to himself was, ' Did Cece have the maturity and the wisdom to decide, under the circumstances, to refuse to talk to the police until she knew better what was going on? Did she have the intestinal fortitude to do that, knowing that the police would take it as a sign of guilt? Or, was her refusal actually the product of guilt?'

After thinking about it for a long time, Dan decided that he didn't know Cece well enough to make that judgment. He wanted to believe that Cece was telling him the truth when she denied any involvement with the murder. Dan had been impressed with her parents from the first time they met. He found it hard to believe that the Tandy's daughter wouldn't have the same qualities of honesty and integrity that he had found in the parents.

That thought prompted Dan to review the papers Wexford had left with him. It seemed inconceivable that they were not what they purported to be — Wexford's records of his research on ConnTrust for the past three years. If the SEC investigators came into his office without prior warning, Wexford certainly didn't have the time to fabricate them. Still he could have anticipated such a visit and prepared them to look as if they had been made over time. Dan looked at each sheet carefully. Even though they were photocopies, it was clear that different pens had been used in making them over the years. And it was clear that the records had been kept in different note books because the formats of the pages were different — consistent for several pages and then a change for several pages. Dan concluded that what anyone should determine from those records was that an intelligent broker had predicted ConnTrust was a likely subject for acquisition by another bank and had acted on that analysis by purchasing ConnTrust stock over time expecting to profit. Unless, of course, they had been deliberately prepared to mislead any potential investigator.

But, even if the expected acquisition didn't happen, the risk from investing in ConnTrust stock was small because of its solid balance sheet and its earnings record. Given a stable economy, it would probably grow steadily in value even if it were not acquired. It would just be less profitable than if a merger occurred. From what Dan could see at that moment, Wexford wouldn't be faced with any action from the SEC. More importantly, Wexford's following of ConnTrust stock and his purchases long preceded his daughter's involvement in the legal end of the merger. Those purchases were documented and couldn't be fabricated later as a cover up.

Sergeant Tardif obviously had information from some source, probably the Federal government — the SEC or the FBI — that Wexford Tandy was being investigated for something to do with ConnTrust stock. From what Tardif had specified in the search warrant, he had some information that connected Cece to her father's investments in that stock. With his limited knowledge of the stock market, the SEC rules and practices, Dan had no idea how that could be done — and done so quickly. Even given it had been done, how did Tardif justify his assumption that it was a motive for Cece to murder her boss? Dan was baffled. Over the years he couldn't remember being involved in a serious criminal matter before his client was indicted and arrested. In the usual case, he would be able to get a great deal of information on the State's case from the discovery which the State was automatically required to provide him under Maine's criminal rules of procedure.

Dan concluded that he wasn't going to be able to make any solid judgments from the facts at hand. Joe Goldberg was due to make a report to him in the morning and he'd have to wait. Perhaps Joe would have something new to report. Dan decided to leave his office a little early and to go to Northeast Harbor on his way home. He wanted to get a good look at Carleton Cottage, to see the boathouse and to go down on the pier if he could.

As he drove towards the Island, Dan's mind turned to Adam Wass. His first thought was that Tiger was thankfully in good hands with the young lawyers in Southwest Harbor, Ian and Kara Campbell. So long as their clients agreed, the lawyers could work together and share information on the case — even go to trial together if it came to that. Dan had come to know Tiger well. Southwest Harbor is a small town on the 'back side' of the Island and everyone knows everyone. He had always marveled at how well Jessie Wass had done bringing the boy up — and how well the boy had done without a mother or father, for that matter. He remembered that Tiger had gotten his nickname from his fondness for sports. He played football, basketball and baseball with a dedication and a ferocity that made the name appropriate.

Dan grew up with Tiger's father. He had a feeling of guilt whenever he thought about Steve Wass. He felt sure the feeling was prompted by the knowledge that the Navy he was in during the war in 'Nam was a lot safer than the Navy Steve Wass was in — the Navy's Riverine

Patrol. Those patrols on the rivers of Vietnam had produced most of the Navy's casualties during the war. Dan wondered again if his feelings of guilt from not being in real danger during that war had anything to do with the fact he liked the boy so much. Tiger was often with his own sons growing up and he had followed his career with interest. He was happily surprised when Tiger went on to college after he got out of the Marines. For some unknown reason he hadn't expected it. Dan was even more surprised and happy to learn that Tiger had been accepted at Tufts Medical School after he graduated from college. He had seen him around Southwest during the summer and he knew he was employed by one of the summer families — the Fairbanks — as the captain of their Hinckley.

Yet Dan couldn't remember seeing Tiger with a woman. He had wondered then why a young man so obviously talented and handsome didn't have a young woman hanging on his arm when he saw him in town in the evening. Dan's two boys were a year or two younger than Tiger but the local youngsters often mixed ages for three or four years. He supposed that was the result of the young folks putting off marriage until late these days. Still, he had never seen Tiger with a date when he was with the group. So he was surprised when he learned that Tiger was dating a beautiful young lady, and was astonished to learn from Cece that they were married.

Thinking about it, he didn't blame them for marrying so quickly after they first met. They both were mature enough to know if they could make a good marriage. Dan, like most males, was always attracted to beautiful woman. When he was dealing with one of them, he always had to caution himself not to make any judgment based on that fact alone, and he tried to do that with Cece. Now he wondered if his assessment of her was influenced not only by his strong belief that Tiger wouldn't be involved with murder, but also because Tiger wouldn't be associated with a woman who might be, as well. He knew he had to be careful here and he resolved to be extra cautious since he knew the families and admired them all.

Dan drove through the village of Northeast Harbor and onto the Kimball Road, passing by Saint Jude's where he stopped for a moment remembering Cece's suggestion that Mr. Fairbanks murderer may well have been there at his funeral. Then he drove on to the Shore Road, by the Northeast Fleet's pier and docks and on by Lady Astor's beautiful old cottage, wondering if she were there when the murder was committed and if it had changed her opinion that her cottage in Northeast Harbor was her favorite place to be.

He made the turn onto Manchester Road and parked his Blazer in an opening where he could look up Somes Sound. He got out and walked over to the high bank on the shore so he could get a better view. Just the end of the Carleton Cottage pier was in sight up the Sound. From where he stood, it was mostly hidden by other closer piers. Dan had sailed in the Sound as a boy but his spare time in the summer now was mostly spent at his cottage at Branch Pond on the mainland north of Ellsworth. Just looking up the Sound renewed his acquaintance with the area. He could see that it made sense for Tiger to commute to and from Southwest in his Whaler rather than go by car. All he had to do was to go across the mouth of the Sound, then to cross the entrance of Southwest Harbor and he would be at the town landing in Manset where he kept his Whaler. From there it was only a couple minutes walk to the summer apartment Gordon had provided for him.

Having accomplished part of his mission, he returned to his Blazer and drove on to the intersection of Manchester Road and Sargent Drive. From there he drove west on the Drive and was soon opposite Carleton Cottage. He would have missed the road to the cottage but for the small sign, black with a gold border and lettering, announcing the entrance. There was no traffic so he stopped opposite it and was able to see, in the angle of the road, most of the cottage. It was one of the old cedar shingled cottages in style at the turn of the century. The shingles were weathered to a nice gray and only the trim around the windows and the doors was painted a bright white. Everything else was obscured by the spruce trees which grew thickly everywhere. Dan then drove slowly along Sargent Drive to the first curve. It wasn't far. He stopped again, got out and looked back. He could see that a vehicle coming out of the entrance to Carleton Cottage would be quickly lost from sight. Harvey Lunt's report was confirmed as to that detail. Dan then continued homeward by way of Sargent Drive to Somesville, then onto Route 102 to Southwest Harbor where he turned onto the Seal Cove Road and up the high ridge overlooking the harbor and he was home. His wife Ginger would be expecting him and would have his dinner waiting. The thought made him happy. At the end of a troubling day he always looked forward to Ginger's companionship. He parked the Blazer in the garage next to Ginger's Seville — the one exception to her firm rule never to buy something expensive when something less expensive would do as well. Ginger was waiting by the kitchen door and Dan took her in his arms when he came in and his worries over the Tandy case were put aside for the rest of day.

As he drove up to Ellsworth from the Island the next morning, Dan wondered what Kara Campbell had found on Gordon Fairbanks' lap-top. He knew she planned to spend the past couple of days looking into the IBM's hard drive and reviewing everything Gordon had placed in it. Joe Goldberg had taken the lap-top to the computer expert in Bangor that Monday morning so that the password could be determined. The expert found Gordon's password almost immediately and Joe had delivered the lap-top to Kara that afternoon. When he reported this to Dan, Joe said that he had had a talk with Sergeant Tardif that afternoon and that Tardiff would only tell him that they were making a lot of progress and expected something to break soon. Tardif wanted to make sure Joe kept track of Wass and Tandy and to be prepared to bring them in when called.

Over the years Dan had more than one innocent client who spent a lot of time in jail waiting for trial only to be found not guilty. It always seemed unfair but that was the way the system worked — or didn't work. He was fearful that the present situation might add a client to that list.

Ian Campbell had a trial scheduled for that Wednesday morning so it was only Kara, Dan and Joe who met at Dan's office at 8 a.m. Joe and Dan were waiting as Carrie brought Kara into the conference room. Both Dan and Joe rose to greet Kara, searching her face for a clue as to her success with the computer. Kara gave them a charming smile exposing gleaming white teeth and increasing the deep dimples in her cheeks. She told them she wished they would get over the habit of rising to greet her and Joe replied that they all needed the exercise. There are better ways, she told them with a giggle and sat in the chair Dan held waiting for her.

Carrie was there instantly with Kara's coffee. After she had refilled the other cups, Carrie left, closing the door behind her. Dan and

Joe were silent, waiting expectantly for Kara's report. Kara put the laptop on the desk, gave the power cord to Joe to plug in and, that done, she booted it up.

"I've made notes of the files I want to show you," she said. "Dan, we need you on this side of the table if you want to see them."

Kara brought up the first file on the screen and they all read it.

4/13 ConnTrust. Reviewed financials with Ralston. He still insists on Pooling Accounting. Wants the advantage of earnings accretion. Northeast insists on Purchase Accounting. Told Ralston if he wants a merger he had to back off. Typically, he's wild.

Then the second:

4/30 Ralston met with John Gropus at Northeast. No one else present. Ralston reports they reached agreement. It's going to be Purchase Accounting. Ralston was elated. I asked what changed his mind. He laughed and said it was between him and Gropus. I suspect a side deal which has to be illegal. I now know Ralston is capable of it. If I learn of it I'll report the facts to SEC immediately.

The third:

5/27 In Torrington for two days with ConnTrust CPA's. Financials coming together. Ralston antsy. Told me Gropus was having second thoughts. Couldn't get details. Obvious it's the side deal. Should demand to know. Will wait until disclosure documents are closer to being final.

The fourth:

6/15 Ralston called. He's wild again. Told Gropus he's back to Pooling Accounting. Gropus threatens hostile acquisition. Ralston demands we find ways to stop it.

The fifth:

7/7 Told Ralston acquisition by Northeast can't be stopped. He's out of the loop. Told him to get other representation. Immediately backed off. Says he'll figure something out.

The sixth:

7/30 Ralston called. Merger back on using Purchase Accounting. Ralston wants it ready for notification of shareholders by 8/14 after market closed for weekend. No explanation given.

At that point Kara stopped bringing up the files and said, "I don't have a clue what the accounting terms are."

"I don't either," Dan responded. "We'll soon find out though. Cece will know. Are there more?"

Kara brought up the next file.

8/3 In Torrington 2 days. Met a Leigh Cranston from ConnTrust at lunch. Her request. Wanted to see me alone. Did at my motel. She's ConnTrusts in-house stock transfer agent. Hates Ralston. Think they were in long relationship — not sure, wouldn't say. She's got something on him or she'd be gone.

Showed me his stock transfer records. Not in his name — name is Ralph Younger. Leigh says Ralston's parking the stock. Thinks it's Ralston's son. Has no SS numbers. She suspects he has deal with Northeast for purchase of his stock right after merger complete. Ralston has told her he wants out of banking after the merger. Cranston says he has a new young woman and he wants to play.

Leigh told Ralston he needed to make the required report to SEC. Told him she would do it. Ralston told her that if she did he'd kill her. She thinks he meant it. She's really scared of him. Wanted me to know and wants my help. Told her I had to think about it.

The next file:

8/12 Told Ralston we'd be late by a week. He's surprisingly relaxed.

Then the last:

8/17 Wrote my friend Gerry at SEC and had it hand delivered asking for receipt. Told him that the merger between ConnTrust and Northeast Holdings was now firm and gave him details to show Ralston was parking ConnTrust stock. Told him to keep the letter safe but to try to protect Fairbanks & Burke if possible.

Got call back immediately. Gerry said he was starting investigation immediately and his people would be visiting us so no one would know where the information came from. He couldn't promise not to disclose at some point. So be it. I have no choice. The law is the law.

Now the fun begins.

"So now we know for sure who alerted the SEC," Joe said.

"But where does that get us, I've been wondering ever since I broke this out," Kara said.

"It gives us a live person to talk to though," Dan said. "Joe, you have to see this Leigh Cranston. I'll bet she can help us a lot, if she'll talk to you."

"I'll go today. But I need Mr. Fairbanks notes printed out to take with me."

"Carrie can do that. Now we have the password we can print any file in the lap-top," Dan assured him as he called Carrie on the intercom and asked her to come in.

"We still don't know why the investigators visited Mr. Tandy," Kara said.

"We don't know a lot of things," Joe agreed. "We don't know if and when Ralston found out that Gordon made the report. If he thought Gordon was about to make the report that certainly is a motive for him to commit murder. And I suppose if he found out after the fact, it may have been revenge."

"He certainly knew about Mr. Tandy's purchasers," Kara said.

"But that was easy to come by," Dan said. "When the SEC demanded transfer records of large and ongoing purchases, that name would surface. Ralston certainly would have reviewed that before it was given to the SEC."

"I'll bet the name of Ralph Younger didn't appear," Joe said. "I'll try to get those records from Ms. Cranston. I'll bet she will have copies at home to protect herself, if she's as smart as I hope she is."

They talked a while longer waiting for Carrie's return with the printouts. They decided to wait for Joe's return from his mission to Connecticut before they reported progress to their clients. Dan was concerned that his client was so bent on protecting Mr. Burke and her law firm that she might let something slip. Until he knew all the players, he said he wanted to keep his cards close to his chest. As the meeting broke up, Dan, for the first time since he took on the representation of Cece Tandy, began to feel progress was being made. Still, he realized, they had a long way to go before he could be sure who had who killed Gordon Fairbanks.

CHAPTER THIRTEEN

A working mission out of state wasn't Joe Goldberg's cup of tea. In the ten years since he had retired from the Maine State Police and started his own detective agency the only such missions had been done at the behest of Dan Hardy. He couldn't be persuaded to go for anyone else. His agency had prospered from its beginning. Within a year he found he had to have help to keep up with the work. Luckily, one of his trusted fellow State Police detectives, Jim Murphy, had been thinking about retirement at the time and was happy to join Joe. He had added one other man since, but he resisted letting the agency get any larger. It was difficult for Joe to turn down work but he decided he would just have to refer some of the cases to another agency.

If a client's finances permitted, it is good practice for investigators to work in pairs, especially when interviewing. In that way they always have another witness to hear what was said. At Joe's urging, Jim Murphy, reluctantly agreed to interrupt his own work and accompany Joe to Connecticut. Joe assumed that Ms. Cranston had already talked to government investigators and he was worried that she might not talk to him. He decided not to call ahead, fearing that even if she agreed to see him, given time, she might change her mind before he could drive to Torrington. It was imperative that he talk to her because she had information they needed badly. She had initiated the talk with Mr. Fairbanks, he hoped that was an indication she would discuss the matter with him. He thought it best to find Ms. Cranston's house and be there when she came home after the bank closed for the day. He'd start by telling her that they were investigators on the ConnTrust case and hope she would assume they were government agents. But he couldn't lie to her and, if she asked, he would tell her up front who he represented and why he was there.

Joe's computer could find the telephone number of Leigh Cranston but it could not give him her address. He had the telephone number before he and Jim set out on their mission. They left Bangor early on Wednesday morning. Jim drove Joe's black Chevy Caprice, taking interstate highways most of the way. Joe took over the driving in heavy traffic on Connecticut's Route 202 going into Torrington, arriving about 3 p.m. They had debated whether they should rent a car with a New York license plate to further their cover but Joe decided they didn't have time. Joe stopped at the first phone booth which came into view, intending to find the Cranston street address from the phone book. There was no book. Three phone booths later they located one which had a phone book still hooked to it and Jim found the Cranston street address. While Joe gassed up the Caprice, Jim bought a street map of Torrington and they soon passed by the Cranston house. It was on the edge of the city in an older neighborhood but the homes were well kept. They found a place to park near the end of the street to wait and watch for a car driving into the Cranston yard.

Joe sat there going over the facts of the case with Jim. Jim had been able to give up cigarettes but not cigars, so even though there was a chill in the air on that late September afternoon, the windows of the Caprice were down. School was out. The neighborhood had its share of youngsters, some riding their bikes and others rollerblading in the street. One boy, about ten, skated by on his rollerblades and then turned and came back to the car.

"You guys policemen?" he asked, his face almost inside the car.

"No we're not," Joe answered.

"What are you doing here?"

"Talking."

"Okay," he said, and rolled away fast to catch his friends.

They had been parked there in front of a house near the Cranston driveway for about a half hour. They were watching carefully, but they didn't see any sign of life in the house. Finally Jim observed that they might be on a wild goose chase. From the suggestion Gordon Fairbanks had made in one of his last notes, Mrs. Cranston could already have been fired and moved out of town. Joe told Jim again that if they had tried to call and get her consent for a visit, she probably would have refused. Just then an older Chrysler Sebring convertible drove into the Cranston yard. A woman who appeared to be in her early forties got out, briefcase in hand, and went into the house. They waited a couple of minutes, got out, locked the Caprice and walked the half block to the Cranston home.

The bell was answered on the second ring by a teen age boy who immediately asked them what they wanted. Joe asked if his mother was home and he said he guessed so and yelled for his mom. Leigh Cranston appeared in a moment.

"Ms. Cranston, we're investigators and we need a moment of your time," Joe told her. "May we come in?"

"Investigators?"

"Yes ma'am..."

She hesitated a moment and then led the two into a modest living room.

"I thought I answered all your questions last week," she told them as she motioned them to sit, taking a seat on the couch opposite the overstuffed chairs she had indicated.

"Well, we have only a few," Joe said. "This won't take long."

Joe had given a lot of thought as to how he would proceed. He hoped to learn quickly if she had been interviewed on a previous occasion and that problem had been solved.

"I have very limited knowledge of this whole thing, you know..."

"We understand," Joe agreed. "I'll come right to the point. We are wondering if the list of stockholders you provided — the bank provided — was complete..."

"Well, I was only asked for a list of those holding one percent or more of the stock."

"Right, but we have reason to believe that some names are missing."

"Like who?"

"Like Ralph Younger."

"Oh my God!...sorry. So you know!"

"Why wasn't his name on the list?" Joe demanded.

"What are my rights here?" she asked in a panicky voice. "Do I have to answer these questions? Do I need a lawyer?"

Joe had anticipated that question at some point and he was prepared for it. He knew Cranston had to have smarts to hold the position of transfer agent at the bank and at some point she'd ask it .

"Mrs. Cranston, first I should tell you that the information about Ralph Younger came from Gordon Fairbanks."

"Oh my God ! But he's dead!"

"True, but he kept a journal and he made a summary of his conversation with you,"

"So...are you SEC investigators? You certainly aren't the two I talked to last week"

"We are not SEC investigators. We are working on the Fairbanks murder."

Mrs. Cranston was silent for a while, wondering where this was going to lead.

"Mr. Fairbanks was such a nice man...I really liked him. I trusted him completely. I was so upset...are you from Maine?"

"Right."

"When I first learned that Mr. Fairbanks had been murdered I started to go to the police...I was so upset... I wanted to help."

"It would help us enormously if you would start at the beginning and tell us all you can about the ConnTrust merger."

"Well, Ralston made all bank employees sign an agreement not to disclose any information we got at the bank."

"Understood. But we are talking about a murder here."

"Yes, of a man I met only briefly, but a man I immediately liked. And the man I work for is an asshole... sorry." Then after a pause, "Well, this may not all come out in any kind of order. I've been stewing about what I should do for months. After he was murdered I knew I should have gone to the police but I was deathly afraid."

"Afraid of ...?"

"Ralph...Ralph Ralston. He threatened to kill me if I told anyone what he was doing. And I know he's capable..."

"How well do you know Mr. Ralston?"

"Well enough! After my husband and I divorced I was basically on my own. I got this house and its mortgage. I had to plan for Donny's education because my ex wouldn't help. When the transfer agent who had been with the bank forever retired, I was offered the job. I'd been Ralph's personal secretary. Oh God, this is so hard..."

Joe waited for her to compose herself and Jim had a chance to catch up on his notes. Jim had wanted to ask her if they could tape the interview but Joe said that it might make the lady clam up and they couldn't risk it.

"Well, if this is going to make any sense you have to know the whole thing so here goes. Ralph was divorced for several years by then. He was a doctor you know. A medical doctor. He had been on the bank's board and soon after the divorce he gave up medicine and became president of the bank. Everyone knew he played around. That's why his wife divorced him. They had one son — Ralph Junior — he's out west somewhere. I started at the bank as a teller but when Ralph learned that I had gone to secretarial school he asked me to be his secretary. It was better pay and more interesting. And I learned a lot...too much! When he offered me the job of transfer agent, he made it clear that there would be a *'quid pro quo'* he called it — he wanted to 'date' me. I had to look up *quid pro quo* to be sure. I became the bank's transfer agent, got a big raise and Ralph began to share my bed. Ralph treated me very well...until he tired of me."

There was another long pause while Leigh Cranston thought about what she would tell them next.

"When he took up with a younger woman he had met on a Caribbean Cruise he started giving me bank stock...a bonus for my good work he told me. He just told me to transfer 100 shares to my name from the treasury...that's what they call the account where stock waiting to be issued is kept. It really is just on the bank's stock book. I asked what entry I should make to justify the transfer to my name. Usually there is an offsetting entry showing that the stock was paid for. He simply said 'none...don't make any. No one will be the wiser.' That happened five times. Now I know all he wanted was to put me in a position where he could blackmail me. When that became obvious even to dumb me, I transferred the stock back to treasury...actually I simply deleted the original transfers. I'm sure it can be traced in the computer's memory but you'd have to know what you were doing and so far nothing has come up.

"I told you that to show how devious he is. Now, getting back to the present. When the regular secretary who records the Board of Directors meetings is sick, I take her place. That happened a couple of times last fall. At that Board meeting I learned that Northeast Holdings — a Massachusetts bank — was in talks with our bank on a merger proposal. Almost the next day Ralph came to my office and told me to transfer 5000 shares of the bank's stock from the treasury to a Ralph Younger. He told me that he was exercising part of his stock options and not to worry about the accounting — he'd see to it. I asked him for at least a social security number or a Federal ID so I could report the transfer to the IRS at the end of the year as required. He said he'd get it for me. He never did.

"Before the end of the year he told me to transfer another 10,000 shares to that account. He said it was his bonus for the year. Then he gave me an ID number to use and told me to print out the certificates and send them to a brokerage firm in San Francisco. He said the shares would be going to his son. A few days later I got the transfer order and the shares were transferred to a 'street name' at the San Francisco brokerage. The bank belongs to a service which provides us with changes to government regulations and I keep up on them, so I asked him — in the light of the pending merger — if he had made a disclosure to the SEC that he had purchased the shares as the regulations required. He told me that it was none of my business. I offered to fill out the form for him and it was then he sat down at my desk right in front of me, looked me dead in the eyes and told me that if I ever told anyone about the transfer — the SEC or anyone else — he'd tell them about the illegal transfers I had made to my own account. I told him to go ahead — I'd long since transferred them back to treasury. He was really angry then. He got up in my face and said he'd kill me if I told anyone. Then he repeated it and asked me if I understood. I said I did and he left.

Leigh paused for a moment. She was visibly upset and shaking. Then she continued, "I was really scared...really scared! And after I thought about it, I knew I wouldn't do anything. I knew with my limited education I could not get a better job anywhere. I just had to go along with him. About two weeks ago he came into my office with the subpoena from the SEC. He was really upset. He threw the SEC demand for information at me and asked me point blank if I had 'caused the problem.' I finally convinced him that I hadn't done anything — that I didn't have a clue what was going on. Then he repeated his threat — he'd kill me if I stepped out of line. He told me to get the information the SEC wanted together and give it to him as soon as I had it all and to make sure no one else saw it.

"We have a good computer system but it took the rest of the day to get it all together. It was on his desk in a sealed envelope the next morning. He came back to my office as soon as he got in and read it.

He ordered me to re-do the papers and eliminate the Ralph Younger account. I tried to protest and he asked if I had forgotten what he told me the day before. I was scared so I just said I'd do it and I did."

"So, as far as you know, the SEC knows nothing about the Ralph Younger stock?" Joe asked.

"They do not. The only one I told was Mr. Fairbanks. I asked him what I should do and he said he had to think about it and he'd get back to me. He never did. Then I learned he'd been murdered. I thought right away that Ralph was some way involved with it."

"What happened after you gave the altered information to Mr. Ralston?"

"I assume he gave it to the SEC. A couple of days later, the notices of the proposed merger that we were required to send to the stockholders were back from the printer. I had extra help getting them mailed. It took all of my time."

"And Mr. Ralston...where was he?"

"At some point I knew he was back from Maine. I don't remember exactly. I haven't talked to him since he threatened me the last time. We haven't seen him at the bank for several days."

"Is that unusual?"

"No, not really. He comes and goes these days."

"Can you get me the name of the brokerage firm in San Francisco?"

"Sure."

"And there is something else we need badly. We need copies of everything you gave Mr. Ralston to give to the SEC."

"I've gone this far — I might as well give you a set of the copies I made and have here at home. I figured I should have a couple of sets for self protection...just in case Ralston tried to say I hadn't given him all he asked for...or told me what not to include for that matter. I have all the original copies — the pages containing the Ralph Younger stock and the ones where those were deleted. "

Leigh Cranston left them and went to another part of the house, but soon returned and handed Joe a folder containing several pages of documents.

"It's all there," she said. "I hope it helps."

"Mrs. Cranston, I'm not a lawyer and I can't give you any advice, but I think you should consult one right away," Joe told her.

"I've been wondering about that. Am I in trouble?"

"You could be. It depends on what you told the SEC investigators when they talked to you. If they asked you a specific question and you lied to them it's a federal offense...a crime actually... even if they didn't make you take an oath to tell the truth."

"Oh my God!"

"You have to take your lawyer's advice, but usually it helps if you go to the police before they come to you."

"I'll do it. I know who to go to. I'll do it tomorrow."

Joe gave her his card and told her he would call her at home the next night to get the name of the brokerage firm in San Francisco. She read the card and then asked if he was really a retired Maine State Police lieutenant. When he assured her that he was, she took his hand and thanked him for coming and telling her what she should do. She said she would have the information for them when he called. They thanked her again for all her help and left.

It was then after 6 p.m. Joe wanted to talk to Dan and then, if he agreed, to go on to New York City to talk to Cece and give her the information they had acquired. He was being cautious. He feared that there was a possibility the FBI or the SEC had a wire tap on Cece's phone and he didn't want to risk a conversation on it. He had no idea where that conversation would lead. Joe called Dan on his cell phone. Dan was impressed that Joe had convinced Ms. Cranston not only to talk to him, but to give him the information and the copies of the stock transfers. He told Joe that what Ralston apparently had been doing in the industry was called 'parking' and if it were coupled with a merger to avoid the law, as in the case here, it was a serious federal crime. Preventing a disclosure of the fact was certainly a motive for Ralston to murder anyone he suspected might do it. The fact that Ralston had threatened Ms. Cranston that he'd kill her if she disclosed what he was doing, made the theory all the more believable. Since the transfer of ConnTrust stock was an in-house operation, Ms. Cranston was probably the only other person who had the information. How Ralston surmised that she gave Gordon Fairbanks the information was another story and they might never know the answer. One thing they knew for sure was that he had it and gave it to the SEC.

Dan gave Joe his blessing to make a quick trip to New York City to see Cece and talk to her about what they had developed from the interview. Joe got back in the Caprice and told Jim to head down Connecticut 8, the turnpike south to Bridgeport, where they would find a motel for the night and then go into the city and find Cece the next morning. Joe had never been on a case that frustrated him as much as this one had.

"Jim, I have a feeling I'm in this thing way over my head." Joe said.

"I don't believe that," Jim reassured him. "It's just because this involves a subject neither of us knows anything about. We've been in these kinds of situations before and we learn and get to the bottom of things eventually."

Joe hoped he was right but at that moment, there were so many possibilities he wasn't so sure. Joe felt sure that Sergeant Tardif was about to make an arrest and he was greatly troubled with the thought of Cece being in jail for a long time waiting to go to trial for murder. Joe made it a practice not to let himself get close to the people he was working for, but the first time he met Cece he was truly impressed. It wasn't her good looks nor her keen intelligence that impressed him. It was the deference with which she treated him. He couldn't bring himself to believe she was a murderer — or Tiger's accomplice.

CHAPTER FOURTEEN

As soon as the investigators were settled in a room at a motel on the outskirts of Bridgeport, Joe called Cece at her apartment in the City. He quickly assured her that there was nothing new to worry about. He said they were in Connecticut to talk to a witness — that the witness had been helpful and, hopefully, they were making some progress. He needed to talk to her and, if possible, to Kevin Burke. Cece agreed to meet them at the Fairbanks office at 8:30 a.m. She said she would talk to Kevin and ask him to join them. She knew Kevin was greatly concerned about Gordon's murder and expected he would be willing to meet.

Joe and Jim were in the City at 7 a.m. They found a parking garage uptown and took the subway to Wall Street. They met Cece in the reception area of Fairbanks & Burke at the appointed time. She took them to her office on the floor below and Joe explained why Jim was with him. Before they could begin, Cece asked how the interview Dan had with her father had gone. Joe gave her the facts of that conversation in detail.

"Your father had records which confirmed that he had been following ConnTrust stock for more than three years. There were detailed records not only of the stock prices, but also an analysis of the bank's quarterly reports showing its good performance and growth. Mr. Tandy had started buying ConnTrust stock a couple of years before the bank merger was announced and over ten months before the parties began to talk. By the time they left, the SEC investigators seemed satisfied, but your father couldn't be sure. Dan is quite sure that your father isn't a target, but, even so, Dan advised him to engage a lawyer who specialized in the securities field to represent him."

"Joe, if Dad isn't a target, doesn't that destroy Sergeant Tardif's theory that Tiger and I murdered Gordon?" Cece asked.

"Well, if it holds up, it destroys that as a motive. But the State doesn't have to prove motive under Maine law," Joe answered. "Tardif starts with the proposition that you two were the last to be with Mr.

Fairbanks, and that Tiger had the ability to inject the poison. If he wanted to, he could conjure up any number of scenarios for a motive."

Joe then went on to tell Cece what they had learned from Mrs. Cranston. He was nearly finished when Kevin Burke joined them.

After some small talk, Kevin said. "I spent the afternoon with Gerald Burstine at the SEC. He called and wanted to see me to ask me some more questions. The way those questions were phrased gave me the impression Burstine suspected someone high up in the bank was buying its stock and 'parking' it for a sale after the merger was final. During the process, he assured me that the SEC was making progress with its investigation of the ConnTrust merger but that it has decided to allow the merger to go forward. The SEC has satisfied itself, that whatever the problems are, they are limited to a few individuals and the merger is in the best interests of the stockholders. Depending on what eventually develops, the SEC will either go after those individuals with a civil action to recover the profits they made and return them to the corporation, plus a fine in triple the amount recovered. Or they might bring criminal charges under RICO, if the facts warrant."

"Mr. Burke, we are sure that Mr. Burstine knows for a fact that Ralston was obtaining large amounts of ConnTrust stock and 'parking' it," Joe told him. "He had it transferred directly to a broker in a street name..."

"How do you know that?" Kevin interrupted.

"We've promised not to disclose the source at this point, but I can tell you it is from a person at ConnTrust who has access to the stock records. "

"I wonder why the SEC hasn't gone directly to the transfer agent for ConnTrust and subpoenaed the records?" Kevin asked.

"They have. They did that immediately, don't you remember?" Cece asked.

"I thought that was only for transfers of over a certain percentage of the bank's stock as well as the other information they wanted," Kevin replied.

"It was stockholders with over one percent and transfers totaling 2500 shares during the last nine months. Either way, that would certainly include what Ralston was 'parking,'" Cece reminded him.

"We now know that Ralston's transfers were not included in the returns he made in answer to the subpoena," Joe told him.

"How do you know that?" Kevin asked.

Joe looked at Cece as if to ask for her help.

"Kevin, you know Joe and Jim are working for Tiger and me, and Joe isn't comfortable in disclosing what they have learned. But I can tell you. Yesterday they met with the transfer agent for ConnTrust and she told them that Ralston had threatened to kill her if she disclosed the fact that he had transferred stock to an account not in his name without disclosing it to the SEC in accordance with Section 16 of the Act. But as of yesterday, the agent had not corrected the information given the SEC," Cece said.

"I'm happy to know that. It answers a lot of questions for me. But it does create a problem. Now that I ...the firm has that information we'll have to tell the SEC. It's not protected by attorney-client privilege. It didn't come from our client," Kevin said.

"It came from an employee of our client. It's the same thing. But it didn't come in the ordinary way — so I guess you're right," Cece said.

"I hope you can delay that," Joe interjected. "The lady was scared to death of Ralston but I think we convinced her to see a lawyer and then go to the SEC to try to avoid being involved herself. We owe her that much anyway."

"Even if you wait 'til afternoon it would help," Jim said. "There is some more important information she promised us and we need a bit of time," Jim said.

"Okay, I can wait that long," Kevin promised.

"May we ask you a few questions, Mr. Burke?" Joe asked.

"Cece told me you wanted to talk to me and I agreed. That's why I'm here. You have to be quick though. I'm on my way to Torrington to meet with the ConnTrust Board of Directors in an emergency session. Apparently the Board hasn't gone along with Ralston firing our firm. I've decided to stay with them a while longer and find out what is going on. I don't know what the meeting is about but I can guess," he answered.

"We understand that Miss Rosen is on the west coast and we hope you can tell us her address," Joe said.

"I wish I could. I can't...I don't have it."

"You haven't heard from her since you came back to the City from New Brunswick?"

"No...Why do you want to know?"

"Mrs. Cranston — she's the transfer agent for ConnTrust — gave us copies of everything she got together for Ralston to give the SEC and the missing pages as well. She also gave us a complete list of stockholders and the amounts of stock held by them, as well as dates of all purchases of the bank's stock in the last six months. It isn't a long list. ConnTrust is a small bank by most standards. Its stock is traded over the counter but it isn't widely traded. Mrs. Cranston pointed to several purchases of one or two hundred shares at a time by a Julius Rudniki, for the benefit of the Jacob Rosen Trust. The name didn't mean anything to us. Mrs. Cranston said it was a guess on her part, but from something Ralston said, she assumed that the bank's consultant, Miss Rosen, had something to do with that trust."

"Oh my God! That could explain it!" Kevin said.

"Explain what?" Cece asked.

"Okay...time to level with you..." Kevin answered. "Every time I tell a lie it catches up with me. This was a private matter and I didn't think it mattered to anyone but me.

"I had to fight to keep Sarah in Northeast Harbor for Gordon's funeral. She wanted to leave as soon as she heard he was dead...even before we all knew he had been murdered. She left right after the funeral. I went to Saint Andrews alone."

"We suspected that already, Mr. Burke," Joe told him. "I checked with the hotel there and found that you had registered alone. Of course you may not have told the clerk Sarah Rosen was with you, but we doubted it. We wondered about it though, and when we saw the Rosen name on the stock list we wondered even more."

"How much stock did the trust buy?" Kevin asked.

"A thousand shares total," Jim answered.

"One thousand shares. Well, that's about $37,000. There are 3,000,000 shares of ConnTrust stock outstanding. One per cent is 30,000 shares — the trust purchases are way below the amount to require a report or even constitute wrongdoing," Kevin said.

"Still, if it got out, it would destroy her credibility as a consultant," Cece offered.

"True," Kevin agreed. "But I don't think it explains why she left so quickly. She told me she had to get away...that she'd be in touch. She didn't tell me where she was going, only that she was going to the west coast. I think she was still in love with Gordon — that she took up with me just to try to get at him. That last day we went sailing with him she was so angry she wouldn't carry on a conversation with him...or me for that matter. She kept staring at him and then, seeing his eyes were on Cece in her bikini, she couldn't conceal her anger. She practically ran off the boat when we came in. When I eventually caught up with her, she was in our car, still so angry she wouldn't talk to me."

"What did you do then?" Joe asked.

"We drove back to our rented cottage in Sawyer's Cove. I grilled steaks. Sarah wasn't one to have more than one or two drinks, but that evening she had several. After we ate, she had another and then went to bed in the spare room. We hardly spoke all evening. I read awhile and went to bed ...in the other bedroom.

"I sleep soundly and my hearing isn't good. Too many rifle shots in the service, I guess. Anyway, it must have been two or three in the morning...I didn't have my watch on. I heard a car come in the yard and I got up. It was Sarah. I hadn't heard her go out. She waited out there in the car for what seemed like an eternity. Finally she got out of the car and came into the cottage. She looked liked she'd been through a war. I laid it on all the drinks she had. But she was walking okay and her speech wasn't bad.

"I asked her where she'd been and she said 'Oh just driving around...I couldn't sleep.' I thought that was strange but I didn't want to argue with her. I went into the other bedroom. Sarah was right behind me throwing off her clothes..."

Kevin paused for a moment, then continued hesitantly, "This is getting pretty personal... I don't..."

"But Kevin, we need to know everything you can tell us," Cece told him. "As badly as we don't want to believe it, under the circumstances as we now know them, Sarah could be involved..."

"I can understand why you say that," Kevin answered. "I've been wondering myself... Okay... I'm sure you know Cece, that Sarah and I have enjoyed each other often since we began our relationship...but that night she was a wild woman. I couldn't satisfy her, try as I might. She finally wore me out.

"I began again to think we were falling in love. From the first time we dated, we really enjoyed each other's company...and the sex was fantastic for both of us. At least that is the way I saw it. But the next day Sarah was cold as a dead haddock and when we got the call that Gordon was dead she went into a funk and wouldn't talk. I had known for years that they were lovers but when they broke up over something I was never made privy to, I thought it was over. Sarah said it was over and I believed her. I laid her behavior that day to remembering old times. Hell, Gordon was my best friend and I wasn't exactly with it either.

"Sarah was never the same again. As I said, I made her stay for the funeral. I had an awful time getting her to go to the brunch at Carleton Cottage afterward and then she insisted on leaving early. As soon as we got back to our cottage at Sawyer's Cove, she packed her things and said I had to drive her to Bangor so she could fly back to New York. She couldn't stand to be on the Island another minute. I didn't question her. When she gets in that mood, no one does. Anyhow. I drove her to Bangor and she caught a flight out. That is the last time I saw her.

"There was a long letter from her waiting on my desk when I returned after Labor Day but she didn't say where she was, only that she was on her way to the west coast and she'd be in touch soon. I'm still waiting. Okay...that's it. I have to leave now or I'll be late. I'd like to be kept informed though. I don't know how I'll react when they find out who killed my best friend."

With that, Kevin got up and left. As soon as he was gone, Joe asked Cece if he might call Mrs. Cranston at the bank in Torrington. He told Cece that Mrs. Cranston had promised to get them some information and he hoped she would give it to him on the phone. Cece gave him the number from her rolodex and he dialed it and soon he was talking to Mrs. Cranston. She told Joe she was happy he didn't wait to call her at home that night because she was worried that her lawyer, who she was to meet in an hour, would make her change her mind. She immediately gave him the name and city of the brokerage he asked her for — Stavitz & Company, San Francisco. He'd have to look up the street address. All she had was the computer transfer information. Joe thanked her again and told her he hoped her lawyer would advise her to go to the SEC immediately. She told him she was going to call the SEC investigators she had spoken to, even if her lawyer advised against it — it was the only thing that would satisfy her. Then she said a hurried thanks and goodbye and hung up.

It was too early for lunch but Cece was still uneasy talking specifics in her office, even though Kevin now told her that Fairbanks & Burke wasn't bugged. He had asked Gerry Burstine a direct question and had been assured that his office was not under surveillance. Cece told Joe and Jim it was coffee break time and invited them to go down to a shop on the street and have coffee and a bagel with her.

The bagel shop was crowded but they found a table in back where Cece was sure none of the other lawyers in her firm who might drop by could hear them. After they ordered, Cece asked their assessment of the new developments.

"I haven't had time to really think about Sarah Rosen," Joe responded. "Until a half hour ago she wasn't even on my long list of suspects."

"She certainly is now, though," Jim added. "The short list."

"Well, Ralston certainly knew about it," Cece reminded them. "Remember the threatening letter he sent to Gordon? But Sarah had to have a motive other than the ConnTrust merger. The amount of stock her trustee purchased — if in fact that is the case — doesn't rise to any standard the SEC would go after her on. Ralston knew of the purchases and must have known she and Gordon were lovers. He threatened Gordon with revealing the fact that Sarah's trustee was making the stock purchases. Gordon may have told Sarah about the threat and told her he was going to the SEC. It's way out, but that could be a motive, coupled with her jealousy."

"Okay, I'll accept that as a possibility," Joe said. "But let's look at it from another angle. Where would Sarah Rosen get the poison — the sodium pentathol? Did she know how to inject the stuff even if she could get it?"

"Tiger says it doesn't have to be injected," Cece told him. "It can be ingested as well."

"Oh, that's right. But she'd still have to get it in a concentrated amount," Joe argued. "I checked. It isn't something you go into a drug store and buy off the counter."

"Okay," Jim said. "Here's what we know about the lady. She lives in New York City. She's got an MBA from Wharton, right Joe? She's a specialist in corporate mergers. She's known Mr. Fairbanks since they were at Harvard together. They often worked on the same merger projects. They have had a sexual relationship which had been ongoing for years but broke up recently for some reason. At some point after that she got into a similar relationship with Kevin Burke. Both she and Mr. Burke were in Northeast Harbor the week before the murder. They were on the Fairbanks yacht the day of the murder. They were invited to stay for a lobster dinner when they all came in from sailing that afternoon...right Miss Tandy?"

"Right Jim, but please call me Cece."

"Okay. Miss Rosen wouldn't accept the invitation and they left for their rented cottage on the back side of the Island. She was really moody and wouldn't talk to Mr. Burke. She had a lot to drink. She wouldn't go to bed with Mr. Burke when he retired for the night, but used the other bedroom. She must have gotten up and left right after that. He heard her drive into the cottage yard when she came back at two or three the next morning. For some reason, by then she had a burning desire for him. Love does strange things to people. Was she celebrating her former lover's death by being passionate with his best friend?

"Rosen tried to avoid the brunch at the Fairbanks' cottage... Carleton Cottage is it?...after the funeral and they left early. Within hours after that, she made Mr. Burke drive her to Bangor where she got a plane to New York City and he hasn't seen her since.

"Apparently Mr. Burke didn't want anyone to know she had left so precipitously, so he went to Saint Andrews in New Brunswick for the weekend. He told everyone that Miss Rosen had gone with him. His excuse for lying is that it's a private matter and no one's business. It's obvious he didn't want his friends to know Miss Rosen was using him — that she was still in love with Mr. Fairbanks and his murder had affected her to the point she couldn't function — that all she wanted to do was to leave Maine — and New York for that matter."

"I think that's about it, Jim," Joe agreed. "Most of Mr. Burke's story can be corroborated. Cece, do you agree that Miss Rosen was upset for some reason? That she left the brunch at Carleton Cottage early?"

"I agree to both of those things," Cece answered.

"As soon as I knew that Mr. Burke said they had gone to the Algonquin Hotel in Saint Andrews, I checked, and only he was registered. He confirmed that without knowing that I knew it already. We have to rely on his truthfulness for the rest," Joe said. "What do you think, Cece?"

"About his truthfulness?" Cece responded. "I think Kevin is a man with strong principles. You don't survive as a merger lawyer without them. You could see how embarrassed he was when he admitted he had told a little white lie. He wasn't trying to deceive anyone with it, I'm sure. I buy his explanation that he was trying to excuse Sarah. He did, as you say, tell us the truth before he knew you'd checked on him."

"Well, the bottom line is that we now have another suspect to check out," Joe said.

"Cece, Joe and I need your input on the ins and outs on the fact that Mr. Ralston was 'parking' — if that's the term — ConnTrust stock," Jim said. "Is that important?"

"It is very important. That's the term — 'parking.' It simply means that an insider buys securities and places them in a name that is difficult to trace for the purpose of a later sale. In this case, Ralph Ralston is what is defined by law as an insider. An insider is a person who trades securities on information he has, but which is not available to the general public. By definition, an officer of a company is an insider. Apparently he purchased...or at least acquired, a large quantity of ConnTrust stock when he learned the bank was going to be merged. He knew that under the terms of the merger, a huge profit to holders of ConnTrust stock would result. That is prohibited by the Insider Trading Sanctions Act of 1984, as well as generally by the Securities Exchange Act of 1934 — the SEA. That's just part of Ralston's problem.

"Section 16[a] of the Act requires an officer to file a report to the SEC of all stock purchased while a merger of his company is contemplated. From what Ms. Cranston told you, Ralston didn't make that filing. But the worst charge Ralston could face is a criminal charge."

"I thought these things were always civil... civil penalties and triple damages," Jim said.

"If the government can prove repeated transactions and a conspiracy, then RICO comes into play — the Racketeering Act. That's what sent Michael Milken to jail. We know the first part can be proved from what Mrs. Cranston told you — that Ralston purchased, or somehow acquired, or caused to be transferred for his benefit— several large amounts of his company's stock. If someone else was involved in what he was doing, there would be a conspiracy," Cece told them.

"This is probably pure fantasy," Joe said, "but I wonder if Miss Rosen was in the scheme with Ralston. Mr. Burke told us that he thought she was heading for the west coast. Ms. Cranston just gave me the name of the broker she sent Ralston's stock to in what she called a 'street name.' The broker is in San Francisco. It's probably far out, but I still wonder..."

"It's something we need checked out, Joe." Cece told him.

They discussed how that might be accomplished and the more they talked about it, the more impossible the task seemed.

"One step forward, and two back," were Joe's parting words as the meeting ended.

CHAPTER FIFTEEN

As he drove his Eldorado up to Torrington for the afternoon meeting with ConnTrust's Board of Directors, Kevin Burke was unusually morose. As his thoughts wandered back over his life he realized that, for the most part, it was a happy one. That was especially true of his days at Harvard Law School — days which for him, in spite of the constant challenges, were ones of pure joy. His life up until then had its ups and downs — from the high of being a football star at Yale to the low the following year spent in Vietnam leading his Marine platoon. His deep patriotism had soon been shattered, and it was only his loyalty to the Marine Corps that kept him performing. He saw no justification for the U. S. being involved in Vietnam. It pleased him that even the politicians who backed our involvement then, now agreed that it was a terrible mistake.

In less than a year Kevin was shot by a Vietcong in an ambush. Close to death his faith in God was all that kept him from going over the edge. He now remembered the indescribable feeling of happiness he had when he had recovered sufficiently from those wounds to fly back to the States. Eileen Murphy had been his one and only sweetheart from the time they both were in high school. Shortly after he returned and had mended sufficiently from his war wounds, he and Eileen were wed. Soon after that he followed his life's ambition and began Harvard Law School. Eileen had been a constant joy then — sober, loving and adoring. He thought ' I had the world by the tail — and lost it!

With the help of his son, Kevin Jr., he had been coping with the trauma of his divorce and the slow and subtle alienation of his two younger sons. Kevin Jr. was then a lawyer, an associate in Hale & Dorr in Boston, happily married to a woman of Irish descent, Kathleen Boyle. Kevin Sr. adored Kate and had spent a lot of time with them after the divorce — to the point that he was afraid he was intruding in their lives. Yet he couldn't stand to be in his New York apartment alone on weekends. When Sarah Rosen had her fallout with Gordon earlier that year, it had been a godsend for him.

It had started innocently. It was one of those many times when the ConnTrust merger seemed beyond saving. Gordon's usual calm demeanor had escaped him. There had been a confrontation with Ralston and Kevin was sure they were going to lose a big-paying client. Sarah had taken Ralston's side and Kevin suggested that they all needed a breather before the situation became totally beyond redemption. Kevin knew Gordon was right in his analysis of the situation and that Sarah didn't understand his position. Gordon expected her to understand the legal intricacies of an unusual merger and he expected too much. After all, Sarah wasn't a lawyer. Kevin abruptly told Gordon he was going to take Sarah to lunch and Gordon got the message.

They were in Torrington. They drove to a small restaurant on the outskirts of town. The drive took time but the two didn't speak. Kevin was patient. He realized that it would take a while for Sarah to cool off. The waiter was a clown and soon Sarah was talking to him. When the waiter left, she asked Kevin what Gordon's problem was and that gave him the opening he had been looking for.

"It really isn't Gordon's problem, Sarah," he replied. "The issue is extremely complicated from a legal standpoint. What you see is a simple accounting problem. What Gordon sees are government regulations which prevent your simple accounting approach from being viable for a CEO, bent on self aggrandizement."

Kevin used the entire time during the lunch to explain in minute detail the complicated legal problem the merger faced and finally Sarah understood. It was then that Kevin saw Sarah as someone other than a very tough and very smart business woman. When she saw how wrong she had been, she dissolved into tears. When she regained control of her emotions, she told Kevin that if she had not been so angry at Gordon she would have listened to him and perhaps understood where he was coming from. Then she told Kevin about the argument that caused their parting — that she had told Gordon he was throwing away his wonderful life by chasing after a woman much too young for him, and one who probably didn't want him anyway. She reminded Gordon that over the years Beth had put up with his constant flirtations with women but she couldn't be expected to be so understanding forever.

"I probably was too hard on him," Sarah said after a pause in her story. "I reminded him he always said that his love for Beth was undying...that he would never leave her for another woman. Recently he told me he knew Beth had only a year or two to live so I told him Beth would surely find out what he was up to, and that he must want her gone because it would surely kill her. That was when he got so angry he started to strike me, but instead he got up out of my bed, put on his clothes and left."

Kevin seemed not to understand. He asked who the woman was. To his complete surprise, Sarah told him it was Cece. How could he have missed it, he wondered. Yet Sarah was positive about Gordon's new infatuation and the fact that they had broken up seemed to confirm it. It was the first time Gordon had not shared his innermost thoughts with him. Kevin knew that Gordon admired Cece greatly because he often sang her praises to him. But those were always in the line of admiring her ability as a young lawyer and never about her beauty or her sex appeal.

When Cece first came to work at Fairbanks & Burke, she had worked for Kevin. When Gordon asked that she be assigned to him, Kevin had first refused but when he saw that Gordon wasn't going to give up, he gave in. Now reminded, he observed during the weekends of work on the merger and the times afterwards while they were all in Northeast Harbor during the summer that Gordon's eyes were always on the young woman, and that Gordon always seemed to want to be near her. Kevin was now sure Sarah was right, and he understood how badly she felt. He knew that Gordon had been an important part of Sarah's life over the last several years and now that part was missing. He had gone down that lonely road himself.

They stayed in Torrington that week to be close to the source of the financial data they needed for their work on the merger. Sarah asked Kevin to go to dinner with her after they finished up the next day. Once Kevin saw Sarah's other side, he found that he really enjoyed her company. After their talk at lunch that day, they were often together — but Kevin often wondered how much of that was caused by Sarah's desire to show Gordon he wasn't the only fish in the ocean.

Kevin had real trouble adjusting to his divorce. His Catholic upbringing taught him that 'once married always married.' He was aware of the fact that these days it was relatively easy to get an annulment in the Catholic church — especially from an errant wife who was also an alcoholic — but at first he was determined not to go that route. Underneath it all, he had hoped that Eileen would sober up and come begging for a second chance. It hadn't happened.

Still a handsome man in his early fifties, Kevin had not lost any of his desire for sex. And certainly Sarah had not lost hers. The attraction for one another increased daily and by the end of that week their pent-up ardor ended in passionate love making, completely satisfying for both of them. At first Kevin felt guilty after each wild encounter. It was as if, for the first time in his life, he was cheating on his wife. Sarah realized what was troubling Kevin so she told him — with the same convincing sincerity she had used with Gordon— that as much as she had come to love him, she had no intention of marrying him. She enjoyed her freedom too much — and besides, he wasn't a Jew.

These thoughts about Sarah caused Kevin to realize how much he missed her. He wondered where she was and why she hadn't called or written at least. Where could she have been those several hours she was away from their little cottage in Sawyer's Cove the night Gordon was murdered? He couldn't bear the thought that the woman he was falling in love with could murder his best friend.

Without realizing how he arrived there, Kevin found himself in the ConnTrust parking lot. He retrieved his briefcase from the back seat of his Eldorado and made his way into the bank, his thoughts now suddenly full of worry as to what the meeting was all about. His review of all the documents his firm had prepared had disclosed not even a small problem with the firm's work, so he knew it had to be something else.

Kevin announced himself to the receptionist and was directed to the elevator and to the fourth floor board room. He was greeted by a woman seated outside the closed doors and was told that the directors had been in session for some time. He was expected, however, and she would tell them he had arrived. She soon returned and told Kevin they would be with him shortly. He was offered a comfortable chair and he sat down to read the morning's edition of the *Wall Street Journal.* Half an hour later the woman's phone rang and after answering the call, she rose and ushered him into the board room.

As he quickly looked around the table, Kevin saw only one face he recognized. It was Walter Goselin, the bank's local legal counsel. There were nine other men around the table. Only one was young and he sat next to Goselin, suggesting he was also a lawyer. The man at the head of the large board room table asked Kevin to sit, pointing to the only empty chair. He introduced himself as Joel Watson, vice-president of the company. Then the other men introduced themselves in turn.

"We've asked you here because we need explanations," Watson said.

"I'll do my best," Kevin assured him.

"First, I'm sure you've noticed our president, Mr. Ralston, is absent." Watson continued. "I should say ex-president. The board has today relieved him of that position. We have been assured by Mr. Goselin that we have the right...even the duty to do that, even though he is not present. No one at the bank has seen or heard from Ralph for a week.

"Our concern, of course, is for ConnTrust. I'm sure you are aware that the SEC is conducting an investigation of the bank. Actually, Walter has been told that neither the bank nor the Board of Directors are the subject of the investigation. They told him the investigation is concerned with individuals... within this bank, specifically Ralph Ralston. We've asked you here because of our concern with the bank's merger with Northeast Holdings. It is something all of us feel strongly about. We want it to go forward. We all agree that it is in the best interests of all of the stockholders. Walter told us that your firm's work has not in any way been questioned, either by him or the SEC. That is why the Board wants you to continue with us. We are aware that Ralph tried to fire you but he had no right to do that.

"By the way, please accept our condolences for the loss of your partner Mr. Fairbanks, who all of us knew and respected very much."

"Thank you...all of you," Kevin said. "It has been..."

Kevin almost lost himself, hearing once again how people related so positively to his partner after only a short acquaintance.

"Mr. Burke, we know you were working closely with Mr. Fairbanks on the merger and will be able to answer our questions. Actually it is really only one question. Do you know of any reason whatsoever that might cause the SEC to stop the merger from going forward?"

"I have to give you a caveat. What I'm about to say is based on my current knowledge of the situation," Kevin started. "I can tell you that when the firm first learned that the SEC was conducting an investigation of the merger, we commenced a thorough review of the entire proceedings and from that review we are satisfied that everything is in order. That of course is subject to change if we find that the financial information we were given was not factually correct."

"Do you know what caused the SEC to commence the investigation?"

"Only rumors. I understand they had a tip."

"We've been told it was a tip and it came from your firm."

"I am not aware of that. But it could be true."

"We've been told that Mr. Fairbanks wrote a letter to Mr. Burstine at the SEC."

"I can't deny that or confirm it for that matter. I just don't know. I do know that if Mr. Fairbanks came by information that someone in the merger process was doing something illegal, it was his duty to make it known to the government...in this case I suppose, without knowing the details, the SEC."

"But what about your firm's duty of confidentiality to its client?"

Mr. Watson's face was beginning to show frustration and anger. Kevin looked at the others who were all sitting in rapt attention. He waited a moment to answer.

"Perhaps I can answer that best by posing a question to you. Who exactly is the client to whom our firm's duty of confidentiality is owed?"

Watson thought a moment — then a light seemed to go on and he answered, "Why the bank — ConnTrust — of course."

"Right! Fairbanks & Burke represents the corporate entity ConnTrust. If in that representation we come across information that someone in the bank is doing something that adversely affects the interests of our client it is our duty to take action. That action depends on what that someone is doing. If possible, the report is made to the CEO with a request for action to cure the problem. Obviously, if it is the CEO who is the actor, a different route has to be taken. And if the act is criminal, we have no choice as to what route to follow."

There was a deep silence around the table, broken only by the sound of several of the men sitting back in their chairs.

After several moments Joel Watson said, "Suppose that a person high up in an organization had knowledge that a merger of that organization was going to take place and that there was profit to be made by the shareholders. Suppose that person bought a significant amount of stock in the organization and had the stock placed in someone else's name. Is that the kind of action which would cause that organization's lawyers to make a report?"

"Assuming that the person is an 'insider' — the SEC has yet to specifically and completely define that term — he must report his purchases to the SEC. If he doesn't, it's a civil matter — he can be required to return his profits to the company and be subject to a fine in an amount equal to triple the profits he made.

"Take this case. An insider places company stock in someone else's name intending to sell it soon after the merger is complete — in any case in less than two years after the merger. The insider doesn't make the required report. That can be treated as a criminal offense under the RICO act. That's similar to what happened to Michael Milken. So, in the first case — failure to report purchases of stock to the SEC — we would, if possible, try to get the report filed and failing that we'd go to the directors, and if no help came from them, we'd then be required to go to the SEC or we'd be in violation of the law ourselves. In the second case — it's called 'parking' — prudence requires us to go to the SEC or the FBI, or both as soon as we know of it."

Kevin spent an hour answering questions along the same line. When he had finished, the entire board rose to shake his hand and thank him for his help. Walter Goselin followed Kevin out and told him that the board had asked him the same questions and he had tried to answer them but they wanted to hear it from their New York counsel. Kevin asked him directly what Ralph Ralston had done to have the board remove him. Without answering, Goselin asked him to wait while he went back in the board room for his briefcase. He opened it and drew out a folder and handed it to Kevin.

"It's all in there," he said. "Call me if you have any questions. I have to get back in there. Thanks again. I'll be in touch."

Kevin put the folder in his briefcase, bade goodbye to the receptionist and left the bank. In the parking lot after he had gotten into his car, he opened his briefcase and retrieved the file he had just been given. At that moment, his only interest was to find out if the Rosen

Trust was involved. Sarah had told him that her father had left most of his fortune in trust for her mother and, after she died, the trust would continue for her until she was fifty. Then, but only if she had either married a Jew or remained single, it would be hers outright. She told him that her mother had died several years ago and in a year she'd be fifty and the money would be hers. It was part of her explanation of why she would not marry someone who was not Jewish.

The envelope contained an alphabetical list of all stockholders in ConnTrust with the dates of purchase or transfer. Kevin found the Rosen Trust entry and was able to confirm what Joe Goldberg had told him — that the purchases for the trust amounted to only a thousand shares. He knew Sarah was well familiar with the SEC rules and would not have been concerned about an action on the government's part, even if it could be proven that she had given her trustee information about the pending merger. He felt a great weight fall off his shoulders. Still, if the fact of the purchases became public, it certainly would end her career as a merger consultant. Kevin knew that Sarah didn't have to work but he also knew that she would be devastated by that event. He drove out of the parking lot and found his way out of town, his only thought was to find Sarah so he could talk to her and try to get to the truth. Greatly troubled, Kevin knew he wouldn't be able to function properly until he knew whether or not Sarah was involved with Gordon's murder.

*C*HAPTER *S*IXTEEN

Joe intended to call Dan Hardy on his cellular phone as soon as he felt comfortable using it and still pay attention to his drive out of New York. It wasn't until they had passed all the Stamford exits that he auto-dialed Dan's office. Carrie answered the ring.

'Hi, Joe," she said, recognizing his voice.

"Hi, Carrie." he replied. "I'm in Connecticut on my way home. I need to meet with Dan as soon as possible when I get back there."

"Dan's in court," Carrie told him. "I know he'll be free the first thing in the morning. I'll make sure you get to see him then. I know Dan is anxious for your report."

They chatted for a moment, making small talk as old friends will, and then they hung up.

The next morning Dan arrived in his office at his usual hour — 7 a.m. Carrie had asked Ian or Kara to meet with them and Ian arrived right behind Dan. They just had time to start the coffee when Joe joined them. Joe began immediately to give the two lawyers a full report of what he and Jim Murphy learned from Leigh Cranston in Torrington. Carrie soon came in with their coffee and some of the donuts she brought in every morning. By the time Joe had finished his report, she had made copies of the materials Mrs. Cranston had given them. Ian wanted to talk about Ralph Ralston who now was the prime suspect as far as he was concerned, but Joe asked him to wait until he had finished the rest of his report.

The two lawyers were not surprised when Joe told them about the Jacob Rosen Trust under which Sarah Rosen was the beneficiary. At the prior meeting they had discussed the Ralston letter to Gordon Fairbanks in which Ralston had implicated her and Cece in illegal stock trading. But they were really surprised to learn that Sarah Rosen had left the cottage in Sawyer's Cove for several hours on the night Gordon was murdered, and that she did not go to Saint Andrews with Kevin as he had originally said.

"What do you suppose Sarah was doing during those two or three

143

hours she was away from the cottage that night?" Ian asked.

"And what significance should we attach to the fact that she left Northeast Harbor precipitously right after the funeral?" Dan asked. "Why doesn't she at least tell Kevin where she is now?"

"We've been asking ourselves the same questions," Joe answered.

"I wonder if Kevin was being completely truthful with you and if he had more information he had not given Joe or Cece," Ian said. "After all, Kevin lied once before about Sarah's activities right after Gordon Fairbanks was murdered, so...can we really trust him?"

"I was watching him closely when he spoke to us and if I were a betting man, I'd bet he was leveling with us," Joe responded. "We know that he has been in a relationship, as they say, with Miss Rosen and I know that Mr. Burke is troubled by Miss Rosen's actions. As far as we know, she has no one else for an alibi as to where she was that night. If he was really into protecting her, he never would have told us that she left the cottage in Sawyer's Cove for several hours the night of the murder."

"It makes her suspect but it doesn't prove she was the murderer," Dan said. "I suppose there may well be an explanation for what she was doing for several hours that night. She could have just been driving around the backside of the Island or watching the ocean somewhere, trying to get her anger at Gordon under control. We know that she was very upset with him that afternoon. We don't know the reason why she refused to have dinner with him. We are told Miss Rosen was convinced Fairbanks was having an affair with Cece. We know he had shared Miss Rosen's bed for years when his wife was in Maine and he was in New York. And you said Kevin Burke seemed to think she was still in love with Fairbanks — even after their breakup.

"What troubles me most is that none of us know Sarah Rosen that well. Even Cece, who has worked closely with her these past months, can't tell us much about her personal life. You'd think that a woman with her intelligence and apparent maturity wouldn't be capable of murder. But love does strange things. She is nearly fifty, yet she has never married. I honestly don't know if a woman in her situation would act the same as a married woman would when her husband is found to be chasing a young woman. I know about married women from personal observation. A good many of the divorces I've handled have been caused by the husband leaving what appears to be good marriage to take up with a woman half his age. In those cases the wife is almost always severely traumatized. If Miss Rosen thought of herself as being married to Fairbanks, she certainly could have been angered enough by what she supposed was going on to have murdered him."

"I can't fault that thinking," Joe agreed. "We've added her to our list of prime suspects and we need to get all the information we can about her. We especially need to know what she knows about pentathol and if there is a source for her in the potent strength needed to act as it did in this situation. The problem is — where is she?"

"I will be speaking with Cece tonight at the apartment she shares with Tiger in Medford," Dan said. "I don't think we need to ask them to come up to the Island this weekend so I'll tell her that. I'm sure she knows we would like to know where Miss Rosen is and I'll ask her to try to get Burke to tell her right away if he hears from her. He may, or he may not. But that appears to be the only way we are going to find her."

"I want to get back to Ralston," Ian said. "From the beginning I've felt that he may well have the most believable motive for the murder. He was the last one to be with Fairbanks that evening — if our clients are telling us the truth. We know Ralston knew Fairbanks was aware that he was doing something illegal with respect to his bank's merger and had threatened to go to the SEC with the information. We're talking big money here. The way I figure it, it's at least $150,000 just on the increase in value of the 20,000 shares he had transferred in the months before the merger was announced. I'm sure Fairbanks told him what the civil penalties could amount to. Cece says it's triple the profit — so $450,000. More to the point is the possible criminal charge against him under RICO. I'm sure Fairbanks told him about that, too. Now we learn that his Board of Directors has removed him as president of the bank. We know they have enough evidence that he was violating his duty to the bank to do that. They wouldn't dare remove him without just cause. We know he is a medical doctor and would have the knowledge and ability to administer the pentathol. I feel sure he would know where to get a quantity of it in the proper strength. Finally, he's disappeared..."

"His disappearance could be prompted solely by the SEC investigation," Joe suggested.

"But I agree Ralston is a prime suspect," Dan said. "Let's see if the materials Leigh Cranston gave Joe shed any light on that."

They spent the next hours going over the materials Mrs. Cranston had given Joe. The purchases of stock by Coffin & Company — Wexford Tandy's brokerage — were listed and then compared with the information he gave Dan. What he told Dan was completely confirmed as to amount and date. The purchases by the Jacob Rosen Trust were listed as well. Again, it didn't appear that the purchases would begin to amount to anything the SEC rules prohibited, even if it could be proved that Sarah Rosen had told her trustee of the impending merger.

"How do you suppose Ralston knew that Sarah Rosen was the beneficiary of the Jacob Rosen Trust?" Ian asked.

"It would be nice to know," Joe agreed.

"I don't think she was close enough to Ralston to have told him," Dan said.

"He also knew that Fairbanks would want very much to protect her," Ian said. "He must have known about their relationship too. He must have found out somehow. Ralston is one smart cookie, that's for sure."

Dan turned the discussion to what their next move should be. Joe said he thought that Miss Rosen would soon turn up. His judgement was that she was way down on the bottom of the list of suspects and he couldn't justify spending money to find her. It was obvious they didn't have the resources to conduct a manhunt for Ralston either, even though he was now their prime suspect.

"I have trouble believing that Sergeant Tardif isn't looking for Ralston," Ian said.

"I think he would if he had all the information we have," Joe replied.

"At some point soon we will have to give it to him," Dan said. The State's theory is that Cece murdered Fairbanks to keep him from reporting her father and herself to the SEC. These documents and Mr. Tandy's notes ought to prove to anyone that Wexford was dealing in the stock long before the merger was even thought of. That leaves Ralston as a prime suspect. I think it prudent to give what we have on Ralston to Sergeant Tardif right away. I want to hold back Wexford's notes, though. I want to save that for rebuttal if this ever goes to trial."

After weighing the pros and cons they decided that Joe would try to find out what progress Sergeant Tardif was making. If he wasn't completely aware of the SEC investigation and how deeply involved Ralston was, Joe would give him copies of what they had to prove Ralston's involvement. Joe then called the Orono State Police Barracks and caught Tardif just as he was leaving for Augusta. Joe told him that he had some new information for him and asked him to stay put until he could get there in half an hour.

Corporal Carsillo greeted Joe as he arrived and took him into Tardif's office. Joe had prepared his plan carefully. First he asked the two detectives how much information they had been able to obtain with respect to the SEC investigation. Very little, he was told.

"It may be that you have all the information I have and more besides," Joe told them. "I know you had to have a basis for your search warrant of the Tandy cottage on Long Pond. At the time you got the warrant, you must have had some information from the SEC investigators...right?"

"Of course we did," Tardif answered. "I guess I know you well enough to know you aren't trying to accuse us of obtaining an illegal search warrant."

"I am not," Joe assured him. "I guess it's my turn... I know that you have been concentrating your efforts on our clients — trying to prove that the murder was prompted by a desire to protect Miss Tandy — or her father, or both — from being accused of insider trading in the stock of the bank whose merger she was working on. Right so far?"

"Okay," was all Tardif would say.

"You told me when this first came on your plate that you suspected Tiger Wass had committed the murder because he thought that Fairbanks had his eye on Miss Tandy and was trying to get her away from him. You must know by now that it wasn't a lover's quarrel," Joe asserted.

"Maybe. We know the Mount Desert PD had a call in the middle of the night this summer because Fairbanks was at the Tandy cottage attempting to get Miss Tandy to leave with him and Wass stopped it. But we have now obtained a copy of the marriage license and its completed return to the State, so we know Wass and Miss Tandy were married. But that still could somehow be the motive." Tardif hedged.

"Okay, we'll leave it at that, even though we all know that theory is not going anywhere."

"So what do you have for us?"

"Start with the assumption that a man by the name of Ralph Ralston was the last person to be seen with Mr. Fairbanks."

"Okay. He's the president of the bank...ConnTrust. The one in the merger. The one your client's father was buying stock in. We have that basic information."

"Ex-president. The bank's board fired him."

"Oh?"

Joe opened his briefcase and took out the copies Carrie had made. He had the papers in the order he had decided to give them to Tardif and he handed him the first two pages Tiger had recovered from the compartment on *Sea Chaser* — the cover note and the short note to Cece. Those were quickly read, Nick Carsillo reading over Tardif's shoulder. Next he handed them a copy of the first Fairbanks letter to Ralston. They both read it twice.

"What does this mean... 'you'll go to jail'?" Tardif asked.

"Fairbanks apparently had been told that Ralston was doing something called 'parking stock'. It's where an 'insider' puts stock in someone else's name for transfer right after a merger takes place...if I understand it right. I understand that Ralston is an 'insider' by definition. That's because he is...was...president of the bank."

"You can go to jail for that?"

"No, as I understand it, that's a civil matter with the SEC. The jail part comes in under RICO..."

"The racketeering act? It applies to bank mergers?"

"Right. As I understand it, there has to be a conspiracy — two or more involved — and repeated transactions. Fairbanks apparently knew there was a conspiracy. Note the reference to the president of Northeast Holdings, the other bank in the merger...John Gropus. Apparently Fairbanks knew that Ralston had transferred stock more than once at least. To make it work, Gropus had to be in on it. Fairbanks would have figured that out early on."

Tardif read the letter again and then said, "I see you have more..."

Joe gave them Ralston's response and the next letter Fairbanks sent him. In that letter he reminded Ralston that his firm represented the bank — not Ralston — and told him to make the required report to the SEC or he would have to withdraw and report the matter to the SEC. Again, that letter was read twice.

"That one is clear enough. More?"

Joe gave them the next in the series — the letter to Fairbanks from Ralston. In it Ralston made the threat that if Fairbanks informed the SEC, he would also inform them that Fairbanks' 'lady friend's' trustee and Cece's father were both trading in the ConnTrust stock. The two detectives read that letter quickly.

"These are very interesting," Tardif told Joe. "They back up our theory that Miss Tandy was giving her father information on the merger and Fairbanks was going to the SEC and expose it all."

"These are copies. They may be faked," Tardif said.

"At the moment you have to take my word that they are genuine. Dan Hardy has the originals and he says they are protected by the attorney client privilege. He will make the originals available for testing when and if it becomes necessary," Joe answered.

"But you could have ..."

Joe got up, took the file with the remaining papers from Sergeant Tardif's desk and started to leave.

"Hold on, Joe!" Tardif said, realizing he had gone too far. "I apologize. I didn't mean you. I meant your client or someone who helped them could have fabricated these. I don't even know where they came from or how you got them. They certainly were not at the Tandy cottage on Long Pond. We took that place apart! "

"That's right. They were not there. They were on Fairbanks' boat...the *Sea Chaser*..."

"We tore that apart too."

"I will show you the secret compartment they were found in, if you want. For the moment, just take my word for it, okay."

"Okay. What's next. I see you still have more."

"The ones I'm going to show you now were down-loaded from Mr. Fairbanks' lap-top. The computer was found with the letters I just showed you in the compartment on Fairbanks' sailboat."

Joe gave them copies of the six short notes Fairbanks had made detailing the progress of the merger talks. These were quickly read.

Then he gave them the long note concerning Fairbanks' talk with Mrs. Cranston. They read it carefully and then Joe gave them the last note from the lap-top — the letter to Gerry Burstine at the SEC. That was read quickly. Then they read them again.

"So that's where the SEC got their information!" Tardif exclaimed.

"Apparently," Joe agreed.

"Joe, I don't pretend to understand the legal references or the accounting bit and I've been out of the loop there since I first talked with the SEC. A few days after Mr. Fairbanks was murdered, I got a call from a Jack Griffin who identified himself as a SEC investigator. He gave me enough detail so I knew he was genuine. When I agreed that I was in charge of the investigation of Mr. Fairbanks' murder, he told me he wanted to fax me some information and after I had a chance to read it, to call him back. The fax came quickly. It was a summary of transactions in ConnTrust stock made by a Wexford Tandy, a broker in Coffin & Company in Portland. I called him right back and he told me that the SEC had information that there had been several violations of the federal securities laws in connection with the ConnTrust merger. He said they had learned that Miss Tandy had been working on that merger with Mr. Fairbanks' law firm. When they got the stock transfer records from the bank they noted the name of Tandy and checked it out. Somehow they determined that Wexford Tandy was your client's father. They thought that in the light of the murder that I ought to have the information. I used that information to get the search warrant."

"That's what I figured."

"Joe, we have known each other a long time and I know you are as honest as the day is long, so don't take offense...okay" Tardif said. "I still have trouble with whether the original of these are genuine."

"First off, I'm sure you haven't had time to analyze them," Joe responded. "When you have you will see that the letters implicate our client as well. They show that Fairbanks had been told by Ralston that his assistant's father had been trading in the stock. Ask yourself why someone who was forging these letters would implicate herself in them. Secondly, the notes from Fairbanks' lap-top had never been seen by our client. We had to have an expert find Fairbanks' password to get into it. Miss Tandy was in New York City when we down-loaded those notes.

Thirdly, we checked out as much as we could. We talked to Mrs. Cranston and she admitted she had given Fairbanks the information he referred too. Finally, you have, yourself, information from the SEC that confirms the Ralston involvement. It seems to me that you have all the corroboration you need."

"Okay. So how do you tie this all in?" Nick Carsillo asked.

"Well, as you know, our clients talked with Dan Hardy and Ian Campbell the night you brought them in to the Hancock SO. They told them and then me their story and that was long before we had the information I just gave you. It was found when Tiger Wass took the sailboat over to Hinckley's for the winter. He was getting the boat ready for storage and he remembered the secret compartment. He built it himself at Mr. Fairbanks' request. That's when the letters and lap-top were found.

"They have told us their story of what happened the day of the murder several times. From the beginning, everything they told us has checked out. The merger had been announced and Ralston was in Northeast Harbor to be with the lawyers in case the media had questions. Everything was going well, so Fairbanks took the merger group and his step-sister, Kelley Morse, out for a sail that afternoon. There were our clients, Cece Tandy and Tiger Wass — Tiger, as you may know was his boat captain — Kelley Morse; his law partner, Kevin Burke; Sarah Rosen, the bank's merger consultant ; and Ralph Ralston, then president of ConnTrust. They came in from sailing in the late afternoon that day. Mr. Fairbanks' caretaker, Harvey Lunt, had lobsters waiting on the pier. Mr. Fairbanks intended to boil them up on the boat and have the group to dinner. For some reason, the only ones who stayed were our clients and Ralph Ralston. Ralston was still with Mr. Fairbanks when our clients left in Tiger's Whaler to go over to his apartment in Southwest Harbor about nine that evening."

"Lunt says they didn't leave until about eleven or after."

"I know he told you that."

"Then he called to tell me he was mistaken. I think you talked to him in the meantime. I believe that what he told us first was the truth of the matter."

"But he told me the first time he wasn't really sure. After we talked the second time he said he was sure it wasn't Tiger's Whaler he heard. That is why he called me to meet with him. He wanted to know if he would be in trouble if he went back to you and told you the truth. I assured him he wouldn't be in trouble. Anyway, if we assume for the sake of argument that our clients are telling the truth, Ralston was the last one with Mr. Fairbanks before he was murdered."

"Okay, let's assume that. How did this bank president inject sodium pentathol into Mr. Fairbanks?"

"Ralston is a MD... a medical doctor. I have checked that out. He's licensed in Connecticut."

A look of amazement came over Tardif's face. Carsillo stopped taking notes.

"Where does Ralston live?"

"Torrington, Connecticut. That's where the main office of ConnTrust is located."

"Do you know where he is...where we can find him?"

"No. We know he hasn't been seen at the bank for a week at least."

"Do you have something else for us? I see more papers..."

Joe took the remaining pages from his folder and handed them to Tardif.

"We got these from Mrs. Cranston, the stock transfer agent at ConnTrust. They do their stock transfers in-house. I'm not sure that the SEC has this set yet. The set they were originally given wasn't complete."

"How so?"

"Ralston had ordered Ms. Cranston not to disclose the stock purchases and transfers he had recently made, so they don't have them. This set does."

"How in hell did you get these?"

"Luck. We had Mr. Fairbanks' note about talking to Ms. Cranston, so Jim Murphy and I made a visit to Torrington. We talked to her at her home. At first she didn't want to talk to us. Ralston had threatened to kill her if she disclosed the transfers he had made, but when we told her we were investigating Mr. Fairbanks' murder, she was more than willing to cooperate. Everything we have checked out has been consistent with Fairbanks' notes and what our clients have told us."

"Oh, I'm sure...but, Joe, I have to tell you we are really getting the heat to do something on this case. The family — at least Andy Fairbanks — has been on our back constantly. The media has been calling everyday as well. Our Chief called me yesterday and said that even the Governor has been asking him about our progress and wants to be kept up to date. Until now, your clients have been our only real suspects. We'll try to check this Ralston guy out, but we are going to have make an arrest in the very near future so be prepared."

As he left, Joe wished Dan had given him permission to give Tardif copies of Wexford Tandy's notes and show him that they compared exactly with the ConnTrust records and that they showed purchases long before the merger talks began. Still he couldn't argue with Dan's trial strategy to save those for rebuttal.

*C*HAPTER *S*EVENTEEN

Joe and Dan arrived at Dan's office in Ellsworth at the same time Monday morning. Dan stopped at the small kitchen to start their coffee, then they retreated to Dan's office. Joe quickly brought Dan up-to-date on his meeting with Rob Tardif. Dan was only too well aware that the media had been paying a lot of attention to the lack of progress in solving the Fairbanks murder. That day's *Bangor Daily News* had an article on the front page and after Joe told him of Tardif's parting words, Dan gave it to him to read.

Northeast Harbor — Police here are still unwilling to discuss any details of the Gordon Fairbanks murder. They say that solving the crime is their top priority but they will not say if any progress is being made. Sergeant Tardif, the State Police detective in charge of the investigation, told the *News* that there are several suspects, all of whom are under active investigation, but beyond that he will not comment.

Sources close to the investigation told the *News* that the authorities believe the murder is connected to the recently announced merger of ConnTrust, a Connecticut bank holding company, with Northeast Holdings, another New England based bank. The stockholders of both corporations have agreed to the merger and the SEC has not indicated it has any objection to it.

However, the *News* has learned that the SEC is investigating the activities of Ralph Ralston, the former president of ConnTrust and it is understood that the investigation concerns insider trading in that bank's stock.

The *News* has also learned that the State Police conducted a search of a cottage at Long Pond on Mount Desert Island a few days after the murder took place but details are not forthcoming.

The family of Mr. Fairbanks has voiced concern with

the lack of progress in the matter. Mr. Fairbanks' son, Andrew Fairbanks told the *News* that the police know who murdered his father and he can't understand why an arrest hasn't been made.

"One guess who Andy Fairbanks says murdered his father," Dan said.

"That's easy — our clients," Joe replied.

"Well, so far Tardif is playing by the rules," Dan said. "He just hasn't enough viable evidence to present the case to the Hancock County Grand Jury, even though it would probably follow its usual routine and hand up an indictment on the flimsy circumstantial evidence Tardif does have."

"Tardif may not be able to stand the heat much longer though," Joe said. "Let's review what evidence we know he has involving our clients and see if he might have enough to get a true bill from the grand jury."

"Okay. For starters, he has evidence to show Fairbanks was murdered. I suppose he can show that our clients were with Fairbanks the night he died. He can get that before the grand jury through Harvey Lunt. Lunt wasn't in the area when our clients left but the Grand Jury gets only one side of the case. He has the call to the Mount Desert PD reporting a fight at the Tandy cottage and the neighbors report that Fairbanks was there. His car was still there when the police arrived. He's got the fact Cece's father was trading in ConnTrust stock while she was working on the merger and the fact that the SEC is investigating that. His evidence is only circumstantial and awfully weak as far as we know. Still, before a grand jury, it probably would fly."

"I agree. He knows he will have to have a lot more to succeed at trial"

"Right. You saw the autopsy report but you don't remember the pathologist reporting that he found any evidence that the sodium pentothal had been injected — right?"

"That's right. I've kicked myself plenty for not being careful to look for that. As I remember it, it was just a statement... the pentothal was injected. It was only one sentence."

"So if that doesn't stand up — if the autopsy report doesn't pinpoint a vein where an injection was made — and we go to trial, we can show that sodium pentothal can cause death if it is ingested...that its effect is slower but otherwise has the same result. Then we can argue that Fairbanks committed suicide. It seems to me we ought to be able to create enough doubt with that argument to get a not guilty verdict."

"We won't know until we see the report and we won't have that until our clients are indicted. But that may be the main reason Tardif is holding off," Joe suggested.

"He has to prove that someone gave Fairbanks the drug intending to kill him. The State will have no trouble with intent. That drug is so potent in lethal strength that the act of giving it to a person proves intent. So far he has focused on our clients because he thinks Cece has a motive to kill Fairbanks — to stop him from going to the SEC and reporting her father's trades and her own involvement. Now that the State can present the fact that they are married, the jury wouldn't have any problem believing Tiger injected the poison to protect his wife or his father-in-law for that matter. They have Harvey Lunt's statement that our clients were the last ones with Fairbanks that evening. That places them at the scene of the crime. So if the autopsy report shows real evidence that the sodium pentathol was in fact injected, we've got a fight on our hands."

"Tardif certainly hasn't found the source of the drug, or if he has, he can't connect it with our clients or he would have his indictment by now," Joe asserted.

"I agree. And that is a real problem for him. He has to have that proof at trial, at least."

"What else has he got?"

"Only the things we gave him. The Tandy stock purchases strengthens his hand with respect to motive, but the Ralston transfers weakens it by pointing to another suspect who was with Fairbanks earlier in the day and was still in the area that evening. If we put our clients on the stand, they will testify that Ralston was with Fairbanks when they left him that night. "

"The jury will discount that as self serving so we have to have corroboration. I checked and Ralston was still registered at the Regency Inn in Bar Harbor until after the funeral."

"You didn't tell Tardif about Sarah Rosen?"

"No, I didn't think we should at this time. It's too far out without more to go on."

"He knows nothing about Kelley Morse?"

"I don't think so. If he did, he'd have a source for the pentathol. He's got a motive problem there though. I'm sure he doesn't know about her and Fairbanks being lovers. We don't know for sure ourselves. It's just speculation at this point."

"We need to check it out."

Before they could decide on that as the next direction for Joe's investigation, the phone rang. It was Joe's associate telling him that Leigh Cranston was on their other line and wanted to speak with him. Jim plugged Joe in on that line so they could have a conference call. Leigh was calling from her home. She was obviously upset. She said she couldn't talk on the phone, she was afraid it was bugged. She said something important had come up and she wanted to talk to Joe in person. She wanted to meet him in Worcester, Massachusetts that evening. She could be there by 6 p.m. He told her he'd be at the Holiday Inn in Worcester at that time. She agreed and quickly said goodbye. Joe reported the conversation to Dan and left for Worcester.

Dan wasn't overly concerned about the costs of the on going investigation. He had kept Wexford Tandy informed of the money being spent. Tandy had assured Dan that he would pay whatever was necessary to protect his family and not to spare the investigation for want of funds.

Leigh Cranston was early, arriving at the Holiday Inn at 5:45 p.m. Joe had been waiting in the lobby and came over to greet her. She seemed relieved to see him and for a moment a smile crossed her face, soon to be replaced by the worried look she had as she came into the motel. Joe had secured a room for the night and asked if she minded accompanying him there. That brought the smile back and she allowed that she thought he was harmless. Then she laughed nervously.

"I'm sorry to ask you to come all this way," Leigh told Joe as soon as they were in the room. "I think what I have learned is important and you are the only one I dare tell it to."

"I was glad to come. What you told us last week has been an enormous help," Joe told her.

"I had an appointment with my lawyer," Leigh said. "He told me not to talk to anyone. He said that if I went to the SEC I would be in trouble because I was so involved. He made me promise to talk to no one but him."

"So the government doesn't know about Ralston?"

"Not from me at least."

"I saw the lawyer last Friday afternoon. I was so shook up when I left him I couldn't go back to the bank. Stock transfers have slowed to a trickle now that the merger has been approved and when I'm not at the bank, Robin Granger is able to take care of my work. Robin is a vice president in charge of operations for the bank.

"This morning I went in early. I've been worried sick about my job. I don't know what I'd do if I lost it. My ex doesn't help with Donald. He left me in debt and there is a huge mortgage on the house."

"I'm sorry to hear that, Leigh."

"Sure, but you don't need to hear about my problems...It's just that I'm so worried."

"I understand, but from what you tell me the bank hasn't grounds to fire you. You just did what the president of the bank ordered you to do. You had no concrete knowledge that what he wanted you to do was illegal. It was his responsibility to make the reports to the SEC. And you didn't make any personal profit from it. Didn't your lawyer tell you that?"

"Not really. I'm not sure he knows anything about the laws concerning securities. He's a criminal lawyer."

"Well, I'm not a lawyer either. I think you should find someone who knows about security laws."

"Mr. Fairbanks certainly did...but he's gone."

Leigh choked on the thought. Joe wondered what kind of man Gordon Fairbanks was to have made such a lasting impression on a woman he had talked to only a couple of times.

"Mr. Fairbanks is the reason I'm doing this. I couldn't help feeling that Ralph had something to do with his murder and now I'm even more sure."

"Why is that?"

"Well, as I started to say, I went in to work early this morning. I wanted to check on the transfers which were done after I left Friday. I brought Friday's transaction up on my screen and I found these...,"

Leigh handed Joe a sheet of paper. "Stock transfer records," she told him.

Joe studied them carefully. The first entry was a transfer of 50,000 shares of ConnTrust stock from the account of Ralph Ralston to the account of Ralph Younger. Joe quickly calculated the value in his head — $2,500,000 at that day's market price of $50. The next entry was a transfer of 70,000 shares of the stock from the Ralph Younger account to an account in the street name of the Stavitz & Company brokerage in San Francisco. The third was a transfer from the Stavitz account of 70,000 shares to a Julius Rudniki. Why was that name familiar, he wondered. Then he remembered from the talk with Kevin Burke that that was the name of the trustee of the Jacob Rosen Trust under which Sarah Rosen was the ultimate beneficiary. Joe had a feeling that finally he might be hitting pay dirt but the information led in at least two different directions.

He stopped studying the transfer records and thought about the implications. First, Ralston transferred 50,000 shares of his stock to his son's account. Then he transferred 70,000 shares from his son's account to the Staviz brokerage in street name. Then Sarah Rosen's trust bought 70,000 shares from the same brokerage — a brokerage in San Francisco. Sarah Rosen was on her way to the west coast. How did those pieces fit ? Either Sarah Rosen and Ralston were working together or that sequence of events was the most unusual coincidence he'd ever seen.

When it was obvious that Joe was ready for her to continue, Leigh handed him an other sheet of paper and said. "Wire transfers."

The first entry was a wire transfer of $ 3,487,450 from Stavitz & Company to Ralph Ralston's checking account at ConnTrust. The next entry was a wire transfer out of the country to three numbered accounts in the Bank of Antigua. The three transfers totaled $ 3,501, 010.

"That last transfer wiped out Ralph's checking account at the bank," Leigh told Joe. "After I had gathered that information, I pulled up all of Ralph's account records. He had cashed in all of his money market accounts on the 15th. He wasn't in the bank after that. I'm not even sure he was in the bank that day. My friend Sally, who handles IRA's and the bank's pension plan, told me that Ralph had tried to withdraw his IRA and his pension funds. He was on the phone to her and she told him she couldn't do it for him. He wasn't there to sign the forms and there was a time limit anyhow. He was wild but he couldn't get her to do it. No telling what would have happened if he had been in the bank."

"So how did he have the transfers made Friday?"

"This is really weird. You remember I told you that he stopped our relationship a while back? I understood it was for a younger woman who he met on vacation and who wasn't from Torrington."

"I remember that."

"Well, I was mistaken. She was right under our nose. It was Robin Granger!"

"How do you know that?"

"She was the one who handled everything on those sheets. We have to record the ID of the person making transfers of stock or money on the wire. The transfer won't go through without entering the person's code. That way the bank has a record. I checked after I called you on a pay phone near the bank. When I came back everyone was talking. We learned that the bank's directors had fired Ralston. Then I found out that Robin had called Joel Watson, the acting president, and told him that she was resigning from the bank. She told him not to try to find her — she wasn't in the states. She hung up before he could ask anything else. We always wondered why Robin was given the job of Operations Officer with her limited experience. She was good at it though, I've got to give her credit for that. She knew how to make wire transfers of large sums of money out of the country!"

"Do you think she's with Ralston?"

"I'm sure of it!"

"How can you be sure?"

"You're going to think I'm awful."

"No way. You had a mission and I'm impressed...really impressed. Tell me about it."

"I went to our accounting department and talked to one of my friends there. They keep a record of all our long distance phone calls. They have a device on our system that keeps constant track of them. We pulled up Friday's records and found three calls to an area code overseas. It was to Antigua ! Then we spent some time finding the name of the number called. It was the Saint Johns Hotel. We looked it up. Saint

Johns is the capital of Antigua.

"I went right to Mr. Watson with what I had discovered. He was really nice to me. He thanked me and said I deserved a raise. Then he asked me to give him the information on a printout which I did. That's when I made a copy for you. He must have called the SEC because I had a visit from Mr. Griffin this afternoon. He didn't say much, but I know someone had informed the SEC of Ralston's transactions while the merger talks were going on."

"How do you know that?"

"Because he had the information on the 5000 and 10,000 share transfers and he wanted me to pull up the screen they were on and make a copy for him. Then he wanted to see the screen of Friday's stock transfers and I showed him that. Then he went to operations, and I don't know what he got from them."

"Do you now have the address of Stavitz & Company?"

"Yes, I got that for you."

Leigh searched in her briefcase and found the address and gave it to Joe.

"Leigh, we — my clients and I really appreciate all you have done for us," Joe said. "I'm sorry that you had to drive all the way up here to meet me."

"It isn't a problem. I wanted to be way out of town when we talked. I'm really upset about this whole thing. My sister lives here so I'll spend the night with her. And if it helps find the person who murdered Mr. Fairbanks..."

Joe offered to take Leigh to dinner but she was expected at her sister's. Joe told her he'd stay in touch and asked her to call if she came across anything she thought would help. Then she was off.

Joe watched her go, thinking how a little bit of kindness on the part of Gordon Fairbanks had opened the door to the important information she had been providing them. It was the one bright spot in his investigation of the murder. But he realized that he was far from solving the case and he knew time was running out.

CHAPTER EIGHTTEEN

One of the things Joe had hoped to leave behind when he retired from the State Police was having his meals alone while he was on the road. The hotel's menu was the usual fare and without thinking, he ordered the 'catch of the day,' remembering only after the waitress had left that he wasn't in Maine. It didn't matter. His mind was not on the quality of the food and he ate without tasting. While he was eating, he read again the information on the printouts Leigh had given him. Obviously, Ralston had planned very well. It seemed clear that Ralston was then in Antigua. Joe suspected he would not remain there very long. It was obvious that Ralston left the country because he knew his scheme was now known to the government, and if he stayed he'd be arrested.

What wasn't clear was the reason he thought he would be arrested. It could be that he had murdered Gordon Fairbanks and feared that the police were about to make him their prime suspect. Or it could be that he was running from the charges he knew the SEC would bring if they learned the real truth about his dealings. Or, it could be both. The records which Leigh Cranston had prepared in answer to the SEC subpoena would not have disclosed those dealings because Ralston made her alter them. Now it seemed likely that Ralston felt sure that the SEC had been given the true records or soon would have them. In either event, they would have enough solid evidence to make an arrest. Either scenario would explain his flight. Perhaps both were true, but with the information Joe had at that moment, one guess was as good the other.

Joe finished his meal and hurried to his room to call Dan Hardy at his home. Dan had been expecting the call. He wasn't surprised at Joe's report nor was he surprised to learn that Ralston apparently had fled the country. It certainly complicated their situation and made the decision as to what to do next extremely difficult. Dan said he wasn't happy that his and Ian's clients might have to bear the expense of Joe going to Antigua. It was a mission that might well be fruitless, even if Joe was lucky enough to find Ralston and talk to him. It was something that the authorities ought to be doing in any event. They had the resources.

"The Maine State Police ought to be able to get the FBI involved since flight to avoid prosecution is a federal crime," Dan told Joe. "Maybe they are involved already. Can we find out?"

"I can call Rob Tardif," Joe answered. "I have his home number as well, as the number at the barracks. I'll do it and call you right back."

Joe called the Orono barracks first and the dispatcher, an old friend, told Joe he could reach Tardif on his pager and he'd have him call back. Joe told him it was very important or he wouldn't ask. It seemed like an eternity but Tardif finally called back.

"I hope this important, Joe," were Tardif's first words. "This is the first night I've had out since Fairbanks was murdered."

Joe apologized and then told Tardif what he had learned from Leigh Cranston. Tardif was not impressed.

"That is interesting information, Joe," he said. "But I think it is a great leap from his securities fraud scheme to his being involved with the Fairbanks' murder. He's supposedly intelligent. How could he believe that murdering Fairbanks would cover up his fraudulent stock dealings? I think he is running from the security law charges and he had nothing to do with the murder. And how would Ralston know that we had any reason whatever to make him a suspect?"

"I can't answer that without more to go on. We're getting new information every day though."

"What do you want me to do, Joe?"

"Ralston is in Antigua right now, I'm sure of it. He won't be there long. When he goes again, the chances are he'll never be found."

"That's probably true," Tardif agreed. "But I know my boss won't go for sending me down there, as much as I'd like to go."

"What about the FBI? If they get this new information they have enough to get a warrant for securities law violations. If they arrest him, at least he'll be where you can find him if it turns out that he was involved with the murder."

"That is true. It could be days before we can get them involved but it's worth a try."

Then Tardif told Joe he really did appreciate what he was doing and that he'd report everything he had been told to the Assistant AG who was helping with the Fairbanks investigation. He was sure that he would report what they now knew to the FBI immediately, even if they both were afraid it would be too late by the time they could act. Joe thanked him and then called Dan to report the conversation.

"It seems to me that we don't have any choice but to get you down to Antigua," Dan said. "I've been thinking about it. I knew when I mentioned it, that the State Police can't get the FBI involved in a state criminal investigation unless there is a federal violation as well. Getting them the facts of flight to avoid prosecution can't be done quickly enough to do any good in this case. So Joe, you have to go to Antigua. While I was waiting for you to call back, I called our travel agent in Bangor and I have seats for two people out of New York tomorrow. You will fly to Miami and then to the island."

"Two people?"

"Yes... two people. You and Roberta."

"Clever! Ralston is there with his new love and you think if we find him she may help get us acquainted."

"Right."

"Have you talked to Roberta?"

"She's packing right now. She flies out of Bangor International at 8 a.m. and will be at Kennedy by 11:00 or so. Delta flight 1010. You can meet her there. She will have the rest of the flight tickets. We won't know until the morning if you have reservations at the Saint John's Hotel but my agent thinks she can arrange it without any trouble. She says she will have some place for you to stay in any event. She's got time. You'll have a layover in New York tomorrow night because your flights don't connect."

"Okay. I've never seen the man I'm looking for. It's a good thing I have ConnTrust's' last annual report. I've checked. There are good pictures of both Ralston and Robin Granger in it."

"Great. I never thought about how you would recognize Ralston except from a description Cece might have given you. I doubt she knows Miss Granger."

"I'll leave for New York City early tomorrow morning and bring Cece up-to-date. I'll call before I leave the country."

Joe had been out of the country while he was in the service but he had never been in the Caribbean. Roberta had been after him for the past several years to take her to one of the islands but there was always some on-going work that made him reluctant to agree to a trip that had to be made on a certain date and for a certain length of time. He wished he'd been privy to the conversation when Dan asked her to go. It probably took Roberta all of five seconds to say yes. He was looking forward to this assignment in spite of the fact that he doubted anything would come from it.

Joe was almost asleep when he remembered that he should call Cece and warn her he would be visiting her the first thing in the morning. When she recognized his voice, she said she'd be happy to meet him at her office. she'd be there about 7:30 a.m. even though she wouldn't expect him before 9:00.

Joe never required more than six hours sleep, an attribute which he found stood him in good stead in police work. At 4 a.m. he was sharing Interstate 395 with the truckers. He made good time on 395 and on 95 until he neared the New York State line. By then the morning traffic into the City was heavy and intimidating. He had checked his maps and had decided to stay on Interstate 95 and then take Interstate 678 to JFK airport where he would leave the Caprice in long term parking until he and Roberta returned from Antigua. He'd take an airport shuttle bus into the city.

Cece was surprised that Joe was in her office a little after 8:00. Kevin Burke was with her when her secretary buzzed to announce his arrival. Kevin left so they could be alone to talk but said he would be available if they wanted to talk to him later. Cece was happy with Joe's report. She felt that progress was finally being made, even though the news of Ralston's departure from the country was certainly not welcome. Cece assured Joe that her father would approve the cost of his going to Antigua and quickly dismissed his offer to pay for his wife's accompaniment. She told him that having his wife go with him was a stroke of genius. She had gotten to know Ralston quite well over the past months and she doubted that Joe would be able to talk to him, even if he were lucky enough to find him. She had observed that Ralston seemed suspicious of any male he didn't know but that he had no problem talking to a woman whether he knew her or not.

"I may not be here when you return," Cece told him.

"Oh?"

"Andy Fairbanks has asked the partners to fire me!"

"On what grounds?"

"Andy is sure that Tiger and I murdered his father."

"To stop him from reporting you and your father to the SEC?"

"Right. Kevin just told me what is going on. He said he flatly refused to bring it before the executive committee. Now Andy has gone behind his back and he may have to bring it before them anyway. Oh, it's not your problem and I don't want to talk about it. I've been thinking that when this is over I want to get out of this city anyway. Eventually Tiger and I are going to live in Maine."

"In God's country."

"Right. Joe, I want to bring Kevin up-to-date on what you just told me."

"I guess you should," Joe reluctantly agreed, still worried about the possibility that Sarah Rosen might be involved but deciding that the new information might help Kevin Burke to continue his resolve to protect Cece.

Cece called Kevin and he told her he'd be in her office in a few minutes. While they were waiting, Cece made copies of the records Leigh Cranston had given Joe. When Kevin arrived, Joe told him what he had learned from Ms. Cranston on his last meeting with her. Then he gave Kevin the records he had from her and he watched as Kevin read them.

"God damn it!" Kevin exclaimed when he read the entry of the last purchase. "Rudniki bought the Ralston shares! I can't believe it! Why in hell would he do that!"

"And he bought them through a San Francisco broker. What do you make of that?" Joe asked.

"I don't know..." Kevin answered. "ConnTrust stock is traded over the counter. There isn't a lot available but the bank should know who has some for sale. Maybe he called and they told him where some could be purchased... I just don't know."

"The merger was known by then," Cece offered. "The price had already changed."

"Maybe he was covering a short sale," Kevin said.

"Do you know Rudniki?" Joe asked.

"I've met him. Rudniki was a close friend of Sarah's father. He was her father's stock broker as well. Sarah told me he was the only one her father trusted to be the trustee of the trust he set up with his lawyer. But from what I see here, the purchase was by Rudniki & Company for its own account. Small brokerages often take a position in a small-cap stock. He could have been covering a short sale or he could be buying to hold the stock. As soon as the merger is finalized, ConnTrust stock will be exchanged for Northeast Holdings stock and he'll probably make a profit on it. Northeast has been doing very well."

"He could change the ownership to the trust later," Joe said.

"True," Kevin agreed. "You're thinking Sarah may be involved. She may be but it doesn't make sense. As a matter of fact, if she was involved with Gordon's murder, it's stupid — just plain stupid! And stupid she's not."

"Have you heard from her?" Cece asked.

"Yes, I have," Kevin said. "I forgot to tell you earlier. My mind was on what to do about Andy. Have you told Joe about the Andy problem?"

"Yes, I have," Cece said. "I told him it isn't his problem."

"It might be," Joe said. "I can understand why a son would want the person who murdered his father brought to justice. But it seems to me — and to Sergeant Tardif for that matter — that Andrew Fairbanks has gone overboard on it. He calls the Orono Barracks every day and demands to be told what progress is being made. The dispatcher is now shielding Tardif from his calls. Andy knows that is happening and has been extremely abusive. It makes me wonder if he is trying to divert attention...if he himself is hiding something and wants to be kept informed so he will know what his course should be. It may sound way out, but in this business you have to consider all possibilities."

"I never thought of that," Kevin said, "Andy had done some peripheral work on the ConnTrust project. I wonder if he was trading."

"But he knew that if his father found out he was using insider information, he'd sack him without a second thought," Cece pointed out. "Gordon was a fanatic about that."

"And he should have been," Kevin said. "That is why he felt compelled to make the initial report to the SEC. By the way Joe, Ms. Cranston didn't contact the SEC so I gave Gerry Burstine copies of the first set of papers she gave you, and I have to get these to him right away. I can only hope..."

Kevin didn't finish the sentence. He picked up the phone and called his secretary and asked her to come down to Cece's office. She appeared almost immediately and Kevin gave her the latest reports and asked her to fax copies to Gerald Burstine at the SEC office. When she was gone the conversation continued.

"You said you had heard from Sarah," Cece reminded Kevin.

"Yes I did. It was just a postcard."

Kevin produced a card from his shirt pocket and handed it to Cece. It was postmarked in Flagstaff, Arizona. The photograph was of Lake Michigan taken from Lake Shore Drive in Chicago. Cece turned it over and read Sarah's small cramped writing.

Dear Kevin,

Sorry this has taken so long. No excuses. I just needed time to think. I'm still in shock. You know how much I loved him, even though it was over between us.

Now I have you to love. I miss you terribly. I'll call you from the coast. Until then, keep my love warm.

Sarah

Cece gave the card back to Kevin who then gave it to Joe who read it quickly and then read it again slowly.

"What do you make of it?" Kevin asked.

The question was to both of them, but Cece answered first.

"Obviously, Sarah is not functioning well. She's upset. She's searching for something — some direction for her life I would guess. One thing is clear, Kevin — she loves you."

"It may be just an early infatuation with a woman I admire and who admires me — but I think her love is reciprocated. Right now, I'm full of worry for her, so it's hard for me to judge."

Cece knew from prior talks with Kevin that he was being torn by his Catholic upbringing. That even though he had his priest's blessing on his divorce, he felt down deep that he was still married to Eileen. He was being torn as well by his youngest son's refusal to talk to him. Now she knew he had the added worry that Sarah Rosen might somehow be involved with the murder of his best friend. Cece had come to know Kevin well over the last several months and admired him greatly. She changed the subject.

"Joe is on his way to Antigua," Cece told Kevin.

"Isn't that a little far out?" Kevin asked.

"It may well be," Joe agreed. "Dan Hardy thinks we have to do it, and I'm the hired gun. We have given the Maine State Police most of the information we have and their prime suspects still are Cece and Tiger. We tried to get them to get the FBI involved. We gave them the information that we are sure that Ralston has fled the country — that is a federal crime as you know. We think they will come aboard, but time is short. Ralston won't stay in Antigua long, we're sure. He'll move his money somewhere and be gone. If I can find him and confront him, the surprise may produce something. It has many reasons to fail, but on the off chance of success, it is worth a try."

"Good Lord, I'm slow this morning. My mind has been on something else...I've got to see Burstine right away. He has the latest faxes but he doesn't know all the details. I'm sure he'll want to get Ralston back in this country when he learns everything we now know."

After making sure they both knew his itinerary, Joe left to meet Roberta at John F. Kennedy International Airport. Kevin followed him out on his way to the SEC office. Both men were deep in thought, wondering where the new information was going to lead.

Roberta's flight was on schedule and Joe met her as she came off the plane. Roberta was all smiles as he welcomed her with a kiss.

"I can't believe I'm finally going to the Caribbean on vacation," Roberta told Joe.

Joe didn't have the heart to tell her that it might be all work and no play so he gave her another kiss and they walked hand in hand to the baggage belt to retrieve the bags.

*C*HAPTER *N*INETEEN

B efore leaving for Burstine's office, Kevin made a call to Walter Goselin, ConnTrust's counsel, and without disclosing the source, he gave him the new information on Ralston's activities. Goselin wasn't surprised. He had just learned most of what Kevin told him from the bank's new president, Joel Watson. He was worried about what he should do now that he had it. Kevin told him not to worry — with his permission, he'd take care of it. He said the basic information was already in the hands of the SEC but it was important for the bank that he talk to his contact at the SEC. They needed to discuss the situation to determine what the Commission's present intentions were with respect to it. Goselin was quick to agree but wanted to clear it with Joel Watson. Within minutes he returned the call to advise Kevin that Watson welcomed his suggestion.

Goselin told Kevin that Watson had been calling him daily asking him to predict what action the SEC might take with respect to the bank. He said Watson was getting paranoid about the situation, fearing that the merger that both banks wanted so badly would now be blocked by the SEC. Goselin was also getting calls from John Gropus, Northeast Holdings president and soon to be president of the new merged company, demanding that he find out what was going on. He said he had already acquired an enormous distaste for Gropus and wouldn't mind at all when the inevitable happened and he'd be replaced by Northeast's in-house lawyer.

In the meantime, Goselin wanted to do what he could for the people at ConnTrust who he had been with for over twenty years. He had really enjoyed working for the bank up until Ralph Ralston took charge and made it plain that all he wanted for the bank was to have it merge, or be bought by a large bank. Anything, so long as there would be a large profit for him. It just wasn't the same anymore, and if Goselin had had his say, it would never have happened. Over the years, Kevin had seen what changes mergers made in a lot of people's lives — often not for the good — and it always troubled him. Even though the firm and he himself had made a bundle of money doing the legal work for corporate mergers, he was not at all sure that bigger was better. The so-called economy of scale didn't always come to fruition and now he was beginning to see some of the acquisitions made with great fanfare and promises soon unravel. He promised Goselin he'd get back to him as soon as he had anything to report.

Kevin made the call to Burstine and was told that he was studying the faxes Kevin had just sent to him. He told Kevin that he had been working on the ConnTrust matter exclusively for the past week or so and it was giving him fits. There were a lot of pieces missing. He was hopeful that Kevin could help and suggested that they meet for lunch. They had worked on the opposite sides of many mergers over the years. During those years they had come to trust each other and had become friends.

Kevin suspected right along that the ConnTrust matter was receiving some attention at SEC, but he was surprised to learn that it was the sole matter on Gerry Burstine's plate for the past week. He sat for a while wondering what could be the reason. As mergers went, the ConnTrust merger was at the low end of the scale of magnitude. Ordinarily, the SEC would make only a quick review, and unless something caught its attention, there would be no problem. Even under the present circumstances where Gordon had made the necessary report of a suspected insider trading violation of law, it would have been handled at a lower level and processed routinely. The small amount of money involved certainly wouldn't rise to a level which might jeopardize the merger. It was apparent there was something more serious involved and he wondered if Burstine already knew that Ralston had fled the country.

Kevin thought about the Rudniki purchases and wondered if Sarah knew about them. Suddenly he had a pang of guilt. He wondered how much his visit was about the firm's client's problems, and how much of it was prompted by his worry about Sarah Rosen. After he had thought about it, he decided it was both but he wasn't about to discuss the Rosen connection unless Burstine brought it up. Damn her, he thought, why doesn't she call so I can find out what is going on.

At that moment, Jenny, Kevin's secretary buzzed him to say Miss Rosen was on the line. Kevin pressed the button without his usual 'thank you Jenny.'

"Hi, Kevin," Sarah greeted, her voice a whisper. "I'm missing you so much I had to call."

"Hi darling," Kevin responded. "Where in hell are you?"

"I'm in Crescent City."

"In the United States?"

"Of course, darling. It's in California. Northwest coast."

"Well, I miss you too. I've half a mind to fly out there and join you..."

"I need more time, Kevin," Sarah quickly interrupted. "As I told you in my card, Gordon's murder has really affected me. It has made me think deeply about myself — and you too, darling."

"I've been thinking about us, too."

"That's why I've been taking my time driving west. Being alone has focused my mind. I've spent my whole life concentrating on getting ahead. Getting good grades in school so I could go to Harvard. Getting good grades at Harvard so I could get into a good graduate school. Working day and night to be prepared ... to succeed. I keep asking myself where it has gotten me. I've stopped at some of the National Parks along the way...something I've always wanted to do. I've been overwhelmed with their diversity and beauty. It has helped me think. I'm getting myself back together...but I need a little more time."

"We ought to be doing it together, Sarah. I need it too. It's no good doing it alone. Why don't you turn around and come back?"

"I may just do that...come back to New York...tell the people out here that I'm not available. They don't have a contract because I wanted to put in the final details after I saw what the entire project was."

"Well, that's what I want. I want you here, darling. I can't even call you."

"I promise I'll call every other day at least, dear. I've been awful but I knew if I heard your voice I'd want to come running home and that would cancel all the progress I've made."

"Sarah, I'm falling in love with you. I am in love with you. That old saying 'Absence makes the heart grow fonder' is true. I want you here with me. You don't need the work out there..."

"I know darling. I...I thought that I'd never love anyone except Gordon. I now know I can love someone else and I do...I love you more each day, Kevin."

By then the two were so choked up that both realized that the conversation had to end.

Kevin said goodbye and hung up. He stood for a while by the window of his office, gazing out at the city. "Why didn't you ask her about Rudniki?' he asked himself. Then he sat down in his huge executive chair, laid his head back, closed his eyes and began to think. Sarah was very intelligent, one of the most intelligent women he had ever known. Professionally, she was honest to a fault. True she had had the ongoing relationship with Gordon but she had shared that in detail with him. She loved Gordon but that didn't excuse her. He decided that affair deeply troubled Sarah as well. And who was he to judge?

Kevin hadn't realized how much he enjoyed Sarah's company until she left for parts unknown. It wasn't just the sex either, he told himself. But he had to admit that the wonderful trysts they had together played a large part in their relationship. Still, he admired her greatly as a person. Their values, their outlook on life, their work ethic, their favorite books and movies, all matched. Sarah had become a real friend.

The bottom line, he decided, was that Sarah wasn't capable of letting herself be part of a scheme to make a small profit by speculating on a merger she was involved with. It meant violating her professional code of ethics. She was just basically too honest for that.

But that didn't explain the ConnTrust stock purchases. It didn't explain where she was for several hours on the night Gordon was murdered. It didn't explain why she left so precipitously after the funeral. He wanted badly to ask Sarah to answer those questions but he couldn't bring himself to ask them on the long distance phone. He knew he had to find out where she was staying and fly out to talk to her. He knew he couldn't rest until that happened. For the moment however, he was on his way to talk to the SEC — and pray that Sarah's name wouldn't come up.

Kevin met Gerry Burstine at the restaurant they had agreed upon. The ConnTrust matter wasn't discussed. There was no knowing who might be listening in a crowded restaurant in the financial district of the city. They ate quickly and soon were on their way to the SEC offices. Gerry led Kevin into his office and closed the door.

"Kevin, the new information you faxed over to me is extremely interesting," Gerry said as they sat down. "I assume it is authentic?"

"It is," Kevin answered. "Apparently it is new to you."

Gerry didn't respond but asked, "Could I ask how you got it?"

"Sure. It came through an investigator my associate, Carol Tandy, has hired to do some work for her."

"That's because she was the last person to be with Gordon Fairbanks before he was murdered and the police in Maine have her as a prime suspect."

"That's right. Should I be surprised that you know that?

"We have help from the FBI. We also know that Miss Tandy's father has been trading in ConnTrust stock."

"I suspected as much. Anyway the investigator's name is Joseph Goldberg. Early on he had a lead that suggested the in-house transfer agent for our client ConnTrust had been giving Gordon information to the effect that Ralph Ralston was acquiring large blocks of ConnTrust stock and wasn't making the disclosures required by SEC Rule 16 [a]. I suspect that Gordon wrote you with that information."

"He did. That is what prompted us to begin looking at the Northeast merger very closely."

"Mr. Goldberg met with the transfer agent — name's Leigh Cranston — and she gave him the first set of papers I sent you."

"Those were quite different from the report we got from Ralston in answer to our subpoena."

"I know. Apparently Ralston threatened to kill Ms. Cranston if she didn't follow his orders and falsify the reports. She seemed to think he was not only serious but capable of doing it. Anyhow she was frightened enough to follow his directions. For some reason I don't know, she met with Gordon and told him the truth. We know Gordon tried to get Ralston to make a proper report but failed. After that he wrote you."

"Can you vouch for those statements?"

"I can only tell you what I've been told by Cece — Miss Tandy — and her investigator. But it all fits."

"It seems too neat."

"Why do you say that?"

"Did you know that Miss Tandy's father is a stock broker with a firm in Portland, Maine? That he apparently is the principal owner?

That he had been acquiring a significant amount of ConnTrust's stock?"

"I know that."

"And then you know that the State Police in Maine think that she was feeding her father information about the merger...that she knew Gordon had found out about it and she and her boy friend murdered Gordon to prevent him from disclosing it?"

"I know that is what they think...but Cece tells me that she and Tiger Wass, the man she's engaged to, were not the last to be with Gordon that night. Cece says that Ralph Ralston was with him when they left. Gordon took our group sailing that day. We had been working on the merger and it was his way to celebrate finishing our work. I was with them during the day but everyone left after the sail except Cece, Tiger, and Ralston. I understand that Gordon boiled some lobsters for them on his Hinckley and after they ate, Cece and Tiger left."

"That isn't in the FBI report but they apparently haven't talked to you yet. They will be talking to you soon, I'm sure. The FBI has been involved since I got your original fax. From what they have developed so far they think there is a good possibility that there is a RICO violation here."

"That figures."

"The conspiracy may be tough to prove but it is probably there."

"Cece told me the details of her father's transactions and I have seen the records. I understood the SEC also has Mr. Tandy's records. They show that he started purchasing ConnTrust stock long before Fairbanks & Burke were hired by the bank to help with the merger. Cece offered to resign from the firm but I won't let her. I don't see the remotest possibility that there is any truth to the case the Maine police spell out."

"Well, you're right. Our people have visited Mr. Tandy. He was right up front with them... voluntarily gave them copies of his ConnTrust files. As far as a SEC charge is concerned, I think you are right. I've just reviewed his records and compared them to the ConnTrust stock transfer records. They started way before the merger talks, as far as we know. More importantly, they all match."

"We've done the same analysis and agree. Anyway, Gordon thought the world of Cece and she of him. And she just isn't capable of murder, Gerry. From what I've seen of Mr. Wass, he isn't either."

"Well, as much as I admired Gordon Fairbanks, that is not our concern."

"Is the merger in trouble?"

"At the moment I can't answer that."

"I was hoping I could report to Joel Watson that he could relax."

"Kevin, we go way back. I'd answer your question if I could but you know I can't. There is a second reason...I couldn't give a complete answer if I were allowed to. Our investigation hasn't been completed and the FBI really has just started looking into the matter. Your client could take some comfort in the fact that so far we have not put a hold on the merger. It is still going forward for a vote of the stockholders of both companies. But we could stop it anytime."

"That's a help. But from everything we know Ralph Ralston was working basically alone at ConnTrust with his fraudulent dealings. None of the directors were involved. His acts are *ultra varies* — beyond his authority as president of the bank. What he did for his own benefit shouldn't jeopardize the merger. The financial disclosures were all accurate and aboveboard. I think I can vouch for that, even if we did rely on the information ConnTrust gave us. Gordon checked sources for everything they gave us. He was a stickler for that."

"If that continues to prove to be true, there won't be a problem. I can tell you that much because you know it already. It's just that we are in the initial stages of the thing. The new information strongly suggests a RICO violation. It has nothing to do with the Tandy's, however."

"I see. It's Ralston."

"Right...and whoever was in it with him. We have a suspect there as well."

"Based on the information I gave you, Ralston's out of the country. Will you be looking for him and bring him back if you find him?"

"I can't answer that yet. This morning we put a hold on his bank accounts, his stock in ConnTrust, and a lien on his real estate. We do that in cases like this, as you know, because ordinarily it is a civil matter and we are only looking to reimburse the company with triple damages based on the profit the insider has made. But if RICO comes into play, it is a totally different ball game. That is really out of my field. The FBI is in charge of that part of it."

The meeting had covered all that Kevin wanted to discuss. He wanted it over before the Rosen Trust came up. He got up to leave, thanking Burstine for taking the time to talk to him. Burstine returned the thanks and promised to keep Kevin informed as much as he could. Kevin promised to stay in touch and left.

Kevin did not return to the firm's offices, but went directly to Sarah's apartment. He used his key and let himself in. He intended to search in the file drawers he had seen in her den. The file drawers were locked and he didn't know where Sarah kept the keys. Frustrated, he decided that it wasn't a good idea after all so he left for his own apartment.

Kevin was sure that Gerry had not missed the information in the fax to the effect that Julius Rudniki had purchased the ConnTrust shares that Ralston — 'Ralph Younger'— had sold to the Stavitz brokerage in San Francisco. He felt sure, however, that Gerry couldn't make the connection to Sarah. Not yet anyway. In all probability the FBI would find that lead and run with it. If a RICO violation were to be proved, the FBI had to be able to show a conspiracy and that information gave them a starting point. But Gerry had told him that they had a suspect already. He didn't mention who it was. Oh my God! he thought, could it be Sarah?

It was late afternoon by the time Kevin arrived at his own apartment, long before he usually had the one double scotch he allowed himself. He looked at his watch, hesitated, then poured the Chivas over ice without measuring it. He took a long swallow, then went into his den, sat back in his Lazy-boy recliner and tried to decide what he should do. The logical thing would be to do nothing — to wait it out and see what developed. But he wanted desperately to know if Sarah were in trouble. If she was, he wanted to be with her. He told himself that he surely wouldn't do anything to get himself involved in something illegal. But he had to do something. The problem was consuming him.

Kevin had met Julius Rudniki, but knew him only slightly. Sarah had introduced Rudniki to him when they met at a cocktail party during the summer. He thought about going to see him and confronting him. But what right did he have to do that? And if Rudniki were involved in something illegal, he wouldn't be about to admit it anyway.

Then he considered flying to San Francisco and going to the Stavitz brokerage on the off chance he could learn something from them. He decided that would take a clever subterfuge and he had never been able to pull off anything like that. He decided that the FBI would certainly beat him to it and that it was another bad idea to boot. He got up, went back to the wet bar and poured himself another Chivas.

$\mathscr{C}$HAPTER $\mathscr{T}$WENTY

When Dan Hardy called Wexford Tandy to make sure he agreed to the need to send Joe out of the country in an attempt to find Ralph Ralston he also got Tandy's agreement to send Joe's wife with him. When he told Roberta that she would be paid for her help she became quite upset — said she wouldn't go if Dan insisted she be paid — the free trip was more than enough. Dan knew Roberta loved music and especially Broadway musicals. For her though, they existed only on recordings. He called around and was able to get tickets to the new production of *Cabaret* starring Matasha Richardson. Roberta had never been to New York and certainly had never stayed in a hotel as nice as the Grand Hyatt. That evening in the City, Roberta discovered a new world — one she would thank Dan for over and over again.

The red light on the phone in their hotel room was blinking when they returned from the theater. Joe answered the page. It was a message to call Cece at her apartment. It was near midnight but the message said to call no matter the hour, so Joe dialed the number.

"Joe, thank the Lord I caught you," Cece said, recognizing his voice. "There's a change in plans. Ralston has left Antigua and he's now in the Cayman Islands. You and Roberta need to be at JFK by 9 a.m. Can you?"

"Sure. Fill me in."

"Leigh Cranston called Dan Hardy — said you gave her his number and to call him if she couldn't reach you."

"I did that."

"She got a call this afternoon from Robin Granger — you remember?'

"Sure. She's the vice-president in charge of operations at ConnTrust. She's the one who made the transfers when Leigh Cranston was away last Friday. Leigh thought she and Ralston were having an affair and that she is with him."

"Right. That's what Leigh told Dan, too. It turns out to be true...she is with him. Leigh said the connection wasn't good but she was sure that Robin Granger was very upset and really scared. Granger told her that Ralston had transferred his money from the bank in Antigua to one in Grand Cayman. He had chartered a private plane to fly them to Georgetown on Grand Cayman and that they were going to fly out in an hour. She told Leigh that she was having second thoughts about what she was doing. Robin told Leigh that she no longer trusted Ralston — that she was sure he was using her and she was scared at what he might do to her. She'd gone through his bags and found an automatic pistol he apparently purchased in Antigua after they arrived. She wanted someone here to know where she was, said she had no family and she had cut all ties to friends when she divorced her husband and took up with Ralston.

"They are staying at Spanish Bay Reef Resort, way out on the north end of Grand Cayman. We have reservations for you and your wife there, as well as a car reserved for you. Your flight at 10 a.m. is on American Airlines to Miami and then on to Grand Cayman. You have to be at JFK an hour early. Your tickets are at the American counter."

Joe retrieved his note pad from his pocket and reviewed the information with Cece. He told her that he would call her from the island when they arrived. Cece said she would call Dan and tell him she had caught Joe in time to tell him of the changes, and they hung up.

Roberta was listening to Joe's side of the conversation and looking on as he wrote down the details. He explained the reason for the change but he didn't mention Robin Granger's concern about the pistol she had found in Ralston's luggage. In Maine, Joe had a concealed weapons permit but he wouldn't be able to bring a weapon with him on this trip, even if he wanted to. He suspected that Ralston could carry his pistol on his chartered plane but he wondered how he would be able to get it by Cayman customs. In any event, it was good for him to know about it.

After a fitful half night's sleep and an early breakfast in the hotel, they were at the JFK American Airlines ticket counter at 8:30 a.m. They showed their identification and had no trouble surrendering their tickets to Antigua and getting the tickets to Grand Cayman. The flight to Miami was smooth and they both were able to catch a nap. The flight to Grand Cayman was equally smooth and the nap easier to take. When they got off the plane at Owen Roberts International Airport, the rush of hot humid air in their faces was one of many first experiences for both of them.

After they had cleared customs, the young black man who had asked Joe if he could help them with their luggage brought it to a waiting cab. The driver was disappointed when Joe told him they had a rental car engaged. Their man then carried their bags to the car rental area and Joe gave him a generous tip. Joe showed his Maine driver's license to the agent and was given a temporary Cayman Islands driving permit. He was also given a map of the island. The 'car' turned out to be a red Jeep with right hand drive. It had been many years since Joe had driven on the 'wrong side' of the road. That was in England when he was in the Army and stationed there. He found himself concentrating on staying in the left lane of the road so Roberta had to navigate. It wasn't a difficult task. The highway north was well marked and the first five miles was a well constructed roadway. Once they got to the West Bay area they took the Mount Pleasant Road, and then the Conch Point Road to the resort.

They were welcomed with warm smiles and immediately shown to their rooms. Roberta had been marveling at the great number of different flowers growing along the road. She was surprised and happy to find many of the same blossoms in vases everywhere about their suite of rooms. There was a prominent card reminding them of the cocktail hour where there would be welcoming free drinks for them. Joe read the brochure for Spanish Reef and found that the only thing that was not included in the daily rate at this 'all inclusive' resort was the alcoholic drinks. Everything else — meals, beverages, gratuities, taxes, sport equipment, snorkeling lessons were included in the daily rate for their deluxe suite. Summer rates were still on and he couldn't believe the rate —$173 per person. He was pleased that Ralston had picked this resort because he knew that the rates were at the low end for any island in the Caribbean. Joe, a real Maniac, was always concerned that his work was too expensive for his clients and tried hard to keep the costs down.

Roberta unpacked and organized the clothes she brought for the trip in the many dresser drawers. Then they both crashed on separate twin beds for short naps. When they woke, Roberta put on a two piece bathing suit and told Joe they were going for a swim. She had been an exercise nut for years and it showed. Joe couldn't help wondering how many women her age would look so good in a skimpy bathing suit.

The resort had a pool surrounded by tables and umbrellas and it looked inviting, but Roberta wanted to swim in the ocean, so they went to the beach. Roberta had never seen sand so white and water so warm. They swam in the gentle surf for an hour or more. Joe reminded Roberta of the free cocktails waiting for them which finally induced her to leave the water. As they came out, Roberta told Joe jokingly that she had decided to stay on Grand Cayman through the winter.

On the flight down to the island, Joe had shown Roberta the annual report of ConnTrust with the color pictures of Ralph Ralston and Robin Granger and asked her to study them carefully. Then he asked her to change the color of their eyes and hair in her mind's eye. He fully expected that they both had tried to change their appearance but, in the short time they had had, it wouldn't be as dramatic as what could be accomplished by surgery. After they had showered to wash off the salt and sand, they dressed in the lightest clothes Roberta could find in their wardrobe. There is seldom much need during Maine summers for very light clothing. One of the first missions into town would be to correct that problem, she told Joe, but for the evening, what she had brought would have to do.

Most of the tourists at the swizzle bar seemed to be new arrivals. The charming hostess asked everyone as they arrived to wear name tags, to socialize and have fun. The waiters did not wait for a rum punch glass to become empty before filling it again and the gathering soon became festive.

Joe, however, didn't allow himself to remain in a conversation with any one person for long. His eyes were glancing around the pool area, searching for Ralston, but he did not see anyone who had Ralston's build and who was of his age. In the photograph, Ralston was rather heavy set. The picture was basically of his face and only his shoulders were visible. He kicked himself for not getting a better description from Cece. His training had been to concentrate first on a person's eyes and then the face. Everything else was secondary. That training of course was before the color of a person's eyes could be changed by changing the color of their contact lenses and hair dyes were so easy to use. Joe was thankful that the couple they were looking for hadn't had time to have plastic surgery.

The swizzle party lasted over an hour and then it was time to go into the dining room for dinner. Guests were assigned to a table which they would keep for their entire stay. Unless, of course, they were dissatisfied, and then they were able to change for one more to their liking. The maitre'd showed the Goldbergs to a table beside the pool and overlooking the beach. A waiter appeared immediately. He told them his name was Albert and that he would be their waiter throughout their stay. He took Roberta's order for another rum punch, but Joe said he would pass. A light breeze was blowing in from the ocean, the sun was setting, coloring the sky a soft pastel pink. For what seemed like only a moment it changed to a deep red and then the evening turned quickly to darkness. Roberta was amazed at how quickly the sun set and how the air remained so warm even after it was dark. Her face was flushed from the rum punch and she was happy. Joe continued to search the tables for a face he thought might be the one he was looking for.

They had finished their *entrée* — broiled Caribbean lobster tail — and Albert had brought their dessert when Joe noticed that the table on the opposite side of the pool now had two diners. Their faces were hidden by the menus they both appeared to be studying, but Joe could see enough of them to become totally alert. Roberta turned to see what Joe was focused on. He turned to her and whispered for her not to stare. When he turned to glance at the table again he was sure the couple was Ralph Ralston and Robin Granger.

"That's them," he whispered. "They're still here!"

"They look like the pictures in the ConnTrust annual report but they have both dyed their hair and he is growing a beard," Roberta agreed in a whisper. "Mr. Ralston looks years younger with his white hair dyed dark brown."

They finished their dessert, declined the after dinner brandy Albert offered and left the dining area, both stealing another look at the couple at the table across the pool. When they were back in their room they examined the photographs of Ralston and Granger again and were convinced they were right.

Joe called Cece and gave her the news that the objects of his search were still in Grand Cayman. Cece was elated to hear that. She told Joe that Kevin had had a call from to Mr. Burstine at the SEC who wanted to warn Kevin that he'd be getting a visit that morning from the

FBI agents assisting in the SEC's investigation of the ConnTrust — Northeast Holdings merger. Cece was with Kevin at the interview. They had given the FBI agents all they could without violating the required attorney-client confidentiality. There were two agents — Harry Tennet and Whitman Whittier. They seemed to have a very good handle on the basic information surrounding the merger but they were tight lipped about the facts they were trying to develop to prove the RICO violation. Kevin, of course, knew what they needed on that score but he was reluctant to talk about it with them — Sarah being constantly in his mind. Cece had all the information Leigh Cranston had provided and when Tennet asked questions in that area, it was she who responded. It was obvious that the FBI agents felt that there could be several possible conspiracies. Cece related the conversation as she remembered it:

Tennet asked, "Did John Gropus ever waiver in his demand that the purchase accounting formula be used in the merger? "

"Not as far as we know," I answered.

"Why was that so important to him," Tennent asked.

"It's very complicated," Kevin answered. "But basically, the purchase accounting in this case benefited Northeast and adversely effected Ralston. Initially, it would lower taxable net earnings for Northeast. But in the long run, because the assets purchased get a stepped-up basis, it would enhance earnings. In pooling accounting the accounting of assets doesn't change..."

"Enough!" Tennet interrupted. "You lost me completely. The bottom line is that Gropus wants it and Ralston doesn't...right?"

"Right."

"Why did Ralston finally agree?"

Neither Kevin nor I could answer that question. It wasn't because the answer was protected — we simply didn't know.

"Do either of you know Julius Rudniki?" Tennet continued.

"I do," Kevin had to admit. "But as far as I know, Rudniki never had any part in the merger. What does Rudniki have to do with this?

"We can't answer that."

Cece told Joe that Kevin seemed on edge as that subject was discussed and she was sure the agents sensed it as well. Before the agents left, Harry Tennet asked if they would inform the FBI if they heard from Ralph Ralston or found out where he was. It was extremely important that they find him. Kevin promised them that they would be told immediately and Cece had Harry Tennet's number at home. She would call Tennet and call Joe back if she had anything to report. She would leave a message at the front desk if he was not in his room. Joe told her that they were going back to the bar. On the off chance that Ralston might be there, they would try to strike up a conversation with him. They hung up — Cece to make her calls and Joe to continue his mission.

When Joe and Roberta arrived in the lounge they found it crowded. Robin Granger and Ralston were there, sitting at a table for four but two of the chairs were empty. That gave Joe the opportunity to ask the couple if they minded having company. Ralston didn't respond, obviously unhappy with the request but Robin Granger seemed delighted with it and said they would be happy to have someone from the States to talk to. That was an obvious reference to the fact that most of the Spanish Reef's guests were from Europe — mostly British, but others were speaking German, French or languages neither Joe nor Roberta recognized.

Roberta held out her hand and said, "I'm Bobby and this is my husband Joe."

After a moment Robin took her hand and said," I'm...Ruth and this is my husband, Rolly."

They all shook hands. One of the waiters appeared at the table. Joe ordered rum punch for Roberta and a Becks beer for himself. Ralston sat silently drinking his Scotch on the rocks, but Robin — Ruth — was more than willing to engage in conversation. It was obvious from her slightly slurred speech that she had already had a good deal to drink but she wasn't inebriated. She wanted to know where they were from. Joe had anticipated the question and had discussed with Roberta how it would be answered. He knew that anyone from the northeast would recognize their Maine accents so they were limited in their answer. They had decided to say they were from Lincoln, Roberta's home town and with which both were very familiar, yet it was far enough away from Northeast Harbor so as not to alert Ralston that they had any connection to Gordon Fairbanks' murder. Robin didn't have any idea where Lincoln, Maine, was and Ralston didn't offer that he knew where it was either. He simply continued to drink as the other three engaged in conversation. Joe said he was a foreman at the paper mill in Lincoln, off on his annual vacation. It was a subject he felt he could talk about intelligently having learned a great deal about paper making from his many conversations with Roberta's father. It was a good choice. Robin had many questions about the industry and Joe was able to answer them in some detail. The talk had the effect of relaxing Ralston and after he had ordered a refill of his Scotch, he occasionally joined the conversation.

When Robin ran out of questions, Roberta was finally able to ask Robin where they were from. She said they were from Brewster, New York. Rolly was a retired medical doctor. They were on their honeymoon. They planned to fly to Barbados in the morning to catch a flight to London where they would begin their grand tour of Europe. At that point Ralston abruptly rose and pulling Robin up, said that they had to get some sleep in preparation for their long trip. He had taken his room key from his pocket and Joe noted the number —113.

After the couple had had time to get to their rooms, Joe went to the front desk where he was given a message — 'call Cece in New York.' The clerk told him that the woman said he knew the number. Roberta had joined him by then and they went to their room where Joe made the call.

Cece answered and quickly said, "I gave Agent Tennet the information that Ralston was down there in Grand Cayman. He was really excited to know that. He asked me to have 'my man' keep close watch on him. He said that the FBI would have agents at Spanish Reef in the morning."

"I hope they have help from the local police," Joe said. "That's been worrying me. If they can't bring him back to the states, this is all a waste."

"I asked Tennet about that because it has us worried too," Cece responded. "Tennet seemed sure the Cayman authorities would allow them to bring both Ralston and Granger back on the warrants they have."

"What's his plan when he arrives tomorrow?"

"Tennet said he'd find you at Spanish Reef as soon as they can," Cece answered. "He needs you to identify them and then he'd handle the situation from there."

Joe assured her that he would watch the couple until the FBI agents arrived. Cece wished him luck and they said their good-byes.

"Thank God!" he said to Roberta as soon as the phone was cradled. "The FBI is coming down here in the morning. Somebody finally got their attention! Honey, for the first time I'm beginning to feel good about this case!"

*C*HAPTER *T*WENTY ONE

Joe's adrenalin was flowing. His immediate task was to keep tabs on Ralston. That meant finding a place where he could keep watch and still not be observed himself. He assumed that Ralston had a rented vehicle parked in the resort's parking lot with all the other guests' vehicles. Staking out the parking lot was a possibility, certainly. He could simply wait for them to leave and follow them if they left. But what if Ralston left from the front in one of the island's taxis? He would miss them then. He knew that Ralston had come to Grand Cayman in a chartered plane so he assumed he would leave for Barbados the same way. He was sure that the FBI agents would be coming to the island in a government plane so it seemed the better plan would be for him to go back to Owen Roberts International Airport and wait there for their arrival. He would also be able to know, one way or the other, if Ralston and Granger had left the island.

He called Cece again and told her his plan. He asked her to call the FBI and tell them he'd be there at Owen International when they arrived. They could identify him because he would be wearing a light blue T shirt with the words 'Lincoln Maine' on both the back and front. It was a short conversation. Cece had to make the call quickly because Tennet had told her he was on his way to JFK as soon as he hung up from their conversation. Cece said she had his cellphone number and hoped she could reach him. She'd call back and report.

Roberta wanted to go with Joe but he wouldn't allow it. He told her he wanted to leave immediately and she would have to stay in the room to talk to Cece when she called back. He'd call her from the airport as soon as he arrived there.

Joe checked the bar as he left. It was full of people and it took him some time to be sure that neither Ralston nor Granger was there. The man at the entrance offered to bring his car in from the lot but Joe thanked him and said he needed the walk. He then asked the man if anyone had left the parking area in the last fifteen minutes. He was told no one had left in the last hour as far as he knew. Joe didn't offer to explain his question and strolled off to the parking area, got in the Jeep and headed for the airport. He was happy to have the information that no one had left the resort because it allowed him to drive slowly and concentrate on driving on the 'wrong' side of the road. In twenty minutes he was at the airport. After he parked the Jeep, he went inside and found a pay phone and called Roberta. Cece had called back and reported that she talked to Tennet and had given him the message. He said that he expected to arrive at Owen Roberts about 5 a.m. He told her to ask Joe to try to delay Ralston's departure if he arrived at the airport before the FBI got there. Joe wondered how he might do that. He checked his watch. It was 10:30 p.m.

Joe returned to the airport's parking lot and moved the jeep to a place where he could observe cars coming into it and could watch the runway as well. After midnight the airport was essentially asleep. Nothing was moving in the parking area. The runway lights were off. There was some activity around the general aviation hanger but that was it. Joe had trained himself when he first became a detective in the State Police to sleep with one eye open and he settled into that mode. A little after 5 a.m. he became fully alert, awakened by the distant sound of jet engines. The runway lights were on and soon a LearJet landed on the runway. Joe tried to get some identification through his small Nikon birder's binoculars but it was still too dark. The jet taxied to the general aviation area of the airport and shut down its engines. Two men descended the ramp, spoke briefly with the ground crew and went into the general aviation office.

Joe resisted the impulse to walk over to the area and see if by some chance Ralston and his lady friend had gotten by him and were about to board the jet. The area where the jet was parked was lighted well enough so he see through his binoculars if they boarded the plane. He decided to wait and watch. Fifteen minutes went by before the sound of another jet turned his attention to the runway. It landed and taxied to the General Aviation area and parked next to the LearJet. It was a Gulf Stream. Three men quickly descended and went into the same office as the first two. Joe waited.

In a few minutes Joe saw one of the men he recognized from the Gulf Stream coming out into the parking lot. Joe got out and walked towards an area more lighted than where he had parked the jeep. The man stopped walking for a moment and then hastened over to him, putting out his hand as soon as he was close.

"I'm Agent Tennet," he said, taking Joe's extended hand.

"Joe Goldberg here. Glad to meet you."

Before any further conversation could take place a taxi came speeding into the area and stopped in front of the general aviation office. A male passenger got out quickly, carrying a small suitcase. Joe recognized Ralston.

"That's Ralston," he whispered, pointing to the man.

"Oh damn!" Tennet said. "We don't have authority to take him into custody yet. Its in process but these islanders don't work that swiftly."

While that conversation was taking place, Robin Granger got out of the car and stood looking hesitant. Ralston was paying the driver. After he had done so, he walked swiftly towards the general aviation building. Robin started to follow him. On a sudden impulse, Joe walked toward her. She turned and as soon as she recognized him she ran to him.

"Joe!" she shouted. "Oh Joe I need your help!...please!"

By then she was standing in front of him shaking, obviously frightened. Ralston turned, looking for her and when he saw her he shouted at her.

"Come on Robin...what in hell's the matter with you...?"

"Tell him I'm not going with him...please Joe," she whispered as she moved quickly in back of Joe.

When Ralston realized what was happening he turned and walked quickly into the building. Tennet by then had caught up with him and they entered at the same moment. Joe turned to Robin who was now crying as she collapsed into his arms. He held her for some time, telling her she was safe and not to worry.

Tennet followed Ralston through the office area of the building and out to where the LearJet and two men were obviously waiting for him. When they reached the jet, Ralston turned and confronted Tennet.

"Who are you and what do you think you are doing?" Ralston demanded.

Tennet showed him his FBI badge and said, "I'm FBI agent Harry Tennet and you are Ralph Ralston, right?"

"Tell me what right you have to accost me!" Ralston challenged.

Tennet showed him the arrest warrant from the Federal District Court in New York. Ralston examined it briefly.

"Show me what authority you have to use that here in the Caymans, Mr. Tennet."

"It hasn't reached me yet, but it will soon. In the meantime, it will be to your benefit to come with me."

Ralston didn't respond. He simply turned and climbed the ladder into the Lear, yelling at the pilots to get aboard. The older of the two followed Ralston up the ladder. The other yelled at Tennet to stand clear or he would be blown away by the jet engines. He then removed the chocks, climbed the ladder, pulling it up behind him as soon as he was aboard. Tennet had no choice but to retreat rapidly. The jet's engines roared into life and the Lear was quickly on the runway. In a matter of a couple of minutes it was a speck on the horizon, glistering in the light of the advancing dawn.

Tennet returned to the general aviation office where the pilot of the GulfStream was talking to the man behind the desk. Whitney Whittier was with him.

"Ralston's crew filed a flight plan for Barbados," Whittier told Tennet.

"We have to follow them, Whit. Right now!" He turned to the pilot and said, "We can file our plan once we are airborne! Let's go Jack."

"They have to finish refueling so I'll do it now. I'll be right there," the pilot answered.

Joe had calmed Robin Granger and when she saw the Lear take off she willingly accompanied him into the office. When Tennet realized who she was he had a conversation with Whittier out of the others' hearing. Then he hurriedly left with Jack the pilot. Whittier introduced himself to Joe and then turned to Robin.

"I'm FBI Agent Whit Whittier and you are Robin Granger I believe," he told her.

"Oh my God!" was all she could say.

"Are you Robin Granger?" Whittier asked again.

"Yes I am."

Whittier then advised her of her right to remain silent and the other rights she had under the Miranda rule and asked if she understood. She did.

"Am I under arrest?" she asked.

"As yet we have not received the consent of Cayman authorities to do that."

"Well, no matter. I want this over with. I'll go back to the States with you willingly. I suppose I should consult an attorney before I talk to you."

"That's fine," Whittier agreed. "Do you have to retrieve anything from where you were staying?"

"No. Ralston took my bag."

"I'll get us on the next flight back to Miami and then back to New York. If you will tell me the name of your lawyer I'll try to have him meet us when we arrive."

The three then got into Joe's Jeep and drove the short distance to the parking lot at the commercial airlines terminal. Granger didn't ask and Joe didn't volunteer what his involvement was or why he happened to be at the general aviation terminal. It seemed obvious that she wouldn't answer any questions he might ask her. He felt quite sure that she wasn't involved with the murder and doubted that Ralston had said anything of importance to her about it. Whittier thanked him for the ride and managed to whisper out of Granger's hearing that he'd be in touch. Joe left and drove slowly back to Spanish Bay Reef, wondering what his next move should be.

It certainly didn't seem profitable to try to fly to Barbados as much as he'd like to be present when Tennet caught up to Ralston. He had no idea when he might catch a flight there anyway. In any event, Ralston wouldn't talk to him, he was sure. The picture of his defiance when Tennet confronted him a short while before still was etched in his mind's eye. All he could hope for was that Tennet would be able to bring Ralston back to the States and that eventually the FBI would break him down.

Roberta was sleeping when Joe let himself quietly into their room at Spanish Bay Reef. It was too early to call Cece so Joe undressed and lay down quietly on the empty twin bed and soon was asleep. Shortly after ten Roberta decided she had to wake him. She had gone down to breakfast alone, realizing that Joe probably hadn't had any sleep all night. She had awakened several times during the night but it did not occur to her to worry about him. When they were first married she worried a lot when he was on patrol at night. As the years went by and Joe had been involved in many dangerous situations, she had come to realize that he was quite capable of handling anything that might come up.

Joe immediately asked what time it was and then called Dan Hardy's office in Ellsworth. When Dan came on the line Joe gave him a full report. Joe said he wanted to get a flight back to the States at the first opportunity but Dan told him that didn't make any sense. There was nothing he could accomplish in the next few days. Robin Granger wouldn't be accessible because she would certainly follow up on her intention to see her lawyer as soon as she returned to the States. Even if she did have information about the murder, they would not be able to obtain it until Tardif was willing to share it. If the FBI was successful in bringing Ralston back to the States, the same applied.

"You have reservations to return in four days" Dan told him. "Your vacation is paid for and there wouldn't be a refund if you left early. I want you to stay there and get your batteries recharged. You've been at this investigation day and night now for over a month. You can do us all more good staying there for some rest and relaxation than you can by rushing back here and waiting until the FBI or Tardif give us more information."

"Thanks Dan," Joe said. "Trouble is, I don't know if I can relax if I stay. This has been the most frustrating investigation I've ever been in. Every avenue I've followed has gotten us a lot of information but we really aren't any closer to a solution than when we started. I have this feeling in my gut that the solution to our problem is right under our noses back there in Maine."

"That may well be but until we find out what the FBI has learned about Ralston we're at a stalemate. In the meantime, you deserve a little time to relax. I'll make the decision. You are on my payroll — remember? You stay. I'll call if anything breaks."

Joe reluctantly agreed.

Roberta had been listening to the conversation so it wasn't necessary for Joe to tell her the events of the night but he had to tell her what the argument with Dan was about — that he'd been ordered to stay there to 'recharge his batteries' until their scheduled flight would bring them back to the States.

"He's right, you know darling." Roberta told him. "And I'm going to make sure you have fun during the rest of our stay."

With that she quickly slipped out of her clothes and began to undress her husband. Joe was so surprised and delighted he didn't offer to help. This was something new. Usually he was the one doing the undressing. Maybe he could force himself to relax for a few days after all. He decided in an instant that it certainly was not going to be from lack of effort on his part.

$\mathcal{C}$HAPTER $\mathcal{T}$WENTY TWO

$\mathbf{B}$eth Fairbanks had been alone in Carleton Cottage since the week after Gordon's death. Andy was the first of the family to leave Northeast Harbor. He felt sure that a great deal of his success at Fairbanks & Burke had been achieved with subtle help from his father and he was worried about his future now that he was on his own. Soon after he had joined the firm right out of Yale Law School, he was assigned to assist senior lawyers in the firm's most important cases. True, he had worked hard and had a good mind but his father had seen to it that he had a leg up on the other associates. He wasn't particularly ashamed of the fact. Everyone knows favortism for one's offspring is common in the large law firms all across the country. Now he had a deep feeling of unease which went beyond his security at the firm. He wouldn't talk about it, even to Brandy with whom he had always been close.

There were too many unanswered questions for him. He didn't want to believe that Kevin Burke was somehow involved with his father's murder. He had known about his father's relationship with Sarah Rosen early on. Andy had the use of the firm's New York apartment when neither of the senior partners had signed up to use it. He came in one evening unannounced and found his father in bed with Sarah. He quickly left and his father didn't mention it to him, nor did he to anyone else. That was a couple of years back.

For the past year Gordon had set aside each Wednesday noon to have lunch with Andy and on one of those occasions he had mentioned, as if in passing, that his relationship with Sarah had ceased. Later Andy learned that Kevin Burke had taken his father's place, but he still didn't know what prompted the breakup. At the time it had caused him to wonder what had happened, and now, after his father was murdered, it bothered him even more. He knew that both Sarah and Kevin were with his father the afternoon he was murdered. At first he had a hard time believing that either of them was involved. Kevin was his father's best friend — but the law practice they had started was now very high stakes. Andy wasn't a partner at Fairbanks & Burke, so he had no way of knowing if there was trouble at the firm or between Kevin and his father. Sarah could have been a problem between them. She may even have taken it upon herself to settle whatever it was.

Andy knew that Tiger and Cece were with his father well into the evening the night he was murdered. But also he knew only too well that Tiger looked on Gordon with the same love and respect that one usually has for his own father, and he knew his father reciprocated that strong affection. It had been a source of jealously for him for years. Try as he might, he couldn't think of a reason why Tiger would want his father dead.

At the time Cece was hired as an associate at Fairbanks & Burke, Andy had been in a long relationship with a woman lawyer from another firm, but by his choice, that was slowly ending. Andy was greatly impressed from the first time he saw Cece, but, under the cicumstances of the hiring, he thought that Kevin had designs of his own on her. Kevin's divorce was then final. He hired her, so it was a good guess. But he was wrong. Cece began to work with Gordon and it was apparent to him that his father had become her mentor. Andy was jealous knowing that she was working on matters he wished to be assigned too. Knowing his father's attraction to beautiful women and the way he treated Cece, he knew only too well the reason for it. Although he wouldn't admit it, the fact that Cece was a Harvard Law grad was another source of dislike. Harvard had refused to admit him — much to his and his father's dismay. As the spring wore on he came to believe that Cece had something to do with his father's breakup with Sarah Rosen. Andy was well aware of his mother's prognosis and his father's developing interest in Cece troubled him greatly. He blamed it on Cece, even though he could not point to any occasion on which she had shown any indication that she was leading his father on. The final blow to his ego came the day they were all sailing on *Sea Chaser* and Cece had rejected his advances. So it was easy for him to consider her as a prime suspect.

Yet, when he really thought about it, there were no real answers for him as to who was responsible for his father's murder. Unlikely as it might seem, someone at Fairbanks & Burke could be involved and all he could think about was that he needed to be in New York to protect his interest in the firm. He tried to get his mother to agree to return to Greenwich so he could be close to her, but that failed. She knew intuitively what was troubling her son and she insisted that he return to New York, so he did.

Brandy returned to Seattle the day after Andy returned to New York. He wanted to be with Norma, young Brandon and his new born son — Grayson. Beth had also encouraged him to leave as well, telling him Norma needed him and that she was 'just fine.' Before he left, Brandy also tried very hard to get his mother to go back to Greenwich to be near Andy, her longtime family doctor and the New York hospitals. He had seen how tired his mother had been when she was in Seattle and he sensed that she was not nearly as well as she tried to pretend. Beth told him she did not intend to return to Greenwich until the snow flew. She was again very firm about it. As both sons knew, when their mother made up her mind about something, there was no changing it, so with great reluctance, Brandy made sure that Melissa Lunt would be with his mother constantly and he too left .

For several days after that, Beth was able to keep her spirits up. She was only too well aware of how sick she was, but she was determined not to let it stop her from doing what she knew she had to do in the short time she had left. Several years prior to his death, Gordon had established both of them as residents of Maine. In that way they could avoid some of New York's income taxes and avoid completely New York's exorbitant inheritance taxes. Maine's inheritance tax is exactly the amount allowed by the Federal estate tax as a deduction from the amount owed on the estate, so the end result is that there is no additional tax and Maine's income tax is substantially less. Beth had heard from her friends how New York would claim that a person who died there was a resident and try to tax the estate. She had long since decided she would die in Maine.

After her boys left, Beth immersed herself in getting all the information her lawyer needed in order to probate Gordon's estate. It was a monumental task and kept her mind occupied most of the days. Still, since she was basically alone at Carleton Cottage, there was a lot of time for her to think. When her thoughts turned to her medical problem she would quickly turn them back to the past. She had had a full and extremely happy life. She adored her sons and now her grandsons. Her deepest regret was that she would not watch her grandchildren grow up. Her love for Gordon was deep and abiding, but she wasn't a fool. She was well aware that in the past year Gordon had increased his visits to his mother in Saint Albans. Gordon had admitted to her that he had 'taken up' with Kelley when her medical problems had reached the point that making love was too painful for both of them. Under the circumstances, she actually approved. She had spent many wonderful days with Kelley over the years and, even with the knowledge that her husband had renewed their teenage relationship, she still considered her one of her best friends. I'd rather he be with Kelly than almost anyone else, she often told herself and she meant it.

On her last trip to Bangor for her therapy, Beth's Maine doctor had gently warned Beth that her time was becoming extremely limited. When she returned to Carlton Cottage from that trip, she tried to call Gordon's mother with the purpose of asking her to come to Maine for a short visit. Kelley answered the call and told her that Celia and her father were off to a veterinarian's convention and would be gone for a week at least. Beth then told Kelley that her time was really short and that she wanted to see her —could she come for the weekend? Beth told her that she hoped Kevin, Cece, and Tiger would be up for the weekend as well. With some trepidation, Kelley agreed. Her one great fear was that Beth had somehow learned what had been going on. She loved Beth very much and her feelings of guilt had been tearing her apart.

Then Beth called Tiger with the same message and the same invitation for him and Cece. It was then that Tiger told her that he and Cece were married. Beth was extremely happy to hear that and insisted they both come up to spend the weekend. Knowing that Cece would want him to accept, he agreed without first calling her. Then she called Kevin and invited him and Sarah. Inviting Sarah was done to assure her that Kevin would come. She was greatly relieved to learn that Sarah was on the west coast but Kevin would come without her.

Kevin knew from Andy that Beth's time was getting very short. They all had been invited to stay at Carleton Cottage but he was convinced that it would be too much for Beth, knowing how she always insisted on being the perfect hostess. When he told Cece about his concerns, she immediately told him that she and Tiger would stay the weekend at Tiger's grandmother's house. Kevin called Kelley and they agreed to stay at the Kimball Terrace Inn.

Beth was determined that the weekend would be a happy time. She had been on pain medication for a long time but her stamina had lessened as the weeks went by. Melissa Lunt, Harvey's niece, had moved into Carleton Cottage to be with her. Together they planned all the meals and Melissa, a good cook, would prepare them for the guests. Beth planned short trips around the Island to visit for one last time all the places she loved so much. Tiger welcomed the suggestion that he drive them around in the Fairbanks' Yukon. The fall foliage had long passed its peak and most of the deciduous trees were bare. Still, it was a time of year Beth loved. She loved the crisp cool air — even the gray days. She especially loved the brilliance of the stars at night, so the trip up Cadillac Mountain was saved for after the evening meal on Saturday.

Beth's guests all arrived at Carleton Cottage for dinner shortly after 6 p.m. that Friday. Kevin and Cece were flown up in the firm's jet, stopping at Logan for Tiger. Harvey picked them up at Bar Harbor Airport and warned them that they would see a dramatic change in Beth since early September. Kelley drove over from Vermont and arrived just as they were sitting down for dinner. Harvey helped his niece with the meal — steaming the clams and lobsters in the large propane gas boiler he had put together years ago. Melissa had baked bread and apple pies. Beth had insisted on making her famous crabmeat crackers as hors d' oeuvres to accompany the well chilled Chardonnay.

Beth was extremely happy to be with her guests. With the exception of Cece, she had known them most of their lives and she loved them all very much. After the meal, they all retired to the large living room overlooking Somes Sound for an after dinner brandy. Beth initiated the conversation by reliving some of the happy times they all had spent with Gordon. Soon the others contributed memories of their own. They all could see that their reminisces pleased Beth greatly. It was a very good evening for them all. Having these friends to share it with her seemed to be a tonic for Beth and only when Kelley insisted that they all should leave to meet again in the morning did Beth reluctantly agree the party was over for the day.

Saturday was a fine fall day, sun without clouds, warm with a gently breeze from the south. It was obvious that Harvey wasn't happy with the long days for Beth. He spoke to Tiger and made him promise that, on the day's trip, he would bring Beth back to Carleton Cottage as soon as she showed signs of tiring. But Beth was animated as they visited the places she had chosen. Each one brought back memories of Gordon for her, yet she seemed to delight in recounting them. Sensing again the effect the visits had for her, the others joined in her laughter, though for Kelley, sitting in back of the Yukon, laughter was often mixed with tears.

They had the evening meal on the glassed-in portion of the veran-dah of Carleton Cottage, which remained warm from the afternoon sun. Melissa, with Harvey's help, cooked the steaks on the charcoal grill, and served another sumptuous meal followed with a Black Forest cake and vanilla ice cream. Again, Beth's favorites. Then Tiger drove them up Cadillac Mountain. The moon was full and the view from the top was magical, the waters of the bay sparkling, the lights of the town twinkling, the air still warm. Tiger had some difficulty getting Beth to return to the Yukon for the trip back to the cottage. Everyone realized that it would probably be the last time Beth would enjoy the view.

They joined Beth at the cottage for breakfast the next morning, after which they attended the Sunday service at Saint Jude's. For the first time during the weekend, as the priest said a thoughtful prayer for Gordon, Beth could not control her emotions and tears streamed down her cheeks. Kelley put her arm around Beth and tried without success to hold back her own.

When they were back at Carleton Cottage for lunch, at Beth's request, Kevin and Cece brought her up-to-date on their efforts to find Gordon's murderer. For the first couple of weeks after the event, Beth had shut it out of her mind. She couldn't believe that someone had any reason to murder her husband. Then she began analizing all the infor-mation she could get. She gleaned information from the newspapers and organized the evidence, concentrating on the people she knew were present that night and who might be capable of doing the act. Then she called Andy and asked him to send her all the information he had. At first, none of it made sense to her, especially Andy's theory that Cece was the perpetrator. Beth prided herself on her judgment of people and she knew very well that Cece and Tiger were not involved.

Beth welcomed the news that Ralph Ralston was now a prime suspect. She had not liked him from the first time they had met. Her intuition told her Ralston couldn't be trusted and she told Gordon her thoughts about him. His response was that a lawyer wasn't responsible for his clients character but he was responsible to see that he and his firm weren't involved in anything illegal. She was well aware of Gordon's unease in the days before he was murdered but she didn't have any idea what caused it and couldn't get him to talk about it. So she wasn't surprised at all with the new information. Silently, her only hope was that she would live long enough to see the murderer caught.

The guests all planned to leave after the Sunday lunch, but Beth begged them to stay awhile longer. They couldn't refuse her earnest request and it was after 4 p.m. when they finally left.

After lunch was served, Beth insisted that Melissa take the rest of the day off, go up to Ellsworth to take in the movie that she told Beth she was dying to see. Melissa had explicit instructions from Andy that his mother should not be left alone so she was reluctant to disobey him. Still, she had not left the cottage for several weeks and she was eager to be away for awhile. She called her girl friend in Ellsworth and made the date. Milissa would pick her up in an hour or so. After the movie the two women had a pizza and a beer at Pat's and then they went to another movie at the Mall. Milissa was happy to have the time with her friend but she drove back to Northeast Harbor as fast as she dared. She worried all the time she was away that something might happen to Mrs. Fairbanks and she'd be blamed for not being there with her.

It was after 11 p.m. when Melissa drove down the drive to Carleton Cottage. As she parked her car, she was surprised to see a light was still on in Beth's room. With the heavy doses of pain medication Beth was on, she had been going to bed early and usually fell quickly asleep. With the added help of a sleeping pill, she would sleep the night through. Melissa knew something was wrong. She ran into the cottage and up the stairs to Beth's room. The door was ajar and she peeked in. Beth was in bed and seemed to be asleep. She went in and turned off the lamp and halfway down the stairs she decided to go back and check more thoroughly. This time she quietly bent down close to Beth and put her ear near her nose and mouth. Hearing no sound of breathing, she turned on the bedside lamp and felt for a pulse. She could not find one. In a panic she called her uncle on Beth's bedside phone and told him she was sure that Beth had died in her sleep. Harvey seemed incredulous and told her he'd be there in a minute.

When Harvey was satisfied that Beth had in fact passed away, he called John Baker, Beth's local doctor and asked him to come immediately because Beth needed him. Dr. Baker lived only a short distance away and was soon there. He quickly confirmed that Beth was gone. He asked who was at the cottage that evening and finding that no one had been there, he made the required call to the Mount Desert Police and reported the unattended death.

Sergeant Tolman was at Carleton Cottage and in Beth's room within five minutes of the call. He asked Dr. Baker if he could tell him the cause of death.

"I can't be sure," was the reply. "Only an autopsy can confirm the cause of death."

"I'm sorry folks," Tolman told them. "The law requires that I secure the premises. You all will have to leave until our work is done here."

Harvey Lunt took his niece back to the apartment over the boat house to spend the night with him. Melissa was crying off and on and in a bad way. She had come to adore Beth. She had never been treated so well, even by her own mother. She blamed herself for Beth's passing with no one present. Harvey tried to console her, but to no avail. She was convinced that if she had been there, Beth would still be alive — and she was right.

*C*HAPTER *T*WENTY THREE

For the rest of the week Roberta tried to keep Joe's mind off the Fairbanks murder. She was only partially successful. They spent their days either in or on the clear warm waters surrounding Spanish Reefs. Joe was fascinated with his newfound sport — snorkeling around the coral reefs which abounded with fish of every color and stripe. Roberta purchased a book on Caribbean fish and gave it to him. Joe made a list of all the ones he had spotted on the reefs. One day they went out fishing with a group from the resort and Joe caught an eight pound grouper which the chef cooked for them for dinner that evening. They were surprised and pleased at how good it tasted. They explored the island from one end to the other in the Jeep. One day Joe went parasailing while Roberta held her breath on shore. The same day they tried their hand at sailing a Hobie Cat.

More than anything else, Roberta enjoyed the meals at Spanish Bay Reef. It wasn't only that she had a respite from cooking — the meals were always quite different from the fare at home in Maine. When their stay was up, Roberta reluctantly packed their bags and told Joe she wasn't leaving unless he promised they would come back again next year. 'We'll see...' was all he would say. After two smooth flights, they arrived in New York City that Sunday night. Cece had asked Joe to stay the night in New York and come in to the Fairbanks office Monday morning so she could bring him up to date on any new developments.

Joe was in the offices at 7:30 that morning but Cece had not yet arrived. Kevin Burke came in as Joe was about to take a seat in the waiting room and he asked Joe to join him in his office. Over coffee Kevin told him how pleased the government agents were with his help in capturing Robin Granger and in their attempt to arrest Ralph Ralston. They had not caught up to Ralston as far as Kevin knew. Ralston had diverted his charter plane to Aruba and chartered another plane there. The pilot of that plane had not filed a flight plan and Ralston had disappeared. They were still searching for him.

Kevin had been talking to Gerry Burstine almost daily during the past weeks and he was well informed on the progress of the SEC's investigation. Kevin had also talked with Jack Griffin and learned that the FBI had interviewed Robin Granger a few days after she had returned to the States. Granger's lawyer was able to make a proffer of her knowledge of the case against Ralston and he had a tentative promise of immunity conditioned on her interview going well. Griffin was being careful and would only give him general information on what they had learned. There were some specifics, however. Most interesting to Kevin was the fact that Granger told the FBI agents that Ralston blamed Gordon Fairbanks for having the SEC on his back. After they left the country, Granger and Ralston had had an extended conversation in which Ralston made her aware of all aspects of their situation and how they got there. Granger told the agents that during that conversation Ralston was extremely angry at Fairbanks and he told her he was very happy that he got 'what was coming to him.' Granger then asked Ralston if he had anything to do with the Fairbanks murder. At that point he acted very strange but he denied any connection with it. Granger hadn't been able to tell if Ralston were telling the truth but that conversation caused her to begin to fear Ralston. She also became convinced Ralston was using her. He didn't personally know how to make the stock transfers or get the proceeds of the sale out of the country and into an un-numbered account. Once that was done she knew she was simply baggage. She knew he had the gun and she knew he was capable of murder. That's why she left him in Grand Cayman.

Cece came in to Kevin's office at that moment. It was obvious that she had been crying and was extremely upset. She explained that she had been delayed by a phone call from Tiger. Harvey Lunt had just called to tell him that Beth Fairbanks had died in her sleep that night and that the funeral would be on Wednesday at Saint Judes. He also reported that the State Police took charge of the body and were going to perform an autopsy. Lunt had not been very coherent, and was all choked up during the whole conversation. He made Tiger promise he would be at the funeral before he would hang up.

Cece told Joe that she hadn't had time for breakfast and asked him to accompany her while she got a quick coffee and a bagel. Before they arrived at the restaurant they found a phone booth and Joe called Dan

Hardy. Dan had just finished a call from Sergeant Tardif demanding to know if his client was at Carleton Cottage over the weekend. It was clear to Dan that Tardif knew that Cece and Tiger had in fact been at the cottage and that he wanted to get some kind of a reaction from Dan. Dan simply told Tardif that he wouldn't discuss the whereabouts of his client but that in the unlikely event that the Grand Jury indicted Cece he would immediately make her available. Tardif had made a veiled threat and hung up.

"Dan, Beth Fairbanks died last night," Joe told Dan. "Did Tardif mention that?"

"He did not," Dan answered. "That explains the call! He still thinks our clients murdered Gordon Fairbanks."

Joe then related to Dan what Kevin told him that morning. Dan agreed that all the circumstances surrounding Ralston's flight from the States pointed to him as the murderer. He certainly had a motive — to prevent him from being a government witness to his own misdeeds. Even if Ralston was aware at the time that it was too late to silence Gordon, with Ralston's propensity for anger, he could have killed him for revenge. Joe told Dan that he would talk to Tardif as soon as he got back and make sure he had the new information. As long as there was another viable suspect it would be difficult for Tardif to go to the Grand Jury and get an indictment of Cece and Tiger.

Dan asked Joe if he thought it worth while to go through Torrington on his drive back to Maine so he could stop to talk to Leigh Cranston and review all her evidence again. She may have left something out, he said, or something may have come up at ConnTrust that she didn't think important. Joe said it was worth a shot and he'd do it.

Joe called Leigh at the bank before they checked out of their hotel and arranged to meet for lunch. He assured her that she had nothing to worry about — he simply wanted to review some facts with her. She seemed relieved, telling him that she had several sessions with the FBI agents during the past week and she was concerned that they might bring charges against her even though they had assured her none would be brought based on what they then knew.

Roberta had never driven south of Boston and was quite content to have a detour. She was amazed to see that cities and towns seemed to be endless, crowding into each other so one couldn't tell where one ended and the next began. Just seeing the mass of people and the maze of buildings mile after mile made her happy that she lived in Maine. They arrived in Torrington just before noon. Leigh was waiting in the bank's main lobby. She smiled broadly at Joe as he approached. He introduced her to Roberta as she got in the car and the two chatted as Joe drove out of downtown Torrington. Soon they were at the same restaurant where Leigh first talked to Gordon Fairbanks.

During the lunch Joe reviewed all of the information Leigh gave him at their prior meetings. Then Leigh told him everything she could remember about the conversations she had had with the FBI agents. Essentially, it was the same information. The FBI agents showed her a photograph and asked her if she recognized the person. At first she didn't. Then it came to her. It was the same photograph that she had seen in Ralston's apartment during the time she was having an affair with him. It was Ralph Ralston, Junior. She had never seen him face to face and Ralston hadn't talked about him much. The agent was pleased to have her say that she had seen the picture in Ralston's apartment and that it was indeed Ralston's son. The agent didn't say why he showed the picture to her but she knew a good reason and she assumed the FBI did as well. The FBI had followed the stock transfers through the chain.

Leigh stopped in mid sentence, her mouth open, staring at something in back of Joe. He turned quickly to see two men rapidly leaving the restaurant.

"Oh my God!" Leigh exclaimed. "That's them. That's Ralston's son and... that is Ralston with him. No one has a gait like him. And his disguise wouldn't fool anyone who has seen as much of him as I have. It's him!"

"I can't believe he's back in the States," Joe exclaimed. "But it's him all right. He hasn't changed his disguise since we saw him in Grand Cayman! What do you suppose made him risk coming back to the States ?"

Joe got up quickly, rushed to a payphone in the entrance of the restaurant where he made a call to Kevin. He knew it was the quickest way to get the information that Ralston and his son were in Torrington to the government agents. Kevin couldn't believe his ears but quickly terminated the conversation to make a call to Jack Griffin.

Leigh was still in a state of shock when Joe returned to their table.

It took some time for Joe to calm her fears. She was convinced Ralston was back in town on a mission — to carry out his threat to kill her. He certainly knew that she had a part in giving the government agents the information that led to them to attempt to arrest him in Grand Cayman. She was convinced that Ralston had murdered Gordon to shut him up and she knew she'd be next. Joe was finally able to convince her that Ralston had bigger fish to fry than to come after her. When he was sure she'd be all right, Joe drove Leigh back to the bank and they resumed their journey home.

The trip back to Bangor was uneventful. As soon as their bags were in the house Joe called the Orono State Police barracks hoping to find Sergeant Tardif still working but wasn't that fortunate. He left a message for Tardif that he had some information he was sure Tardif would be interested in and that he'd be at the barracks at 7 a.m. the next day to talk to him.

Tardif was waiting when Joe arrived. Neither had had breakfast and they agreed to go to the cafe the troopers usually patronized. After they ordered, Joe related the events of the past week, starting with the reasons for the decision that prompted him to go to Grand Cayman. Tardif didn't interrupt, but soon was taking notes. When Joe finished, he sat silently drinking his second cup of coffee.

Finally Tardif spoke. "I had most of that from an up-date from the FBI yesterday," he said. "If, in fact, it was Ralph Ralston you saw in Torrington yesterday, it only makes my analysis more believable."

"How is that?" Joe asked.

"I don't have a clue why Ralston would come back to the States...especially to his home town where he would be sure to be recognized, even with dark glasses and his hair dyed. But I'm sure of this — if he murdered Fairbanks he wouldn't be back in the States under any circumstances. If they are able to get a criminal conviction for violating the securities laws the worst he will get is a heavy fine and a short time in a minimum security federal prison. If he is convicted of murder, he'd be down for life. He's smart. He wouldn't take the risk."

"That's not true if they have a RICO charge."

"He still wouldn't get a life term."

"Okay. You're right. Ralston is smart — that's for sure. But he's got a mean streak in him and he's angry. If they catch him he'll lose all his ill-gotten gains. Don't forget that Robin Granger told the FBI he blamed Fairbanks for his troubles and she thinks he killed Fairbanks. She's seen his wrath directed at Fairbanks and she fears for her own life."

"I understand that, and Ralston is still a suspect. But not the prime one for the simple reason that your clients were with Gordon Fairbanks last and the Tandy woman had a motive for murder."

"Rob, I respect your thinking, but I don't see how you can say she had a motive. The Feds certainly don't think so or they would have given her a 'target notice' before they talked to her."

"That may be, but I believe that Tandy had given her father some information on the merger after he had already been buying the stock. He continued to buy during the negotiations in increased amounts. Joe, I expect that we'll get to the bottom of it soon. "

"Something breaking?"

"You know Mrs. Fairbanks died Sunday night?"

"I do. But she died of cancer."

"Don't be surprised if that wasn't the cause of death."

"You have the autopsy report?"

"Not yet...but we have preliminaries. And again...your clients were the last to be seen with Beth Fairbanks! Odd, don't you think? Just a little bit odd?"

CHAPTER TWENTY FOUR

B eth's funeral was quite different from Gordon's. The family and friends in attendance all knew she had been ill for over a year and those nearby had seen the rapid decline in her health in recent weeks. 'It was a blessing' was the usual comment. Only a few pews were occupied at Saint Jude's. Most of Beth's close friends had returned to their winter homes but some had made the trip back to Northeast Harbor for the funeral. Beth was not one to have a lot of close friends, but the ones she had valued her friendship highly and they were all there. Kevin and Andy flew back to Northeast Harbor in the firm's jet. When Kevin learned from Cece that she and Tiger would be attending the funeral he was about to ask her to come along. Suddenly remembering that Andy believed Tiger and Cece had murdered his father, he felt it best that they make their own arrangements. Celia, Jack and Kelley drove over from Saint Albans. Brandon flew in from Seattle alone, insisting that the long trip was too much for Norma and the two very young children.

Actually, it was a memorial service for Beth. It was intended that she be buried next to Gordon in the family lot in Northeast Harbor, but the autopsy was taking much longer than expected. The police could not or would not say when the body would be released. The family was told that the chemotherapy and all the medications Beth was on had complicated the process. Only Andy was suspicious that something was wrong.

His suspicions were confirmed four days after he had returned to New York City. Sergeant Tardif had called to inform him that his mother died from a lethal dose of sodium pentathol.

"That's the poison they used to murder my father!" he exclaimed.

"Right," Tardif agreed.

"My mother was murdered then!"

"We're not sure."

"Why aren't you sure? She certainly didn't die of natural causes."

"Right, but she could have taken her own life...your father too, for that matter."

That thought had not occurred to Andy and it caused him to end his questions. Tardif asked him if he had been in Northeast Harbor the weekend his mother died. When the answer was no, he asked if Andy knew who had been with his mother that weekend and again the answer was no. Tardif told him he'd be in touch as soon as he had any more information and hung up.

Carleton Cottage had been secured by the police while the cause of death was being determined by the State's pathologist. When Sergeant Tardif got the report he immediately requested and received a warrant from the district court judge in Bar Harbor to search the cottage. As soon as Tardif had appeared at the cottage with the search warrant Harvey Lunt asked if he could call a lawyer before he allowed them in. Lunt's mind was racing. He knew that Tiger and Cece were prime suspects in Gordon's murder and they had been there during the weekend before Beth died. The cottage was secured immediately and the State Police had not released the body, even after Andy had insisted it be released in time for the funeral. He knew he should call Andy but instead he called Dan Hardy. He wanted Cece's lawyer to know what was going on. Dan told him he had to let Tardif in and he should call Andy to inform him what was taking place.

Andy was with Kevin when Lunt's call came in. He was in the process of telling Kevin what Tardif had told him shortly before. When Andy told Kevin that Tardif had asked him who was with his mother the day she died Kevin told him that his mother had asked him to be with her that weekend. Kevin told him that his mother said she knew she was 'winding down,' as she called it, and wanted to have him spend the weekend with her.

"Alone?" Andy asked.

"No, not alone," Kevin answered. "Beth had asked your grandmother Celia, Jack and Kelley, but only Kelley could be there. Jack and Celia were in California at a veterinarian's convention."

"Anyone else?"

"Yes. Cece and Tiger."

"Mother asked them too? Oh my God!"

"I assume so. They were there."

"Cece, Tiger...but not me!"

Andy got up and left Kevin abruptly. He was so angry he couldn't talk. He realized that Kevin controlled his future at Fairbanks & Burke and he didn't dare tell him what was racing through his mind. When he was back in his office he called Carleton Cottage. Tardif answered the call and Andy told him what he had learned. Tardif thanked him and asked him not to tell anyone they were talking nor to tell anyone what he was about to say.

"I probably shouldn't be telling you what I'm about to say," Tardif said. "You must know that everyone who was at Carleton Cottage the day your father was murdered is a suspect...including you."

"You know I didn't murder my father."

"I don't know that for sure because I don't know who did. But it seems unlikely to me and I need your help...okay?"

"You know how hard I have been trying to help. How many times I've called you? "

"Right, but that could have been a concern on your part that our investigation was leading to you. But so far it hasn't, so I'm going to tell you where we're at. At first we were convinced that Tandy and Wass were the murderers. That was based on the fact that Tandy's father had been trading heavily in ConnTrust stock while she was working with your dad on the merger. He stood to make a lot of money on the deal. With me so far?"

"I know all that."

"Okay, then we find out that ConnTrust's president, Ralph Ralston was in Northeast Harbor that weekend and we soon learned that he was in serious violation of the federal securities laws. As the information developed and the Feds were about to close in, Ralston leaves the country. Next we soon get a lot of information from the Feds that would be a real motive for his murdering your dad. So he is a real suspect."

"I can't believe for a minute he did it."

"Well, hear me out. Ralston had an accomplice in his stock manipulations...his vice president at ConnTrust, Robin Granger. Do you know her?"

"No, but I've had bits and pieces of what you are telling me. The firm has been involved in helping the SEC with investigating the matter."

"Right. So this Robin Granger left the country with him. She's back in the U. S. now. Apparently she feared for her life with the guy.

The FBI has talked to her and she believes Ralston murdered your father. They still haven't caught up with Ralston even though they now believe he's back in this country. But he isn't my prime suspect any longer."

"Why is that?"

"My gut tells me that your mother was murdered. I can't be sure because, as I say, it is possible that she took her own life."

"How is it possible? Have you found the source of the poison? Was it injected or did she swallow it?"

"Swallowed it, as far as we know. The pathologist didn't find any evidence of a needle."

"Did you find a note?"

"No note."

"How could it be suicide? Mother would certainly leave a note!"

"I can't answer that."

"Where could she possibly get the drug...the pentathol?"

"That is one of the reasons we don't believe it was suicide. She wasn't driving any longer and Lunt says he took her for therapy but no where else."

"Wasn't Melissa Lunt with Mother?"

"Melissa says she had the afternoon off and later went to the movies. A friend was with her and confirms that fact."

"When did Cece and the others leave?"

"We don't know."

"How long would it take for the poison to act?"

"Well, it wasn't as strong a dose as your father got. It would have taken longer to do its work. Your mother could have had the pentathol for a long time, hidden it in a place where no one could find it, waiting for the time she would use it."

"If she swallowed it, wouldn't there be a glass with residue of the poison on it? And if that glass has fingerprints on it, won't that be proof enough?"

"The kitchen sink was full of dishes. Apparently Melissa Lunt left before the group had finished lunch. We are in the process of checking that out but it will take a lot of time. "

"I understand. But it seems to me that Cece and Tiger should be your prime suspects."

"They certainly are among the prime suspects. We are following through on that. We had eliminated Ralston as a suspect in this one because, as far as we knew, he was out of the country when your mother died. Now with a report that he is back in the country we have to check that out."

"That makes sense. So who murdered my dad? Who is your prime suspect at the moment?"

"I've got to check out the information you just gave me. If you assume that the person who murdered your father is also responsible for your mother's death then the trail logically ends with those who were here at Carleton Cottage on both occasions. Check me out. They would be Kevin Burke, Kelley Morse, Cece Tandy, and Tiger Wass. Correct?"

"Well, I wasn't there last weekend but if Kevin is telling the truth, that's right."

"Of course, your mother had a motive. I've been thinking about her a lot."

"Wrong. Mother was with my brother in Seattle when my father was murdered. She flew back the next day."

"Okay. But she could have had help."

"That's ridiculous!"

"Maybe. Maybe not."

"You think it possible that my mother took her own life but you don't think my dad did. Why?"

"With respect to your dad, at first our pathologist thought the poison was injected. Now he isn't sure. If it had been injected it was surely murder. The poison acts so quickly the needle would have been found. Now we aren't sure of anything. Your father could have drunk the stuff from a paper cup, thrown it overboard knowing the wind and tide would take it away quickly. By the time we got the pathologist's second report, it was too late to make a definitive search.

"This has been one of the most difficult assignments I've ever had, Mr. Fairbanks. My head tells me your father was murdered but I have only a list of people who could have done it, but that is all it is — a list. I need help! Who do you think is the prime suspect?"

"I think it was Cece Tandy."

"Why?"

"Or, maybe Tiger Wass."

"Still, why?"

"Okay. It's only a hunch."

Tardif agreed that there were a lot of hunches but that wasn't the kind of help he needed. Then he told Andy that he had to get back to work and that he'd be in touch. Andy had been trying hard to keep an open mind about his father's murder. He thought about it constantly and tried to be lawyer-minded in analyzing all the facts that came to him. He tried to sublimate his acknowledged prejudice towards Cece, but each time he really addressed the issue, he came to the same conclusion. He convinced himself that Cece and Tiger were responsible — so convinced that he told Sergeant Tardif they were his choice of prime suspects. Now he was convinced that his mother had learned some fact that would confirm his belief, so she confronted them with the fact that weekend and they murdered her to keep her from going to the police. He thought he knew his father too well to think he'd take his own life. What would be his reason? He couldn't be in trouble with the law. He was just too scrupulous a lawyer for that. He knew of his father's relationship with Sarah Rosen but that was over and it didn't seem possible that that could be a cause. And where was the vital evidence — the syringe — the needle — the cup with a residue of the pentathol. That would be true in his mother's case as well. But his mother was too tough to take her own life, he was sure of that. Even if she did, she was too kind not to leave a note.

So it always came back to Cece and Tiger.

*C*HAPTER *T*WENTY FIVE

For a long while after the call from Harvey Lunt, Dan Hardy sat back in his chair, deep in thought. What in the world is going on, he wondered. Why was Sergeant Tardif at Carleton Cottage with a search warrant? Didn't Beth Fairbanks die from her cancer as had been reported? Dan immediately dialed the number for the Campbell law office. Learning that Dan Hardy was on the line, Ian Campbell interrupted the conference with a client he was engaged in and went into his small library to take the call. The two arranged to meet in the late afternoon in Southwest Harbor after Dan finished his day's work in Ellsworth. In the meantime Ian would locate Joe Goldberg and ask him to join them at his office.

Ian called Joe on his cell phone to inform him of the new development. Joe was on his way out of Bangor on a short assignment for another client but he turned around and drove directly to Northeast Harbor. He found Tardif at Carleton Cottage and asked what was going on. Tardif told him he had received the autopsy report and that Beth Fairbanks had also died from the same drug that had killed Gordon Fairbanks. He and his crew were in the process of working up the scene and it was too early to give him any information. Tardif then asked Joe to be sure that Cece and Tiger would be available in the event that he was able to verify his suspicions. He told Joe that the two had been Mrs. Fairbanks' weekend guests and were perhaps the last ones to see her alive. He said it was too much of a coincidence that they were also the last to be with Gordon Fairbanks the night he was found dead. He reminded Joe that Tiger was in medical school and undoubtedly had access to the drug that killed them both. It was obvious to Joe that Tardif was convinced that Cece and Tiger had killed them both.

Joe learned from Harvey Lunt that his niece had been staying with Beth Fairbanks for the past several weeks. He decided he should interview her. He spent the afternoon on the Island looking for Melissa Lunt but he failed until he learned that she was seen leaving Northeast Harbor in her old Volvo right after Beth's funeral. Joe went back to talk to Harvey Lunt. Melissa hadn't told anyone where she was going, even Harvey. Lunt told him it was completely out of character for her to leave without telling anyone where she was going and he was really worried because she blamed herself for not being with Beth that evening. Apparently Harvey had not been told the truth about the cause of death for Beth Fairbanks and Joe thought it best not to tell him. Harvey told Joe that he had a talk with his niece before the funeral. At Harvey's request, Melissa related to him the events of the weekend and the evening before she found Beth in her bed. He knew Melissa was the last to see Beth alive but he didn't seem concerned that Joe was looking for her, especially after he was told that Joe wanted to make sure Mrs. Fairbanks hadn't left a note. Harvey was sure that Beth's cancer was the cause of her death.

Joe went back around Sargent Drive to see if Tardif was still there. He was, but Joe drove by, and on to Southwest Harbor to keep his appointment with the lawyers. When Dan arrived, Joe made a detailed report of where they were at, starting from the beginning. He had just finished when the phone rang. Kara answered and then handed the phone to Joe, her hand over the mouthpiece as she told him it was Tardif. They listened as Joe talked to him. It was a short conversation. Joe said only two sentences : "That's just plain wrong!" and "I'll do it."

"Tardif has obtained secret indictments of murder this afternoon against both Cece and Tiger and wants us to get them both back to Maine immediately or he'll issue an all points bulletin for their arrest," Joe told the lawyers.

"I can't believe he did that!" Kara exclaimed. "He has to have more evidence than we know about."

"Maybe, but I doubt it," Joe said. "Just yesterday he told me he was going to make an arrest soon. I know his superiors have been on his back. All the news media have been on his back, too. This weekend one of the papers suggested that Tardif is incompetent, so he's been itching to make an arrest. "

"Did he say it was for both murders?" Dan asked.

"He didn't say," Joe answered.

"I'll call Tiger and tell him." Ian said. "Then we can call Tardif back and tell him our clients will be back here tomorrow."

Ian left the others to make the call from his office.

"We'll have to file the usual motions and get Tardif's discovery right away," Kara said. "Then we'll know better where we're at. He must have something we don't know about."

"Maybe so, but I'll bet all he's got is circumstantial evidence," Joe offered. "He's probably going solely on the fact that our clients were with both Beth and Gordon a short while before each died. Tardif thinks Cece had a real motive to kill Gordon. But we've got solid evidence to refute her father's involvement. Tardif has to know that. He always looks for a motive — as we all do. He thinks he has one for Gordon Fairbanks murder but what evidence has he got for them to want to murder Beth Fairbanks? It has to be more than that they were with her several hours before she died!"

"In any event we'll soon find out," Dan said. "The court probably won't allow bail and we'll demand discovery immediately. I don't see what else we can do at this point."

"Well, there are a couple of things," Joe said. "I now that Ralston was back in the States as of a couple of days ago. If he flew back here the day I last saw him in the Cayman's he could have been in Northeast Harbor on Sunday, the day Mrs. Fairbanks died. I don't have a clue why he'd want to murder Mrs. Fairbanks unless he thought she had come up with a reason to know he had murdered her husband. It seems highly unlikely, but it can't be ruled out. Why else would he return to the U. S.? We have to see if anyone here saw someone who fits the description I can give of him in his disguise."

"What about the others?" Dan asked. "Kevin Burke was with her over the weekend and so was Kelley Morse."

"Right," Joe answered. "I can't come up with any reason either of them might want to murder Beth Fairbanks and that makes it seem unlikely that either is a suspect. From everything we know, Kevin Burke was very close to her."

"Cece told me sometime ago he adored her." Dan interjected.

"Right," Joe continued. "We've learned that Mrs. Fairbanks had a reason to dislike Kelley Morse. She was Gordon Fairbanks' first love and apparently that relationship had been renewed. But he's been dead over a month now and I can't see how Morse plays into this unless she did murder Gordon for some reason and Beth could point the finger at her. Still, I think it worth while for me to have a talk with her."

"It seems to me that the only logical explanation is that Mrs. Fairbanks took her own life," Ian said.

"But wouldn't she have left a note?" Dan asked. "From all reports she was the essence of kindness and wouldn't have wanted to leave any doubts about her death. And how did she take the sodium pentathol witihout leaving a clue as to how she took it? Where is the glass or cup? Where did she get the poison? She had to leave some kind of a trail. Surely Tardif has checked all that out."

"Tardif was in that process when I was at Carleton Cottage this morning. But he had to have asked that the Grand Jury be brought in before he had finished that task. He had to have something else." Joe said.

"True," Ian agreed. "But what else is there?"

The group spent an hour going over again all that was known to them concerning the Fairbanks' deaths without resolving any important issue. It was decided that Joe should drive out to Saint Albans in the morning and talk to Kelley Morse. Joe made the call to Kelley. She immediately wanted to know the reason for the visit. She wasn't aware that the police thought that Beth Fairbanks had been murdered. That suggestion caused her to cry. After a lot of explaining, Kelley finally agreed to talk to Joe in the morning. Dan, Ian and Kara would talk to Tiger and Cece at length after they arrived the next day. Then the lawyers would take their clients up to the Hancock County jail and turn them in. Maybe something would come out of those talks but none of them expected too much.

Joe had promised Roberta that they would take Buck, their Brittany Spaniel, partridge hunting that Saturday. When he arrived home late that evening he told her that he had to go on a wild goose chase all the way to Saint Albans, Vermont to interview a witness in the Fairbanks cases. Roberta was ready to pout when Joe added that he wanted to her to come along. He told her the weatherman was promising a clear, cool fall day. It would be a fun time and she could help with the driving. Quickly, she agreed.

They got an early start, taking Route 2 to Bethel, stopping only in Skowhegan for coffee and donuts. They arrived in early afternoon to find the Morses unsaddling their Morgan horses. Kelley left her horse for the senior Morses to care for. Roberta was happy to stay with Celia and Jack Morse, watching them do the chores while Kelley took Joe into the den to talk.

Kelley was apprehensive at first and answered Joe's questions mostly with a yes or no. After a while she relaxed and gave him minute details of the weekend she spent with Beth and the others at Carleton Cottage. She said that Beth certainly was upbeat and didn't appear suicidal. The group toured the Island and visited Gordon's Hinckley in the yard. They spent a lot of time reminiscing about their times together, and enjoying the delicious meals Beth had planned for them.

"Everyone seemed to really enjoy the visit, given the circumstances," she finally told him. "Beth told us when she invited us that even though it was a 'farewell party' as she put it, it was to be a happy time. And it was."

Kelley paused and then went on, "I've given it a lot of thought since we talked last night. At first I didn't believe the State's pathologist got it right. They do make mistakes, as you well know from your profession. But then I came to realize Beth could have taken her own life. I saw signs of how much she was suffering even though she had done her best to hide it and she was obviously very well medicated."

"So you think she was suffering so much she could have done it — taken the poison?" Joe asked.

"It's certainly possible. But why wouldn't she leave a note? Why haven't the police found any evidence of how she had ingested the poison? What happened to the glass she drank from? Where did she get the stuff in the first place?"

"I can't answer those questions. But I ask you — what reason would anyone have to murder Beth Fairbanks?" Joe asked.

"I can't believe anyone would. She was the nicest...the kindest women I've ever known. I loved her..." Kelley's voice trailed off as she began to cry.

When she stopped, they talked a while longer. Kelley wanted to know why it was taking the police so long to solve Gordon's murder. Joe gave her all the facts that he had developed, point by point. After he had finished, Kelley told him she couldn't bring herself to even entertain the thought that Cece and Tiger were responsible...nor Kevin nor Sarah Rosen. It had to be that awful Ralston. She hadn't liked him from the first time she had met him. Joe told her that was his thinking as well.

As he got up to leave, Joe thanked her for taking the time to talk to him.

As he left, Joe wondered if Kelley was telling him the truth. She didn't appear to be a viable suspect, but his training and experience taught him never to rule anything out. Joe retrieved Roberta from the barnyard where she had been enjoying her time with the Morses. It was late afternoon, and since the next day was Sunday, they stayed the night in a motel outside of Montpelier. They spent Sunday enjoying the countryside as they leisurely drove back to Maine.

Monday morning Joe was in Dan's office at 7 a.m. to report that his interview had confirmed, for him at least, that nothing happened that weekend that seemed to indicate a problem from any source. Dan and Joe were soon joined by Ian and Kara. Ian reported that neither Cece nor Tiger had noticed anything during the weekend at Carleton Cottage that seemed unusual.

Tiger and Cece were to be arraigned in Hancock Superior Court at 9 a.m. The lawyers had prepared several motions ready for filing. Some might not be filed, depending on the court's ruling on bail, but they had to be prepared for any eventuality. Dan had not been able to talk to Sergeant Tardif and they still didn't know which assistant attorney general was assigned to the cases. It was decided that Joe should make a further effort to find Melissa Lunt while the lawyers expected to spend most of the morning in the courtroom. Joe knew that Tardif hadn't found her and she just might have something useful, even though he knew it was a long shot.

Joe's first thought was to visit Harvey Lunt again to see if he had heard from his niece. He found him finishing breakfast in the small apartment over the boathouse at Carleton Cottage. Harvey told him that Melissa had called late the previous evening. She was with her 'friend' in Lubec. Harvey gave Joe instructions as how to find her there and called to make sure she'd be there when Joe arrived. He assured her that it would be all right to talk to him.

It was after 1 p.m. when Joe finally found the small house that Melissa shared with her clamdigger boyfriend. The boyfriend had a baby girl just at the crawling age and a boy about two years old living with him. Apparently their mother had abandoned them. The house was a two room affair without plumbing and it was almost impossible to carry on a conversation. Joe ended up asking Melissa to talk to him in his car outside the shack. He went over the events of the day and early evening of Beth's death. Joe questioned her slowly and carefully. He found that Melissa had an excellent memory and was able to give him an accurate time table.

Melissa had nearly finished giving Joe her information when Joe asked, "Do you have any knowledge that Beth Fairbanks had some kind of poison hidden somewhere in the cottage?"

"Why?' Melissa asked.

"The police say Mrs. Fairbanks was poisoned," Joe answer.

"Oh my God!" Melissa exclaimed. "I can't believe it!"

"That is what they are telling us."

"So you think I did it?"

"I don't think anything, but they have indicted Cece and Tiger," Joe told her. "Didn't you know that?"

"We don't have a TV..."

Then Melissa told Joe that she didn't want to talk about it anymore. It took all of Joe's considerable powers to convince her otherwise. Joe wasn't sure that he ever did. He changed the subject abruptly, asking Melissa what she was going to do now that her job with Mrs. Fairbanks had ended. She didn't have an answer. She said she had taken up with 'her clamdigger' — Joey — just before she went to stay with Mrs. Fairbanks. Now that she had returned she was sure she had made a bad mistake. She hadn't realized Joey had the kids and now it was obvious that all he wanted her for was to be their mother. She didn't want that and anyway, Joey wasn't the same guy she had spent a couple of weeks with before she went to stay with Mrs. Fairbanks. The kids weren't there then. Back then it was all fun and games, but now she knew it was a lot of lies.

During the conversation, Melissa seemed to warm up to Joe. It was obvious that she was in a bad situation.

"Wouldn't you like to leave?" Joe asked.

"Oh God yes!' she answered. "I'm scared to death of Joey but I don't have a car."

"I could bring you back to your uncle's in Northeast."

Melissa quickly agreed but she wouldn't go back into the shack. There was nothing there she wanted and she couldn't face Joey. Joe started the Caprice and they were on their way.

Soon Melissa seemed at ease, so Joe asked her to tell him more about Mrs. Fairbanks. Was she content up until the last? How did she seem to get along with Kelley Morse? Did Mr. Fairbanks show affection towards her? Melissa's answers were thoughtfully given. She was able to relate observations which confirmed everything Joe had learned. Beth Fairbanks was always upbeat. After Mr. Fairbanks died, Kelley Morse was often at Carleton Cottage with Beth. Melissa hadn't stayed full time at Carleton Cottage until the last couple of months, but she had worked for the Fairbanks for the last two years. She really liked them both. Mr. Fairbanks was so sweet...and yes, he really doted on his wife.

Harvey Lunt was surprised and pleased to have Melissa back in Northeast Harbor. He thanked Joe profusely for bringing her 'home', then took her hand as they climbed up the stairs to the apartment over the boathouse.

The drive back to Bangor was over before it began. Joe was conscious of passing through Ellsworth only because it reminded him that Cece and Tiger were incarcerated in the Hancock County Jail there. Tiger at least. Since there was no facility for women in Hancock County, Cece probably was in the Penobscot County Jail by then. No matter. They were both in jail and as far as Joe was concerned, they had no reason to be. Tardif had simply caved in to the great pressure from his superiors and the media and obtained an indictment on flimsy grounds.

Still, Joe had no better direct evidence pointing to the murderer. He had never been involved in an investigation where so little real progress had been made towards a solution. He had never been so frustrated. Usually he didn't get to know the person whose case he was working on. And if he did, usually the person wasn't one he could relate to anyway. Over the years he found that most people charged with criminal misconduct weren't people he would be comfortable having for friends. But, even given the fact that he had been with her only a few times, he had been greatly impressed with Cece Tandy. And Tiger Wass favorably impressed him as well.

Try as he might, Joe couldn't bring himself to believe that these two young people could be capable of murder. There came a time in every case he ever worked on when a piece of evidence popped up which led to a solution. It was long since time that they had a break. Where was the missing evidence? What had he missed, he wondered. He was sure that the solution was near at hand — but what prevented him from finding it?

$\mathcal{C}$HAPTER $\mathcal{T}$WENTY SIX

B y Sunday afternoon the media learned that two 'suspects' had been arrested in the Fairbanks murder. By evening they had information from a 'reliable source' that the police had strong evidence that Beth Fairbanks had been murdered and that the two were being charged with both crimes. By Monday morning, the *Bangor Daily News* published the names of the defendants but had little exact information on the basis for the police charging them with the Fairbanks' murders. That evening, Channel 5 covered the arraignment of the defendants and had gathered a great deal of information on Cece and Tiger but still no details on why they were charged. Channel 2 had a live interview with Andy Fairbanks who complemented the State Police for their good work and said he looked forward to the conviction of the two defendants, both of whom his father had befriended, and who deserved 'to be put away for life.'

The hearings on the various motions the lawyers filed in State v. Tandy and State v. Wass were held Monday afternoon, immediately following the arraignments of the two defendants. Judge Rollins denied bail for both without comment. He then denied the Motions for Discovery — saying only that, at the time, they were premature. They could be presented again if matters warranted it. Then he granted the state's Motion to Consolidate, and ordered the cases joined for trial. Then, to the surprise of everyone, he denied the defendants' Motions for Speedy Trials.

Both the print and broadcast media were in attendance at the hearings and the courtroom was filled with curious people. After the hearing ended, camera crews were waiting at both entrances of the court room to film the defendants and their lawyers as they emerged and went into the conference room. They were all shouting questions but Dan Hardy's refusal to talk to the media was well known and, as expected, no answers were given.

The rapid action and the Court's orders put the defense lawyers in a bind. Trying two defendants charged with murder together was unusual in Maine and trying murders which had occurred more than two months apart was unheard of. The ruling contravened what the lawyers had been taught about due process. They were convinced that the ruling would be reversed on appeal — but that wouldn't happen until after the trial. Judge Rollins had been appointed to the Superior Court bench only recently. He had no experience as a trial lawyer. Dan knew that he had been ordered into Hancock County only to preside at the arraignments — that he was the only judge available and he would not be the trial judge. Still, if they filed a motion to separate, any other judge would be reluctant to change the consolidation ruling. The problems for the lawyers were compounding at every turn.

The meeting of the lawyers and their clients was short. Cece knew the implications of the judge's ruling but she was more concerned that the 'speedy trial' motion had been denied. The women's section of the Penobscot County Jail wasn't her idea of a great hotel. Ian wasn't greatly disturbed by the consolidation ruling because he knew Dan would have the 'laboring oar' at trial. Kara, always upbeat, was convinced that they soon would get a break in the case. Weeks without one, however, had been the reality and until they got the State's discovery, there was really no place to turn. The meeting was becoming more depressing for everyone. Dan sought a way to end it quickly, and asked Tiger if he had any questions. Tiger had not participated in the discussion. He saw how discouraged Cece was becoming and it worried him greatly.

"This is not the end of the world folks," Tiger said. "I've been in a lot worse situations than this and I'm still alive. We've all got to have faith. Let's not forget the bottom line here. Cece and I know we didn't have anything to do with the Fairbanks murders. I have faith that the system works. We'll get through this, so let's all get back to doing what we have to do."

Tiger and Cece were able to have a quick embrace before the Sheriff's deputies took them away. Dan asked Joe and Ian to join him at his office to plan strategy while Kara went up to the law library to begin the research so the defense team could be ready to attack Judge Rollins rulings.

Carrie, Dan's secretary, greeted them as the came in and said, "I just had a call from Harvey Lunt. He wanted Joe. He said it's urgent that he talk to him right away."

Carrie dialed the number Lunt had left and handed the phone to

Joe. Harvey answered on the first ring.

"Hello... Joe," he said, his voice strained. "I just got the *Bangor Daily*... I've got to talk to you, Joe. Can you come on down here? I... I don't want to drive. I'm too upset."

"You hang tight, Harvey," Joe told him. "I'll be there in half an hour."

Joe was in Northeast Harbor in half an hour. It was a gray day and the sun was setting behind the western mountains of the Island. As he drove by the Carleton Cottage he could see that yellow police tapes still surrounded it. He was sure that Beth was the reason Harvey Lunt wanted to talk to him but he didn't have a clue what it was all about. He drove the Caprice past the cottage and down the narrow gravel road to the boathouse near the shore. He parked beside Harvey's old Chevy pickup, got out and headed for the stairs to the small apartment on the second floor. Harvey had heard him drive in and was waiting in the kitchen door looking down at him. The kitchen was in the back of the building. When Joe reached the kitchen, Harvey pointed to a chair at the kitchen table. As Joe sat down Harvey put a cup of steaming coffee in front of him along with some cream and sugar. From the bread box Harvey retrieved a bag of DJ's donuts, opened the bag, offered it to Joe and then sat down opposite him. Joe hadn't eaten since breakfast so he welcomed the treat. Harvey raised his mug with trembling hands and took a long drink. With a long sigh he began the conversation.

"They arrested Tiger and Cece," he said.

Joe thought, 'Good Lord, is that why he got me all the way down here?'

"Yes, I know," Joe answered.

"How'd they come up with the crazy idea those two kids murdered Gordon... and Beth?" Harvey asked, looking extremely puzzled as well as greatly annoyed.

"The State Police were being pushed hard to make an arrest, Harvey," Joe said. "Sergeant Tardif is convinced that both Fairbanks were murdered. He had evidence that Cece's dad had been trading in the bank stock that Cece and Mr. Fairbanks had been working on. There was a lot of profit to be made by Cece's father if the merger went through. It's all circumstantial evidence, but apparently Tardif convinced the Grand Jury that Cece leaked the merger information to her father and then murdered Gordon...or had Tiger murder him to cover it all up."

"Tardif's a dumb bastard. He really pushed me around when he talked to me...actin' like I was some piece of... you know. An' I jest don't get it. That's a reason for those kids to murder Gordon? Never heard somethin' dumber! They both thought the world of Gordon. Tardif's full of bullshit right up to his mouth!"

Harvey was angry and shouting. Joe continued his explanation.

"Harvey, the police think that Gordon found out Cece had given her father some information on a bank merger they were working on and her father stood to make a lot of money as a result. That was illegal and Gordon tried to stop it. When Gordon knew it was too late, he told her that he was going to inform the SEC so his law firm wouldn't get in big trouble. A leak like that — assuming it happened — could ruin his law firm. That was their business — mergers. They would be blacklisted. No one would hire them if they were convinced the firm could not guarantee secrecy. Worse, it might lead to civil or even criminal charges against him and the firm."

"An' they killed him to put a stop to it! Dumb. Goddamn dumb!"

"They know Gordon died from a lethal dose of sodium pentathol. They think it was injected. Tiger is soon to be a doctor. He'd know where to get the drug and how to use it.."

"Anyone could have gotten it and given it to him..."

"And injected him with it ?"

"Don't need to be injected."

Joe was now on the edge of his chair. How did Harvey know that, he wondered.

He saved the question and instead he asked, "They were the last ones to see him alive."

"That ain't so..."

"Oh?" Joe interrupted.

"That Mr. Ralston's car was still in the yard when I left to go to my sister's."

"And you think Tiger and Cece had left by then?"

"Ayuh...I do. I know for sure...saw them leave in Tiger's Whaler."

"That's not what you said before."

"I was mixed up."

"Well, that confirms what Tiger said all along... that they left before Ralston. He was a doctor before he gave it up and went into banking. Ralston certainly could have murdered Mr. Fairbanks. He had reason too. He was trading big time in his bank's stock and didn't make the disclosures required by law. It's probably worse than that. He probably was involved with a conspiracy with the president of the other bank. We know Mr. Fairbanks knew some, if not all, of those facts and he told Ralston if he didn't go to the authorities, he'd turn him in. We think Ralston murdered him to prevent that."

"Nope...not Ralston either. An' he couldn't 'ave murdered Mrs. Fairbanks. He wasn't even around here then."

"You think the same person murdered both Mr. and Mrs. Fairbanks?"

"I'm sure of it," Harvey said in a low voice.

The statement was positive and Joe began to believe that the old man knew who murdered both Fairbanks. Like most Maine natives, Joe knew that Harvey Lunt would take his time telling him his story so he didn't speak. After a while Harvey continued.

"Ya know Joe, Beth was dying of cancer. She's been goin' back and forth to Bangor to have more chemo every three or four weeks..."

"I know that..."

"I ferried her to Bangor off and on all last summer to have her treatments. They don't have the radiation machine in Ellsworth, ya know."

Harvey's eyes were beginning to water but after a pause he went on.

"I've worked for the Carleton's all my life... ever since I was in school. Worked for Mr. Carleton with my dad as a kid an' then full time when he passed on. Bill Carleton was the finest' kind. I never know'd anyone better'n him. Worked for the Carleton's over fifty years now. Ann Carleton was a saint too. Couldn't find better to work for. An' that Beth...watched her grow up...She was just a kid when I first started here working summers while I was still in school. God, she was beautiful even then and as she got older. She was the prettiest and nicest woman I ever..."

Harvey paused again, tears streaming down his cheeks. He cleared his throat and went on.

"She never knew it... never even suspected it far as I know... that I fell in love with her back all those years ago."

Another long pause.

"I knew I could never marry her...Carletons got money...Lunts got nuthin'. You know how that goes. So I had to be content jess seein' her 'round the place."

Another long pause. Joe wanted Harvey to get back on the subject so he prompted him to continue.

"You said Ralston left last but he didn't do it ...murder Mr. Fairbanks?"

"Nope, he didn't. An' I didn't say he left last. Just said he was still here when I left for my sister's."

"So who left last?"

"Kelley...Kelley Morse. Mr. Fairbanks'... girl friend...lover, I guess they call it these days."

"Did you see her?"

"Damn right I saw her. That's the car I told you 'bout right after it happened. Didn't see it comin' out the road. Almost ran into it when I turned in. Lights right in Kelley's face. Saw her good...no doubt 'bout it."

Joe began to see a very different story emerging from what Harvey had told the police and the story he had told him as well. Still he didn't want to say anything that might cause Harvey to stop his narrative. He'd have to be patient and just prompt him to continue without being confrontational.

"How long have you known Kelley Morse?" Joe asked.

"Can't tell... it's been so long. She was here a lot visitin' Beth. She's been comin' with Gordon's mom and her dad for years. Always comes in August with them. Other times she comes alone. Gordon and her would sail every day. Beth hardly ever went with them. Anyway, she was comin' out the road when I come back form Sis's."

"I was just out to Saint Albans where the Morses live," Joe cut in. "Kelley's father is a vet and she sometimes helps him out. They use sodium pentathol to put animals out of their misery. That's what killed Mr. Fairbanks and my sources tell me that is what killed Mrs. Fairbanks as well. Kelley Morse certainly knew how to give a lethal dose of the stuff and she could have gotten one from her father's office or even his bag if he brought one with him. It is one of those things I was following up on. That is why I was in Saint Albans. You know she was here visiting Beth the weekend she died."

"Cece and Tiger were here, too," Harvey reminded.

"I know..."

"And Kevin Burke..."

"I know."

"But Kelley didn't do it. Kevin either."

Harvey had stopped talking again and was sipping his coffee. Joe thought he was on to something with Kelley Morse so he had tried to hurry Harvey along. He was losing his patience but he waited. This might lead to something, then again it might not, but he had to wait and see. Harvey was uptight but he certainly wasn't delusional. Joe was learning something new every time Harvey spoke.

Finally he asked, "What was Kelley doing there that late at night? It was late, the night Mr. Fairbanks died...right?"

"Ayuh, it was late, almost midnight. 'Bout the same time she left every night since she'd been here. Beth was in Seattle helpin' Brandy and Norma with the new kid. Been there a couple weeks. Kelley come over from Kimball Terrace...that's where the Morses always stayed when they were here. Come over every night 'bout eight or nine. Mr. Fairbanks always slept on *Sea Chaser* when Beth was away. Kelley'd park her car at the cottage an' walk down to the pier. She knew I was here. Didn't try to hide it. August was some hot, you remember. They'd have their drinks in the cockpit..."

Harvey stopped and the beginning of a smile crossed his face.

"You're wonderin' how I know'd from up here?"

Harvey got up and pointed through the big window in the front of the apartment to the float at the end of the pier. Joe stood to see and then they both sat back down.

"Gordon gave me a pair of Nikon binoculars for Christmas, couple years back. They almost make night day. I like to sit on the little porch out front nights when it's hot. They couldn't see me watchin'. Probably wouldn't care anyway. They was always nakid. Sat there close together in the cockpit, nakid n' talkin' an' drinkin' every night for that week and a half. An' Beth out there in Seattle, sick as she was, helpin' her kid. Kinda person she was...Gordon don't give a shit...,"

Harvey was shouting and pounding his fist on the table.

Harvey stopped talking, lifted his mug again with both hands, took a long swallow of coffee and then continued.

"When it was pas' time for boats goin' by, they'd take a mattress from one of the bunks an' lay it on the cabin trunk roof. *Sea Chaser's* a big boat ya' know. Then they'd go at it. They'd play around for a while and then they'd ...go to screwin'. Sometimes Gordon'd be on top and then Kelley. Sometimes they'd stop and switch. They'd do it slow and easy for a while and then they'd go at it like a couple' a kids. When they was done they jest lay there for a long time. Some times they'd do it agin'. Always 'bout midnight they'd go below. I guess they were takin' a shower because the lights on the port side midship'd be on. Soon after that, Kelley'd leave. I always ducked back inside before she come by. She never seen me."

Harvey's voice had turned angry.

"That really got to me. Beth Fairbanks don't deserve that. Not by a god damn sight! All I could think 'bout day and night — Gordon was screwin' Beth's friend. All my life I dreamed... made believe Beth was mine, even though I know'd I couldn't ever have her, an' why I never married. It's a terrible sin to cheat on a wonderful woman like her. She out in Seattle takin' care of Gordon's new grandkid an' all the while she's dyin' of cancer an' he's back here screwin' his god damn fool head off. Goddamn him all to hell! He deserved to be murdered!"

"That's why you said Kelley didn't do it...She loved him too much?"

"Didn't say that. Jest said she didn't do it."

"Okay...but how can you be sure?"

"I know who did. But you got to have all of it...the whole story."

"Okay, go on."

Harvey didn't go on. He got up and re-filled his coffee mug. Then he filled Joe's and sat back down. He seemed to be thinking how he should go on. After awhile he began again.

"Well, 'bout the time I watched that performance every night...Couple a weeks I guess it was... I knew I had to do somethin'. If Beth had been here maybe I'd told her. Even thought 'bout callin' her. Could have...had Brandy's number. Give that up as a bad idea pretty quick though. Hell, I wanted to save her from grief...not cause her more'n she had already.

"I'd go to bed but couldn't sleep thinkin' 'bout it. All the time gettin' madder and madder. I been readin' in the paper about how they executed that woman in Texas. The one axed those people an' bragged 'bout it an' then got religion. I was talkin' 'bout it to my sister and she says ' We got that stuff in the office. The stuff they used to put her away nice and easy.' Sis works in the vet's office in Ellsworth, ya know. Got me to thinkin'. They said it's a easy way to die an' even if I feel like killin' him, I don't want him to suffer too much."

Joe was again on the edge of his chair. It was obvious where this was going and he couldn't believe his ears. Harvey Lunt was the last one in the world anyone would see as a murderer.

"I asked her if she ever done it... kill the animals. Said she done it often. I asked her how an' she said that she didn't like to use a needle, so she just gave them a strong dose in their water dish...So I told my sister that I needed some of the stuff to put my friend's dogs out of their misery. Told her he was gonna' shoot them dogs but didn't have the heart. Told her I wanted some full strength 'cause I don't want no foul -up."

Joe again saw the beginning of a smile which quickly changed.

"Don't have a friend with no two dogs, but Sis don't know it. She said she'd get me some. That's why I went over to their house that night...to get the stuff. Even then I warn't sure I'd use it but when I come back an' almost ran into Kelley, all I could see in my mind's eye was them screwin' away on *Sea Chaser* night after night while Beth was out there takin' care of his grandkid and her dyin'. I lost it right there an' then. Drove down here, got out with the stuff in my pocket an' hiked down the pier an' went right aboard *Sea Chaser*. Didn't know how I was goin' to do it but I figured there had to be a way..."

Harvey stopped and put his head in his hands for a moment and then continued.

"It was easier'n I thought. Gordon was still awake but in his bunk, just lay'n there nakid an' really under the weather...drunk'd be a better word for it. Told him I was jest checkin' on him an' the boat. Then he asked me to get him a drink. 'Water?' I sez. ' Hell no' he sez. 'Get me some real stuff Harvey — pointin' to the galley. I see the Chevas on the counter in the galley. He can't see me in the galley, so I got him the real stuff with a little something extra added an' give it to 'im. Got off the boat real quick then. Didn't want to be around when it happened. Hiked back up the pier an' sat on the bench a long while...Don't know how long. Forced myself to wait. Sis says it happens fast though. "Bout an hour later I went back aboard. Gordon was like I left 'im... only he were gone... I checked real good. Then I took the bottle of Chevas an' the glass...that's all I touched, an' left real quick."

Harvey got up, went to the cupboard over the sink, took out a plastic bag with a bottle of Chevas Regal and a zip-loc bag with two glasses in it, brought them back and sat them on the table in front of Joe.

"You'll want these," he said. "I suspect the glasses got fingerprints on them. I put them in the bag so you don't touch them ."

Harvey didn't say why there were two glasses. Joe didn't ask — he was too stunned. He knew there was more to the story and he'd just have to wait. Harvey sat back down and looked at Joe, saying nothing.

"Okay. Tell me about Mrs. Fairbanks," Joe prompted.

"Ayuh. Need to do that. Don't feel too bad 'bout Gordon. He got his accordin' to the good book. Adultery ya know. People use to stone 'em to death."

Joe didn't have the heart to tell Harvey he had it backwards. It was the old man's justification and it wasn't for him to judge.

"Beth was different," Harvey continued. "She'd be better after the chemo...for awhile at least. Then the pain'd be back worse n' before. Then we'd go up to Bangor agin'. Same thing'd happen. Better...then worse. None of her kids'd be around. Brandy didn't know how bad she was out there in Seattle or I know'd he'd come. I wanted to call him but Beth wouldn't let me. I was with her off an' on, day an' night, helpin' Melissa. She wouldn't let me call Andy either. We both know'd he'd put her in a nursin' home an' she hated the thought of that. So she suffered an' I did too...but mine was some different. Finally, the visitin' nurse told Beth she'd have to go some place where they could give her morphine. Beth put her foot down...told her she wouldn't leave Carleton Cottage. It was the only place she ever loved an' she wanted to die there..."

Harvey stopped...fighting back the tears, his hands still trembling on the coffee mug he was clutching. After a while he went on.

"Beth began to beg me not to let them take her away an' I

promised her I wouldn't. Then one day a week or so ago...time's been runnin' together on me...the nurse told Beth she had called Andy an' he was coming up on the weekend an' take her out to a place they could ease her suffering. After the nurse left, Beth begged me to find a way to let her 'go peacefully to sleep' — is the way she said it. I told her 'bout my sister an' the veterinary clinic an' how they put animals away. She wondered if I could get some of the stuff for her. I told her I'd check it out. She said ' Harvey, just do it...for me...Please. You know how much I think of you... love you really'. Beth said she loved me! That's all I needed to hear."

Another pause and more tears. In a quaking voice he went on, "That afternoon Beth insisted Melissa take the afternoon off. It was okay with me 'cause I needed time. When I came into her room I told her I had some of the stuff. I was scared she'd put two and two together — 'bout Gordon ya know — but she was too sick to think. All she said was she hurt so bad. She begged me to give her the stuff right then an' I did. She put the stuff in her water glass herself...made me promise to get rid of the glass an' not to tell anyone. Then she thanked me for all I'd done for her over the years...she was talkin' in a whisper and I was leanin' down near her mouth. She pulled my head close... gave me a kiss. Then she looked me right in the eye an' said agin' 'I love you Harvey'."

Harvey was still shaking and shedding more tears. Finally he found the strength to go on.

"I watched her while she swall'ed the stuff. She was gone in no time. I took the glass an' the bottle of my stuff an' came back here an' waited. Don't know how long...some time...late I think...Melissa called an' I went up to the cottage."

Harvey couldn't talk anymore. Tears streamed down his deeply lined, weather beaten face, but he didn't make a sound. Joe reached over and put his hand on Harvey's hands, both still tightly clutching his coffee mug. After a couple of minutes Harvey got up, went into the front room and came back with an envelope. He gave it to Joe. It was addressed to Mr. Goldberg.

"It's all in there, Joe. The whole story. I wrote it out for you," Harvey told him.

Harvey put the envelope in the bag with the Chevas bottle and the bag of glasses. Then he picked up his coffee mug, poured in the rest of the coffee from the pot, got his coat from the peg by the door and put it on.

"Let's go Joe. I'm ready. Take me on up to the Ellsworth jail so those fools can let those two nice kids go. Stupid fool police don't have a goddamn clue!"

Joe got up, took the envelope, the bag with the glasses, and followed Harvey down the stairs. Harvey was in the Caprice and buckled up before Joe had time to put the envelope and the bag in the trunk and get in. As soon as the car was running, Harvey tipped up his coffee mug and emptied it.

"Needed a little somethin' for the trip," he smiled at Joe. It was a real smile this time.

Joe drove out the Carleton Cottage drive, happy that he now knew the truth but, angry at himself for not checking more completely on Harvey Lunt. It wasn't only the police who didn't have a clue, he told himself. He was soon on Route 198 heading to Ellsworth. He had been conscious that Harvey had yawned a couple of times soon after he swallowed the last of his coffee and now his head was slumped on his chest.

"Harvey! Oh my God!" Joe shouted.

Harvey didn't respond. Joe quickly found a place to drive the Caprice on to the shoulder of the road. As soon as the car was stopped, Joe leaned over and put his ear near Harvey's mouth. He couldn't hear any breathing. Then he tried to find a pulse but there wasn't one. He unbuckled his own seat belt and put his ear on Harvey's chest and he couldn't hear any heart beats.

Joe's sudden thought was confirmed. Harvey was dead. Being a prudent Downeaster, Harvey hadn't used all the 'stuff' his sister had gotten for him. He saved a little for himself.

CKNOWLEDGMENT

Again, I have relied on my editor, Diana George Chapin for her many suggestions. I find that I defend too much what I have written, and discarding anything is done with great reluctance. Diana almost always wins and she should.

I am also indebted to my friend, Alan Ferguson for background on Saint Albans, Vermont.

My friend and neighbor, Ned Wharton has been a resource and a great help with the final work.

Support from my wife Ginny and encouragement from my children make following my avocation pleasurable.

Printed by Downeast Graphics and Printing, Inc., Ellsworth, Maine